THE GHOST

OF THE

IN

BETWEEN

LEONICIA SORIA

TEKNINJA PUBLISHING

Phoenix, Arizona

B – We are a team. I love you.

TL – You are my inspiration. I love you.

JM – Thank you for sharing your command of the English language with me.

Content Warning

This book contains discussions of suicide, mental health struggles, as well as drug and alcohol abuse.

While the story is ultimately a message of hope, healing, and resilience, it includes content that may be distressing to some readers.

If you are struggling, please know you are not alone. Help is available.

Consider reaching out to a trusted person or contacting a support organization in your area.

In the United States, the National Suicide Prevention Lifeline is available 24/7 at 1-800-273-8255 or 988.

For resources in other countries, please visit https://findahelpline.com.

Take care of yourself as you engage with this book, and know that hope can be found even in the darkest moments.

Prologue

I WAS CONTACTED BY a ghost.

My name is Bella Amescua. I'm a nineteen-year-old Latina studying computer science at Palo Verde State University, right here in Arizona, near downtown Phoenix. You don't know me, and you have no reason to believe this, but I am going to tell you about something unexplainable that happened to me. I was contacted by the spirit of my best friend, Cierra Fallion, who tragically took her own life earlier this year.

Six months after her death, Cierra began texting me from beyond the grave over the course of eight days. Our communications consisted mainly of texts, but there were also two *voice calls*, which I will explain in greater detail if you stick with me. During our conversations, Cierra talked about where she ended up after she died, a place she called The Hyperveil, that I think you are going to want to hear about.

She also revealed some things about the world of the living, specifically two opposing hidden forces that surround us even now, that she referred to as, "the rAnd0m" and "the mesh." While our discussions were unsettling, the things she said about her death, the fate of her soul, and what it all meant for me, have given me the hope and strength to live a better life, as well as the courage to tell you my truth.

Contents

Chapter 1

Calebrea Canyon

THE DAY I MET Cierra started with an argument with my parents. It was the beginning of the fall semester of my freshman year. I was sitting in my room getting ready for an event on the PVSU campus, wishing something exciting would happen to me for once in my life. I grew up in a small upscale community near Phoenix, Arizona, named Calebrea Canyon, where nothing exciting ever happens, especially in matters involving, *me*. I have a mom and a dad and I did all the cliché things young people are supposed to do, nothing mysterious about it, *yawn*. Maybe I was being a little hard on myself, but truthfully, before I met Cierra Fallion, my biggest secret was the sheer tedium of my existence.

From as far back as I can remember, my mostly straight-laced, accomplished, tech-worker parents were deeply involved in my life, constantly hammering me with their rule-following influence. My father was a Marine, and my mother was first in her family to graduate from college. So, I was raised surrounded with all this structure and stability, which is good I guess, but also quite boring. I suppose I could be clever and summarize that my seventeen years of life up to that point had definitely been more paint-by-numbers, and less back-alley spray paint graffiti. Maybe that is why at first glance you probably wouldn't see it, but deep down inside, I always felt like a nerd. A computer nerd, to be exact, *bleep-bloop*.

"You're gonna be late Bell," my dad called out to me as I was putting on the finishing touches of my makeup in front of my bedroom vanity mirror.

I came traipsing out of my room and drifted into the kitchen where my parents were hanging out, drinking their morning coffee. I was trying to be nonchalant so they wouldn't notice my appearance and ask too many questions; however, I had spent the last hour getting extra dolled up, and clearly, it showed. I may be a computer nerd, but I can hide it very well, *when I want to.*

"Isabella, why are you so fancy-dancy?" my mom asked, as she was slightly taken aback by how put together I was looking that morning. Normally, I would have been dressed much more laid-back and casual. My dad did not seem to notice one way or another, which slightly annoyed me. I think my mom sensed this, so she pushed a cup of coffee in my direction, made exactly the way I like it.

"There is a special event on campus today, so there are no classes," I replied. Then I saw an opportunity, and quickly shifted gears. "I think I changed my mind. I want to live on campus," I said, flat out, no punches pulled.

My parents were clearly not ready for their only child, their *mija*, to move out, and I knew that, and I said what I said anyways. That sort of abruptness and bluntness was just my style when I felt like being sorta mean, so my timing and delivery of that statement seemed perfect to me. I was getting all puffed up inside with an overabundance of confidence at the thrill of saying something that I knew would upset my parents, who were *the referees of doing everything proper* in my life.

They both looked shocked, which was satisfying because that was exactly what I was going for. But then it occurred to me that maybe they were more surprised with the fact that school had just started, and there was already a day with no classes. My uncertainty of which was which added to the overall tension in the room.

"Next year, yeah?" my mom asked, with a pensive look, biting her lower lip while brushing her long hair back behind her left ear, revealing her now sad eyes.

"No, *now*," I said while firmly putting my cup of coffee down on the kitchen counter.

I said it with such an authoritative, matter-of-fact tone, twisting my words like a dagger that I had jabbed into my parents' side. I don't know why I felt like being mean to them at that moment, but I did. I guess I was annoyed about all the structure I had around me, because it suddenly felt like a weight that was holding me down from doing something impulsive. Like unexpectedly making up my mind that I was moving out of my parents' house for example.

"Well, it is too late for this year Bell, student housing deadline was last month," my dad interjected with his own confident swagger. His words were like a shield, defending my mother from my bluntness.

It was a fifty-something-year-old-dad checkmate defense, foiling my emotional dagger with cold hard logic. He had a non-emotional, smug look on his face too, which annoyed me even further.

"Not if I join a sorority. They let you move into those dorms right away, *when I am accepted*."

"*If you are accepted*," my dad deadpanned while simultaneously acquiescing to this new information, knowing it was time to accept defeat and regroup. He was so wise and logical to the point where it would bug me, especially when it was something that I found so emotional.

He looks like a brown robot, with that ridiculous and completely unnecessary military style haircut, my inner voice sneered with a little bit of actual venom.

That was a truly mean thought, and it jolted me back to reality, forcing me to feel the heavy tension of the room. I guess it was not often that I got anything over on my father, so I decided to ease up on both of them, as I began to feel the tendrils of guilt slowly creeping into my heart. *My dad is no robot, he is my ride or die,* my inner voice interjected. My heart warmed a little, and the mood began to swing from negative to positive. I decided that I would crack a joke that I knew my dad would appreciate to quickly alleviate the awkwardness that I had created.

"I have been living here with you guys my whole life, and as you know dad, familiarity breeds contempt," I said with a sarcastic smile, while gently resting my hand on one of his very broad shoulders.

He half grimaced, half smiled, because my dad was full of colloquialisms, especially those of a negative connotation, and I think he got a kick out of me using one of his bread-and-butter sayings.

"Well, you know Bell, I guess I'm not surprised, because people rarely change, unless it is for the worse," he deadpanned.

My mother is the kindest and gentlest person I know, and she is not a fan of our cynical sense of humor. So she quickly changed the subject.

"No problem Izzy, when you get back, we can see what we have to do to make that happen," Mom said.

She is such a planner so this act of orderliness must have been somewhat self-soothing for her. This new situation hung out there in time briefly, and we all looked at each other to see if there was anything else that would organically develop in our conversation.

There was nothing left to say, so before things got awkward again, I gulped down one last swig of coffee, hugged both my parents deeply, gathered my belongings, and I went out into the three-car garage. I pressed the garage door button and the motor whirred with a low mechanical growl as it lifted one of the heavy bay doors. I got into my car and it started up with a gusty roar, followed by some modern-day automotive computer bleeping and blooping. As I pulled out of the driveway, I paused briefly and admired the beautiful split-level home that I grew up in. For some reason, I felt like I was saying goodbye to this place, which was silly because I knew I would return later that evening once I was done with my school activities. I shook my head sharply to shake this strange feeling from my brain and regain my focus.

I shifted my car into drive and I started twisting down the long curvy road of our gated community in my white late model Honda as I exited our subdivision of huge single-family houses on oversized lots. I steered out onto the nearby San Tan freeway, and then stepped on the gas with the radio blasting on my way towards downtown Phoenix, and the Palo Verde State University campus. I then sat way back into the driver's seat and got comfortable. I peacefully zoned out listening to the sweet sounds of my favorite Arizona band, The Format, as it blared out on my powerful car stereo. Sorry Jimmy Eat World, maybe I will get you on the drive home.

Chapter 2

Rush

It was Rush Week at the sororities in the second week of August. The fall semester had started the week prior, and the entire campus was humming with Greek Life buzz, coupled with the commotion of countless students scampering towards their seemingly random destinations. I was not lying to my parents earlier, there were no classes because today was Open Rush, where each house was open for visitation by potential pledges known as Rushers, like me.

It was a *hotter-than-usual* Arizona Tuesday morning, and I parked my car in the main four-story campus garage and then started walking towards the Greek Leadership Village, so that I could assess the situation for myself. I was wearing my best baby blue Sunday dress with sleek, strappy wedges that added just the right amount of height, creating a perfect balance between sweet innocence and edgy confidence. It may sound silly, but simply voicing my desire to move out of my parents' house earlier that morning changed my entire outlook on the world. This was obviously not my first time on campus, but my new mindset literally made me feel like I was taking my first baby steps out into the world itself.

After exiting the parking structure, I quickly found myself surrounded by several of my fellow students, many of them carrying signs, sticks, tape, glue, and glitter, leaving a trail of multi-colored particles across the sidewalk in front of me. I paused, and joked to myself that it looked like these guys had looted the local Hobby Shack craft store, and they were now running from the authorities, with all their pilfered booty in tow. In addition to these arts and crafts kids, there was a sundry of girls that I could see. Pledges who did not yet belong to a sorority, dressed in their *Sunday-best* attire just like me. Each of us hoping to find a home in one of the two campus sororities.

It was mid-summer in Arizona, and even though it was only ten in the morning, the temperature had already climbed to a sweltering 106 degrees. I could feel the sweat beading up and trickling down the small of my back. Despite the heat, I was fully dolled up—long lashes, full makeup, and my hair perfectly curled. It wasn't that I was trying to be over the top, but honestly, I've been blessed with good genes. I have long, wavy brown hair, dark eyes, naturally tanned skin, a pleasant smile, and a small waist. At just over five feet tall, I'm not the tallest girl, but I've got shapely legs that give me a confident stride, especially when I'm buzzing with nervous energy, like I was in that moment.

All of which is to say that I can turn heads when I walk by. And I will never forget, as I was strutting my stuff, that I did not feel so bored for the first time since high school. Being excited and unafraid, I wanted to be seen, I wanted the attention, and I was fully living on planet, *look at me*! But, keeping it real, with everything going on around me, nobody was paying attention. It might sound like I'm bragging about myself, but please don't misunderstand—I'm just setting the scene so you can picture how everything unfolded that morning. I mean, like most things in our modern day technologically connected life, the visuals are important after all, as nobody reads books anymore.

The Greek Leadership Village, or GLV, is in the middle of campus, quite close to the parking garage. It has three medium height buildings that are surrounded on all sides by a brick and wrought iron wall that together conceal a great green grassy area in the center, forming a big cohesive walled-in square. I walked past the concrete gates and down the stairs into what serves as a grand entryway to a sunken courtyard. Immediately on my right was one of the three five story buildings, which served as sorority housing. The building across the big square of grass on my left was a frat, while the last building in the far opposite center of the grassy courtyard served as the headquarters for the entire compound.

It was there on the courtyard sidewalk, past the steps and in front of the sorority building, that I initially saw Cierra Fallion. I will never forget the first thing she said to me that day. As I was walking up to a table with some Delta Pi Zeta Sorority propaganda on it, there she was sitting in a chair all by herself, behind a table that was covered by a large shade umbrella. Cierra wore a light-yellow summer dress, with her long blonde hair swept up in a high braid with a few angel hair wisps that circled her face on the sides, all perfectly coiffed. With her hair up like this, you could really see her pretty blue eyes and shapely face, which was a little intimidating in itself. I quickly made a mental note that this girl seemed to be the perfect contrast to me physically as she was fair and blonde, while I am dark and brunette. My observation of our physical contrast made me wonder if her personality was going to clash with mine, just like all the other times I have tried to make friends with new girls and failed for that very reason. Although she was sitting down, I surmised that she was approximately my height as well, which is another data point for you to consider.

My preliminary plan with this girl was to stop and introduce myself using my best manners, starting with the kindest formal greeting I could muster. In my head I was visualizing how interesting, smart, and sophisticated I would appear. I figured I would just impress her and then make some small talk. But my earlier overconfident swagger had passed, and now I suddenly felt out of place, hot and just generally uncomfortable. I thought meeting someone new with whom I shared a mutual interest would calm my jittery nerves. I stood there for just a quick second as I gathered myself, preparing to make a friendly approach with my best foot forward.

Before I got that chance, Cierra suddenly cocked her head in my direction and, in a high-pitched voice, blurted out:

"Hey, what's this bug-eyed bitch doing here?"

It was a deadpan statement, not a question, her tone making it clear she wasn't looking for an answer.

When I heard this insult, I paused momentarily, while I looked right into her eyes. I was equal parts shocked, offended and pissed. I wanted to make sure that this girl saw me allowing all the positive emotion that I had built up earlier to completely drain from my face. I furrowed my brow and clenched my teeth, making a deliberate show of looking all around me before finally settling my gaze on her, squinting in her direction with my angriest expression. This little performance was my way of making it clear that I understood her disrespect was aimed at me—and I wasn't having it. On the surface, I might come across as quiet and nerdy, but make no mistake, I'm still a hot-blooded Latina with a bit of a temper.

Internally, I paused, trying to keep myself from exploding with anger and causing a scene. I crossed my arms and bit the inside of my lip, silently reminding myself to breathe and count to ten. Losing my cool wasn't going to be worth it—just as my dad used to tell me when I was a little brat growing up. In my head I made it to the count of five before my lack of patience forced me to check my internal feelings. Yep, my feelings were hurt, and I quickly felt my blood temperature reach a boil. *Sorry about that, Dad.* I guess what angered me most is that this girl had cut right through all of my defenses so quickly and easily. Like she knocked my wall over and knew exactly how to push my buttons. *How dare she!*

I took a deep breath, uncrossed my arms and marched up to the table to confront her. I slammed my left hand forcefully onto the table, while I put my right hand up on my hip after I allowed my body momentum to swing my small purse around my waist and land gracefully on my posterior. I had already thought of the perfect comeback to make her life miserable, just like she had made me feel.

But then, when our faces met, Cierra quickly crossed her eyes so deeply that her pupils almost disappeared behind the corners of her eyelids near the bridge of her nose, and she said in an exaggerated posh, stuck-up, California girl voice,

"Got a problem, babe? Maybe you are not Delta Pi Zeta material!"

For a moment, everything stopped and there was absolutely no sound, and it seemed as if someone had hit the mute button for the entire universe. *This must be what pure silence is like,* I thought to myself. It was so quiet that I could feel these puffy clouds of tension forming around my eyelids, uncomfortably pushing my eyeballs back into their sockets, making them throb. The tension was so thick, I think I must have been squinting and not even been aware of it. Everything started to fade out into my peripheral vision and for a moment I thought I might actually faint. The only thing I knew for certain was that I was in a complete daze from the double whammy this girl had thrown at me with her earlier rude comment followed by the silly crossing of her eyes and fake posh voice.

I nervously blinked a few times as I looked at her in complete bewilderment. And there she was looking right back at me, with a look of, *well,* I am not entirely certain what was going on in Cierra's head, not then, *not ever.* As our eyes met and we got a full measure of one another, Cierra leaned back in her seat, tilted her head slightly and she cracked a genuine, but muted half smile. Then we both unexpectedly started laughing hysterically! Our laughter bubbled up from deep inside, and we had no choice but to lean back and just allow the hilarity to thoroughly envelop us. It was as if this entire situation had been a well-rehearsed skit performed by two longtime friends that were suddenly reunited. But it wasn't a skit—it had been a bold move on Cierra's part, and one that could have easily spiraled into something physical. The tension had been so thick that, without even thinking, I'd unscrewed the lid of my ice-cold water bottle, ready to step it up if things got worse. Thankfully, it hadn't come to that, I thought as I carefully screwed the lid back on, low key relieved the situation had diffused.

As with many things in Cierra's life during the time that I knew her, she had recklessly and fearlessly rolled the dice and won against a challenge that she had created for herself from scratch. No rhyme or reason, Cierra never tried anything, she just did it, consequences be damned. Reflecting back now, I think this entire situation was really a test that Cierra had devised to quickly and thoroughly evaluate me as a person and potential target as a friend. And if that was her intention, it certainly worked, because subconsciously, I had been examining Cierra, and had determined that she was going to be someone that I wanted to know. I imagined that Cierra sized me up and decided I was her equal (or as close as she was going to find at PVSU). The two of us, laughing in the hot Arizona sun, formed this virtual yin and yang, a perfectly matched, but contrasting pair, that were now singularly intertwined and marching towards some mission we were not yet even aware of. Sometimes I have found in life that you are just on the same wavelength as someone else, and wow, was I ever in tune with this girl. I think Cierra sensed it too, and she honed right in and latched herself onto my soul.

"Hi, I'm Bella." I leaned in and offered my hand gently for a pleasant shake.

"Cierra, with a C, nice to meet you," she replied with a friendly tone, using her real voice for the first time as she shook my hand.

After Cierra and I had properly introduced each other, I felt a shift in my consciousness yet again. Whatever had happened between us, the only thing I knew for certain was that I didn't feel nervous any longer, and I didn't feel like a computer nerd any more either. I simply felt more alive than I ever had before, *in my entire life*. I am not exaggerating when I tell you in no uncertain terms that Cierra had an immediate and massive impact on my life, from day dot.

Cierra stood up quickly from the chair she had commandeered earlier and grabbed my hand while looking directly into my eyes. She said that she needed to use the bathroom. She added that it would be a good idea for me to accompany her, while she was dragging me forcefully along with her in a hurried fashion. Once she determined I was coming along with her willingly, she let go of my hand, and we both slowed to a more deliberate, natural walking pace. We strolled along the lateral edge of the courtyard, down towards the end of the corridor of buildings, to some public restrooms that are housed on the first floor of the headquarters building.

Once we reached our destination, Cierra pushed me through the door of the girls' bathroom, as she entered behind me and slammed her back against the door, as if she was attempting to seal it permanently shut. *This girl is definitely up to something, or she is crazy, or both,* I thought to myself, apprehensively.

"Whew, that place out there was definitely giving me *the ick,*" she said, sorta feigning complete exasperation, which made me grow suspect of her motivations.

She must have sensed my trepidation, because she then reached into her impossibly tiny black purse and pulled out a mini double shot bottle of Fireball whiskey, which only served to put me even more on edge. She completely ignored my reaction as she quickly twisted the cap off this small bottle with amazing speed and precision and dramatically tilted her head way back, draining its contents in one big gulp. A little booze dribbled down her lip and she looked at me a tiny bit embarrassed as she wiped the excess whiskey away with the back of her hand. She did all this while the edge of her right lip was curving into a tiny mischievous smile, revealing a dimple I had not noticed before. The smile abruptly disappeared though, and the look on her face suddenly went completely blank, and she gazed in my direction with an empty stare, like she was deep in thought. Then just as quickly as the first time, she whipped out another mini bottle of Fireball from her purse, and in one motion, the cap flew off and hit the ground while she lurched forward and quickly pushed it in my face.

"It is only ten am, girl!" I protested with both my hands up as I was backing away slowly.

Fighting was no use, because she ignored my objection and skillfully grabbed the nape of my neck and popped the little bottle right into my mouth. I really did not want to drink this booze, so I plugged the opening of the bottle with my tongue and then just stared back at Cierra with my bottom lip jutting out, like I was pouting.

"Come on and drink up already, missy!" Cierra exclaimed in a surprisingly bossy tone. She then paused for a moment as she cocked her head to the side while scrunching up her face, looking perplexed. Her eyes lit up as she came to a realization, and she smiled and said while giggling, "You look like a baby with her favorite binky stuffed in her mouth!"

That line made me want to laugh so hard, but somehow, I was able to keep my composure. At this point, I had no choice but to either chug it or wear it, so I forced the sweet warm whiskey down my throat while my arms were outstretched in front of me awkwardly, as if my hands were reaching to grab onto some object which was not there. Cierra was fast and strong, and her actions were more than a little jarring. *Nothing in my wildest imagination could have prepared me for a girl like this,* I thought to myself.

This experience made me feel a little violated if I am being honest. However, her actions were so comical and unexpected, making me feel keenly aware of being alive in some mystical way I cannot quite explain, in spite of my unease. I guess, using the simplest of terms, I would describe this moment as being beautiful. Indeed, thinking of this experience now, it was thoroughly emblematic of what beauty is—that unique property that grabs you by the shoulders, shakes you, and says *hey, you are a living being, take a look around and enjoy it.* In this tiny bathroom, at this moment, time stood still and I was definitely taking it all in for what felt like the first real college experience I had since stepping on the PVSU campus two weeks ago.

In some way, this whole situation—the bathroom break, the Greek Leadership Village, and meeting Cierra Fallion—while certainly new to me, carried a definite sense of déjà vu. Deep in my subconscious, I felt as though I had lived this moment countless times before, shrouded in an infinite haze of barely perceptible memories, riding through my mind like an invisible wave of gravity. The warm aftertaste of the whiskey in my mouth provided some vague but familiar contextual sensation, making me feel like I already knew this girl. Maybe it was the booze, or perhaps it was simply meeting Cierra, but whatever the cause, for once in my life my naturally tense shoulders relaxed, and I felt comfortable and happy just to be alive.

Apparently, there was no booze left in her tiny purse, so it felt like it was a naturally appropriate time to leave this place. Cierra and I were just a tiny bit buzzed as we exited the restroom. I felt that warm reassurance of alcohol gently heating up my insides while the pleasant but artificial sense of well-being was swimming over me. Yes, I was definitely starting to set sail even from that small double shot of whiskey. We didn't even actually end up going to the bathroom really; this was just a big ruse on Cierra's part to slam some booze and lighten the mood. And that was Cierra in a nutshell, she was definitely always wanting to break the surface tension and lighten things up. Much like me, Cierra's shoulders seemed bunched together with nervous energy and she was so anxious to release it in whatever way she could easily get away with. The difference between us was that she knew how to break through the tension, as opposed to me, not having a clue. I just let it sit there, a constant weight on my back. I guess I was quickly figuring it out though, because here I was in week two of college, already learning more than four years of high school honor courses could ever teach me. *Dad would be so proud,* I thought to myself as I hiccuped with a slightly inebriated grin on my face.

We stumbled out of the bathroom into the courtyard and slowly made our way back to the Delta Pi Zeta table. Cierra resumed her seat underneath the shade umbrella while I hovered with my arms crossed. The hot Arizona sun was cutting through everything with the power of a billion candles, and when it hit the bare skin of my arms, I felt a stinging sensation from the sheer intensity of it. I shook my head slightly in an attempt to regain a tiny bit of sobriety and got serious for a moment. I asked Cierra if she liked the Greek lifestyle, specifically the Delta Pi Zeta sorority and if she thought I should pledge there.

"How the F would I know Babe?" she responded with a slightly annoyed but matter of fact expression on her face.

It then dawned on me. Cierra had just seen the empty seats behind the table when she first got there and decided to sit in the shade. She wasn't a DPZ sister, she was rushing, just like me.

"We might as well join this DPZ thing while we are at it though, I don't want to walk around anymore and this is BORING as hell, Binky," Cierra said to me with half open glassy eyes.

"Binky?" I asked, with no clue what she meant.

"Yeah, YOU, Binky!" she said without even glancing in my direction, but while pointing directly at me. It somehow made what she said sound rather official, as if she were granting me a knighthood or something.

"Sounds good to me, Fireball!" I replied back, and I now understood that I had made a new friend, and acquired a new nickname in the process, too. I glanced right at her when I said that, and I noticed her lip curling up into an ever so slight, smile of approval.

Cierra just oozed cool without even trying.

"Ok, it's settled then, we will pledge our souls here. DPZ is good enough I guess." She breathed in deeply and then naturally sighed.

I shook my head in skepticism and amusement. But then I thought, *she isn't wrong, you know?*

Looking back, that is how things were with Cierra most of the time, good, bad or indifferent. Everything just seemed to fall into place, like I had no say in the matter and neither did she, things just happened. I would compare the time I spent with Cierra to streaming a movie on your computer. The events are already written to a data file and queued up, just waiting for someone to play it back and observe what happens, but with no actual control over the story. Yes, you could play, rewind, fast forward, pause or stop, but the movie never changes and the ending and meaning remains the same. At this point in time, it seemed as if my relationship with Cierra was like that of a freight train just leaving the station, picking up steam, and becoming an unstoppable force. I was not aware in that moment of naive bliss that I was hurtling towards a disastrous destination of sadness and ruin for me, Cierra, and everyone around us. I didn't know it at that point, but eventually many people were going to hear our story and be filled with a profound and empty sadness, too. FML.

Chapter 3

Terminal

CIERRA AND I HAD exchanged information and parted ways about 10 minutes earlier. When I looked down at my smart watch, I realized it was already early afternoon and I had missed lunch. Not that I remember being hungry as the Fireball whiskey that I had consumed earlier had turned my stomach. Normally missing lunch would have made me angry, but for some reason, I was just walking around campus, totally mellow, completely weird. I thought about how my dad had taught me as a little kid that anger is the emotion one feels when something fails to meet their expectations, and that how angry one becomes depends on how powerless they feel. Well, the only thing I felt besides my slight stomach discomfort was an unfamiliar mix of excitement and fatigue. Again, *weird*.

As I stood there pondering the legitimacy of being mad about an empty stomach, an extremely cute boy walked by. This caused me to dump my inner thought process and stand there with a completely dopey look on my face. He was about six feet tall, had longish brown hair, a chiseled chin and was *really* fit. That certainly woke me up from my small Fireball buzz and made my stomach discomfort mostly disappear. I caught myself gawking at this boy, and that made me a little annoyed at myself. I grimaced and then shook my head sharply, attempting to at least have the appearance of a proper young lady with a modicum of restraint.

Seeing that boy got me in the mood to do some campus exploring. I was not stalking him, I swear. Besides, he had already disappeared from view. I walked back to the parking garage so I could change into a spare set of casual clothes that I kept in the trunk of my car, folded neatly in a gym bag. I had done cheerleading in high school and had figured out back then that it was always a good idea to keep some extra clothes handy so that I could quickly change into something more comfortable. I looked in my bag that had been stashed for months, and bingo, there were some jean shorts, a baby doll t-shirt and tennis shoes. I am so smart, I thought to myself as I happily changed in my car. The parking garage was somewhat dim and my car had dark tinted windows, so this was a pretty low risk/high reward maneuver.

I locked my car and started walking. My destination was right at the heart of the PVSU campus, where there was an old building that was built beneath a rocky bluff. The entire structure was underground, so you had to walk down two flights of stairs at the front to get to the entrance. I learned quickly upon enrolling at PVSU, that the students called this building The Pit. I made my way down the stairs and stood silently for a moment before going inside. I was thinking about what was inside this building, and how it was the only reason I decided to attend PVSU in the first place.

When I was a little girl, maybe five years old, my parents gave me my first computer, an old hand-me-down Apple MacBook. It was very small and my dad put a deep blue skin on it, my absolute favorite color, making it perfect for me. That computer was my world the first summer that I got it. I remember playing this one particular game for countless hours on it with these penguins on an island. One of my friends had told me that if we all stood on one side of an iceberg and made our characters jump up and down, we could flip it over. I don't even know if I believed that, but I spent hours trying anyway.

One day, something very special happened.

"Bell, come quick!" my dad had yelled from the other room.

I rushed over, and there on my little MacBook was the familiar face of my Grandma Antonia. It wasn't a photo or a video, but she was moving and she could see me too. It was my very first video call, and that moment is forever etched in my memory. As a little girl, I couldn't believe my eyes—seeing my grandma, who lived so far away, right there in front of me. Even though it was something completely new, it also felt strangely familiar at the same time. I was instantly fascinated and wanted to know everything about how this incredible connection was even possible. That was the day that I became a computer nerd.

I smiled warmly to myself as I was enjoying this fond memory. Just then, some sweat beaded down the small of my back and brought me back to reality. I realized I was just standing there in the hot sun daydreaming in front of the building without going inside. I grimaced slightly as I opened the heavy glass door and was greeted by a whooshing sound and a blast of welcome cool air from the Palo Verde State University Library. I immediately picked up on the comforting and familiar musky smell of the old books inside. However, I did not come here to read.

In addition to its unique architecture, this building is home to the only quantum computer in the entire state of Arizona. It is one of the few in the entire country, actually. I am not going to nerd out on you and explain the ins and outs of what a quantum computer is and what it can and can't do, other than to say, a quantum computer is quite literally spooky magic. It can do things that are nearly beyond human comprehension. I might even suggest that quantum computers perform some of their calculations on a level beyond the physical realm or within an unseen dimension we cannot detect.

Two years ago when I was a junior in high school trying to figure out which college I would attend, the fact that PVSU had a quantum computer available exclusively to computer science majors right here in my own backyard was the single most important factor. It literally made up my mind for me. Now, I could just VPN in and access this computer via a terminal from anywhere in the world, even my phone. But I have to tell you, there is something special about this building, and the room that holds this extraordinary piece of technology. It is like the whole floor is alive, you can feel the electricity in the air, and there is some hard-to-quantify quality that surrounds you here.

I noticed something from the corner of my eye. It was that cute boy that I had seen earlier. There he was near the stacks of books in the middle of the room. He was standing with his right shoulder propping himself up against a pillar. I looked in his direction and gave him my super brief, once over eye inspection and looked away, but he did not even notice me. I was miffed. But then I looked closer, and this boy had a blue paperback book splayed on the palm of his massive left hand, and he was intently studying it. I couldn't see the title, but I am pretty sure it was a technical book on the C programming language by Dennis Ritchie. *What the hell,* I thought to myself, how could such a cute specimen like this boy be reading something like that? As I was standing there pondering what I was seeing, my mind started to drift off. I was imagining going up and saying hello to this boy, and how he would smile and introduce himself, and how we would just hit it off, and then, *who knows?* As I was daydreaming, I got a notification on my phone that snapped me back into reality. I looked down to see what it was. By the time I cleared it, when I went to go look for this boy, he was gone. *Ugh.*

I walked past the stacks of books where he had been standing just moments earlier to see if I could catch a glimpse of where he had gone. I was suddenly enveloped by this amazingly fresh yet earthy aroma that entered my nostrils, and filled up my mind, body and soul. It was like pine, honey and the smell of soil after a gentle thunderstorm. I realized that this was what that boy smelled like, and it made me tingle all over with excitement. Even though he wasn't there, this guy had my full attention. Like a bloodhound, I tried to follow his trail, but the scent tapered off and I determined that he was definitely gone. I was sad, and it made me sigh, *bleep-bloop.*

I continued walking farther into the heart of the building, past several columns of books, towards a slight clearing, and then a massive set of thick greenish blue tinted windows. Behind those windows, stood Cassiopeia, the PVSU quantum computer. She was a glorious mix of huge, sleek aluminum support beams, white coated metal, and plastic. At the center stood a beautiful round column of brass, gold, and copper coils. Steel girders and fittings were housed inside thick clear plexiglass. The inside of that clear dome was chilled to a staggering negative 450 degrees. Cassiopeia is the epitome of super science mingled with art and a tad of the metaphysical, and seeing it blows me away, every time.

To the right of this main room is a smaller hallway and entry into a lab filled with access terminals. I swiped my student ID and gained entry into the lab which happened to be empty. It was always quite puzzling to me that we have this amazing computer here that is not guarded by anyone, and that most people access this system remotely, never setting foot into the building that houses it. It seemed criminal to me that one would use this computer and not actually want to do so from an open terminal mere feet away from its presence. Maybe I am being silly or I am a massive nerd—or both.

I sat down at one of the small cubicles and swiped my ID at a reader that was stationed next to the access terminal. As I was about to start typing on the mechanical keyboard, I was immediately zapped by a particularly strong jolt of static electricity. It hurt and it really pissed me off. As I was looking down at the source of my discomfort, I started studying the keys of the keyboard, and the layout of letters that it holds. I knew, of course, that it was called a QWERTY keyboard, referring to the sequence of characters that appear right underneath the number row. Although the keys appear randomly ordered, there is definitely a reason for them being arranged like that. Someone designed it that way about 150 years ago, to keep the keys from jamming back then, as they were too close to each other mechanically. Hard to understand, but just trust me, it makes sense if you see it. So, even in the smallest things that stand the test of time, there is often an order there that most do not question, but live under the effects of anyway. Sort of like my life, and somewhat of a microcosm of the morning I just had. There is a pattern, a mesh of the way things happen, something that I became more aware of in the future, but still could not quite comprehend or appreciate that morning. At least not in the way that I soon would.

I spent the rest of that afternoon writing a little program to try to simulate the early expansion of the Universe up through the present time. Sounds complex, but it was actually really simple. But in that moment, the real complexity in my mind was finding out more about the cute boy I had seen earlier. I tried sniffing my arm, my shirt, my hand, looking for some remnant of the cologne he was wearing. I realized I was obsessing at that point, and forced myself to think about something else.

I want to mention it here so that I don't forget, but I observed on that day, that sometimes, when I would run programs on Cassiopeia, it felt like the answers it gave me were coming from another dimension. *Probably nothing,* I said to comfort myself.

Chapter 4

Fight or Flight

THAT NIGHT, WHEN I got home and climbed into bed, I struggled to fall asleep. I was agitated from the excitement of meeting Cierra, not to mention the lingering effects of the Fireball whiskey I consumed earlier that morning. My system tends to be fragile, and sometimes even an extra cup of coffee too late in the day can keep me up, stirring restlessly into the night. Now, maybe to you, meeting Cierra doesn't seem like a big deal, and the events of that day might come across as fairly ordinary. But for me, it was significant. I don't often meet people I genuinely like—none that I find truly real, anyway. You might think it's strange for someone so young to be so guarded. But this skeptical, world-weary outlook isn't as uncommon among today's youth as you might think—especially for young Latina girls. In my experience, we tend to carry a seriousness that sets us apart from other kids. It's like the world seems to expect us to be tougher, and too often our struggles go unnoticed. Life is complicated, and you have to learn to grow a thick skin. That's just the way things are.

On top of the usual societal pressures, I also deal with something internally that I haven't revealed yet, which adds to my jaded outlook. To explain it fully, I have to take you back to a pivotal moment in my short, but complex life history. When I was in kindergarten, I made friends with a spunky girl named Grace, who lived down the street. She was kind to everyone, fun to be around, and at that time, the perfect friend for me. Grace was the type of girl who smiled with her whole entire face, and when she beamed at me with those genuine eyes, I imagined we'd be best friends forever. Sadly, that wasn't how things turned out—for either of us.

In the summer after the last year of middle school, to celebrate our graduation from eighth grade, I went to a sleepover party at Grace's house. The evening started off by going out to dinner with her parents at the local pizza restaurant that had animatronic animals, video games, and ticket redemption machines with cheap prizes. I was so caught up in all the excitement that I filled up on way too much grape soda and mediocre pizza that ended up sitting in my stomach like a rock. I didn't let it bother me too much though. as I was having entirely too much fun going completely loco with Grace. After dinner, we went back to Grace's house and we spontaneously decided to go for a little night swimming. All of the homes in our neighborhood had pools. However, for reasons I cannot explain, swimming is only fun when you go to someone else's house to do so. To add to the excitement, we brought out Grace's little battery powered party speaker and spent about two hours jumping in and out of the pool while listening to One Direction and the like.

A few hours later after getting cleaned up, maybe around eleven, we ran out of steam and I slowly crawled into a sleeping bag on the floor in Grace's room next to her bed. Up to that point in my life I had never really even thought about falling asleep, because normally, I would just close my eyes and the next time I would open them, it would be the next day. Unfortunately for me, there was a shift occurring internally that I was not yet aware of. Starting that night, and going forward, sleep was going to be a struggle at a minimum. Instead of drifting off gently to sleep, my thirteen-year-old self just laid there on the floor thinking random and unsettling thoughts. We had just graduated eighth grade and fear of what high school would be like was certainly messing with my head, but that was merely one factor. Everything felt like it was getting jumbled up, and my disconcerting thoughts were starting to manifest a physical reaction, as I felt anxious to the point that my stomach started to hurt. I even heard it churn, like I was hungry, which was impossible because

I was still stuffed with that awful pizza. After some tossing and turning, I did manage to fall asleep, but later, around one in the morning, I woke up all sweaty and totally rattled.

I got up on my elbows in my sleeping bag, and I tried looking around, but it was pitch black. I was enveloped in total darkness. It felt like there was not even a single photon of light swimming in the ether. *How did Grace not even have a nightlight,* I thought to myself. I was thoroughly annoyed and quite honestly, *frightened.* Luckily, I did have my smartphone, so I pulled it out and looked at the screen as it came alive and filled the room with its soothing and familiar bluish light. I wanted to call my mom, but then I felt a strange sensation creep into my mind that I had never felt before, like an unwanted guest.

When I looked at the screen, instead of being drawn in by the icons and the eventual mental reward of checking social media, something else happened. I started focusing on my fingers holding the phone, and they were solid white and stiff. They were so rigid, I felt that I could not even move them. I began to feel this primal fear, from deep inside me, at some base level. There was a nervous raw energy that felt like it was pouring out of my neck, near that place where the back of your skull meets your spine. This sensation, when I think about how I would describe it, is a pure and ancient animal-like awareness, telling your body that it is time to react. Some people refer to this part of their physiology as their lizard brain. Normally you are not even aware of it. However, when this feeling is raw and unchecked with no natural rational filter, it injects pure unadulterated terror into your veins. This is panic.

My entire body started screaming to my brain that it was time to get out of there, and that I should stand up and run. And like some command that I had no choice but to follow, I attempted to comply with total obedience. I dropped my phone, stood upright in one fluid motion, and started bolting. The only issue being, I was in a darkened home that I was not 100 percent familiar with. So rather than exiting Grace's room through her bedroom door, I ended up running straight into her closet doors instead. These two doors were flimsy and hanging in a track with wheels so that they could easily be moved from one side to the other. So, when I hit them, they came flying right off the track and they tumbled down onto the floor with a loud crash. I bounced against them as they fell down and hit the back of the closet, and I landed on my rear end near the front of the closet. The result of all this commotion was a cacophony of noise waking up the entire house.

Instantly, everyone sprang into action. I couldn't even see anybody yet, but I could sense this intense reaction to the crashing closet doors from all throughout Grace's house. Immediately, it felt like every single light in the house had been turned on and everyone that was previously fast asleep was suddenly crowded all around me. Truthfully, I barely noticed them, as my primal reaction to what I was feeling inside was causing me to stand upright again and bolt for the front door of the house. It was an utter s-show, no denying it.

Although I was not aware of it at that moment, this was only my first, but definitely would not be my last experience with panic disorder. This condition frequently gets confused with generalized anxiety disorder, but trust me, these two things couldn't be farther apart. Anxiety is like a slow dripping bathtub faucet that steadily fills the tub until it runs over several hours later. Panic is like being crushed under the entire weight of Niagara Falls in less than a millisecond.

I've been dealing with this condition for years, ever since being diagnosed shortly after this first episode. It may never fully go away, but through years of experience and techniques learned in therapy, I've managed to keep it mostly under control. Still, it has shaped my life in countless ways. But back then, as a thirteen-year-old girl in the middle of the night, it consumed me in its rawest and most terrifying form. At that moment, it felt like nobody understood or knew how to help me.

Grace's parents were trying to be attentive, bless them, but they were clueless. They were trying to hold me down, to assess the situation, and to keep me from hurting myself because I was flailing about. This was exactly the wrong strategy for someone having a panic episode. It definitely made things worse, which I would only find out much later in therapy. I ended up resisting them back with all my might, and I was a feisty, strong little girl, so I know it was not easy for them.

Luckily for me, Grace's older teenage sister Alisha was there, and she had some experience in this area, as her boyfriend at the time struggled with severe anxiety himself. While panic disorder is certainly not generalized anxiety, the two are related mental conditions. My actions provided enough information so that Alisha was able to recognize what was happening to me and react somewhat appropriately.

"Let go of her right now!" she screamed at the top of her lungs.

Everyone gave Alisha puzzled and uncomprehending looks. But then they seemed to sense Alisha's understanding of the situation, and they released me. I stood straight up and headed for the front door of the house.

Alisha followed and she even opened the door for me. "Let's go, Bella," she said as she put her hand gently on my back and pushed me out the door. She did it in such a calm manner, that somehow made me feel like I was being rescued.

When the door opened, a burst of air struck my forehead, and because I was sweating, it felt cool and soothing, which immediately calmed my frantic mind. Alisha and I ran down the street together, and we kept running until I was out of breath. We then naturally slowed to walk in unison.

"Better now, Bella?" Alisha said softly, as she tilted her neck down ever so slightly to be at eye level with me, with one hand on my shoulder, and we continued to slowly wind down.

"Yes, can we go back now." Relieved, my eyes stared right through Alisha, in a daze.

"Sure kid, let's roll."

When we got back to Grace's house, I saw my parents' SUV. They had been summoned while I was running down the street in the middle of the night in my PJ's. Mom and dad helped me gather up my stuff, and as we were leaving, Alisha grabbed their attention and pulled them to the side. I heard her whispering something to them, and my parents' eyes were wide open, but they nodded in understanding, and they thanked Alisha for her help.

Before we left, I went to Alisha and hugged her deeply. "Thank you so much."

"I was at the right place at the right time girl, nothing to it," she said, downplaying her earlier act of heroism.

Thank goodness that Alisha had been there that night. You hear about guardian angels, and it is easy to dismiss that idea in our modern secular life. But I am here to testify that Alisha was certainly put there for a reason, to be my savior. Like I said earlier, that night was my first, but definitely not my last episode with panic disorder. Unfortunately for me, I was to become oh so intimately familiar with this condition.

Panic cannot be reasoned with, as it is not rational like anxiety. It is impossible to argue with someone who is experiencing it. And once it strikes you, it is like a monster waiting outside your door, for the rest of your life. It is always there, and with just one twist of the doorknob, it is free to enter and take over your current frame of mind. Your only hope is to recognize it early when it rears its nasty head, and use self-soothing coping mechanisms to keep it at bay. Even then, sometimes it is so strong that all you can do is yield to it and wait for the clock to run out, hopefully without injuring yourself. Although there is also medication that can help, even that has its own set of drawbacks and is not a perfect solution.

Later that same summer, I had my second episode with panic disorder when I went to the mall with my mom to do some clothes shopping for high school. This one, while not as strong as my initial attack, was coupled with the added dread of having it return, so this made things feel worse than the first time. While in the car, without warning, my brain suddenly told me something was wrong, and that I was in danger and it was time to run. It's like that sinking feeling you get in your stomach when you are nervous, except that your neck has been removed from your body, and your body has been replaced with the contents of the entire world, and you are falling with all that combined weight through the floor. We were halfway to the mall when I tore off my seatbelt and tried to open the car door to get out. The only problem was that we were traveling down the freeway and if it were not for the child locks on the SUV, I might have died. The person that invented child safety locks was my guardian angel that day.

So, I had two strong episodes that summer and various other small attacks that were not as notable as the first ones, which I like to call, "The Big Two." All I can say is thank goodness for my parents, as they have been so understanding and they had the patience and perseverance necessary to get me the help I required. They never got angry at me, even when my outbursts were so inconvenient and made zero sense to anybody, they took their time and truly helped me. They did much research and then brought me to a brilliant therapist named Jerilyn. Over the next several months, this wonderful woman helped lay the foundational strategies that would eventually allow me to get hold of my condition, so I could live with it. All of that therapy takes time and repetition to be effective and I still see Jerilyn occasionally to make sure I am keeping my condition in order. Dealing with panic disorder tends to be a struggle that moves on an incredibly long timeframe coupled with an intricate incremental scale of small victories and sometimes bigger setbacks. The peaks and valleys will even out, but like I said, it takes years of commitment towards getting better.

Young friends do not have the patience or understanding to help each other get through stuff like this. They are just not equipped for it and I don't even blame them. Everyone has their own problems, and have little time or patience to deal with the struggles of others. Grace and I were never quite the same after the night of my first panic episode, unfortunately. She said that she was cool with it, but I could definitely tell things had changed. Grace would no longer spontaneously call me on the phone, stop by my house to visit out of the blue, or even text me like she used to. I had to initiate any interactions, and even then, when we saw each other, it was definitely superficial and awkward. I felt like I was coated in this invisible substance, and Grace was afraid to get any of it on her. When high school started in the fall, the word spread all over that I was having "*issues*." I can only imagine that Grace shared the experience of that night with someone else, and they shared it, until it was a rumor. However it occurred, I don't think Grace was malicious and sometimes things just happen.

As a young Latina woman, I have never experienced anything outside of minor situational racism, but I have definitely experienced discrimination and prejudice from my panic disorder. Everyone knows what racism is, and good people will not tolerate it, not even for one second. That is not true with the stigma associated with a mental illness, even a minor one like panic disorder. Nobody really understands this stuff unless they have personally experienced it, either in themselves or in a loved one. People do tolerate and perpetuate the stigma, and through their ignorance, they can even enable or encourage further distress towards those that are afflicted. Once you are diagnosed and people find out, that information can be used to polarize you. Even worse, your enemies can use it to isolate and bully you.

Grace was never mean to me about it, and I do not think she ever meant to hurt me. Recently we have even begun speaking again. However, there were two girls that made it their life mission to make my existence a living hell my freshman year in high school—Samantha Elsher and Megan Sommerset. I already knew these two girls, as they both lived within a couple miles of my house, and I even played summer league volleyball with Samantha during sixth and seventh grades. However, during middle school, because of districting lines, Samantha and Megan attended a different middle school than me. So, by the time we were reunited in high school those two were fast friends, and I was on the outside, a perfect target for their bullying. Through my own weakness, I allowed myself to be polarized and isolated and there was no guardian angel to save me. More to come on these two later on.

For now, I will say that I am not bitter about the unfortunate situations that I experienced that summer or anything else associated with my panic disorder. In fact, after meeting Cierra, I had an entirely different view on these earlier life changing experiences. I felt like this invisible hand had swept over my entire soul and left me with a warm embrace, blemishes and all. I felt proud of how I did not let panic disorder destroy me. Even though I had just met Cierra, she was immediately my counterweight sent here to be my guardian angel.

Lying there, reflecting on it all, I suddenly realized that my flaws had shaped me into a more empathetic and patient person. They had prepared me for something meaningful—like meeting someone special, like Cierra.

I let out a small relieved sigh that turned into a series of yawns and I fell deeply asleep.

Chapter 5

Rules for Smart People

CIERRA AND I PLEDGED to the Delta Pi Zeta sorority where we both were accepted with little actual effort on our parts. This was surprising, because it has been my life experience that I have always had to fight for everything I ever wanted. Nothing I tried ever seemed to just land in my lap, not like this anyhow. Especially as a freshman in her first semester in college. As unfamiliar as this situation was, the fact remains that we both got into our first-choice sorority for basically just showing up with a pulse. It was so easy that part of me couldn't help but wonder if, much like when I became cheer captain in high school, someone in authority liked my *"look"* and gave me the position to fill some kind of Latina quota.

A month and a half had flown by since Cierra and I met. I remember warmly comforting myself, thinking Cierra's good luck was constantly rubbing off on me, because in my mind I just knew that stuff like this happened for her all the time. I was a little nervous by all this newness surrounding me, but my internal dialogue reassured me that Cierra lived a life of leisure, privilege, excitement and danger, and now these things were going to be made available to me as well. I was just certain of it. Not gonna lie, I loved it too, because right away, the two of us saw eye to eye most of the time and we would just vibe with one another with a smooth ease and absolutely no cattiness.

Our friendship was special. There was never any awkward silence or the need to say things that were superficial or false, just to fill the void, like some people do when they are not completely at ease with one another. She called me Binky, I called her Fireball and we reserved the inside jokes and nicknames just for each other. We didn't let anyone in on what we were thinking and we referred to them strictly by their real names.

I know it is an overused expression to describe someone you deeply admire as being intelligent, but please believe me when I say that Cierra was 100 percent the smartest person I had ever met. I can recall even then in our earliest moments at the sorority and in the classes that we shared, thinking to myself, *how did this girl end up here in this third-tier national university? She should have been at Stanford or Duke, literally.* Not that I was relegated to attending PVSU either. I had options graduating Salutatorian in high school and I specifically turned down a full academic ride to that school down south in Tucson that shall remain unnamed.

Like I said earlier, ever since I was a little girl, I knew that I had to work hard to get what I wanted, and this was especially true of academics. I've had my nose buried in textbooks from the time I brought my first homework assignment home at age five. This repetition and dedication to my studies afforded me a huge level of academic stamina, which also served as my foundation to approaching life in general. I can easily plow through large page fine print textbooks, and while I do not have a photographic memory, I can retain large swaths of information from what I read.

Being a bookworm also taught me the power of observation, about being quiet and using my other senses to study situations in order to glean their true meaning. I put in the work in the quiet hours to get to where I wanted to be. My methodical approach to academics and life were in direct contrast to how Cierra tackled things from what I could see. When she came into this world, she possessed intellectual abilities that allowed her to just wing it most of the time. *Clearly, she was born this way,* I told myself. I wasn't jealous per se, but I did envy the natural way Cierra could just use her big old brain anytime and anyplace she desired to get her way. It did not take me long to figure out that Cierra was definitely what one would classify as being gifted, it was so obvious to me. I think she knew this about herself too; however, Cierra never flaunted her intellect. If anything, she would hide it around most people and minimize it around me with self-deprecation and deflection. Both of us together formed two sides of a gold coin, heads being studious, tails being sharp-witted, combined being dynamite.

In these early days of our friendship, I would often amuse myself by imagining Cierra as a little five-year-old tow-headed nugget. I would picture her innocently raising her hand in kindergarten, only to say something profound, but also morally questionable for her young age, making her teacher blush. I smiled as I pictured this little cherry bomb of a girl possessing an innate ability to leverage her intellect to get her way. I know in my heart that Cierra held a high level of respect towards me as well. It was a mutual admiration society that the two of us had built from the very beginning of our relationship. Indeed, we were two computer nerds in a pod.

My parents only met Cierra one time, when they picked us up late one night after a party where our ride had abandoned us. Even though we had only been friends for a couple months, it didn't take long for them to recognize what a perfectly matched set the two of us were.

"You guys should go out and party in two geeky white lab coats like the Nerd Herd guys at Tech Buy," my dad teased us from the driver seat.

"Oh, that would be sexy." Cierra crossed her eyes at me in the backseat of my parents' Lexus, while leaning in to inconspicuously tickle me.

Even though we were both buzzed from drinking early in the night, for some reason Cierra absolutely reeked of it, like the booze was emanating from her pores. I looked up at my dad's reflection in the rear-view mirror, and even though it was very dim, I could see that he was giving me the *"tone it down mija,"* look. I know my parents could smell the booze on us and I worried that I was somehow in trouble, even though I knew that was not the case, as they were clearly relieved to rescue us. We had a "no drinking and driving call anytime no questions asked" ride program in place ever since I first learned to drive.

"Why don't you come out and party with us sometime, Mr. A?" Cierra jokingly suggested, or at least I think she was joking.

"Oh, I don't know guys, do you think I am Delta Pi Zeta material?" my dad asked, which shocked me and Cierra.

The air was very still in the car after my dad had surprisingly and inexplicably used our little inside joke when Cierra had accused me of not being Delta Pi Zeta material in the GLV courtyard the day we first met.

Then Cierra blurted out, "Look at the two of us, they will let anyone in!"

Everyone had a good laugh at this, despite the slight inappropriateness of Cierra's earlier responses to my father. It was easy to let all of this slide, as I knew that Cierra never had any bad intentions.

In addition to smarts, Cierra was also very pretty, but not in the traditional sense of the word as much of her beauty came directly from her 'rizz. Her platinum blonde hair emphasized her deep blue eyes and made them sparkle in a way that would subconsciously say to you, *Hey, let's party*. She had a dimple on her right cheek that would make its appearance every time she smiled, especially when she would do her sly-half-smile where she curled up her right lip slightly. That smile was accompanied by a vibe that was intoxicating, and her edgy energy would fill up an entire room when she would enter it. I know that is another cliché to describe someone having that kind of allure, but sometimes it is simply the truth. Now typically, I would find these kinds of features from another female to be bothersome, but Cierra had a naturally soft approach that balanced things out, and most often she would draw attention away from us and onto someone else entirely by joking around. Her unpretentious nature had a way of breaking the usual surface tension I would feel around other girls. Her actions towards me were never malicious, and the way she would joke around was like a heartfelt and genuine breath of fresh air that I didn't even know I needed. Again, another unnecessary but totally true cliché that just describes Cierra perfectly.

Coupled with her strong intellect, Cierra had a naturally crafty nature that she would use to play intricate pranks on me and others. These were both mental and practical. Frequently, these jokes would be truly surprising and occasionally even borderline disturbing in nature when they caught you off guard. Sometimes, deep in the pit of my stomach, I would get uneasy around Cierra, because my intuition said that there might be something she wasn't telling me and that I shouldn't fully trust her. This feeling was rare, however, and it would quickly subside.

Most often Cierra and I would spend our time giggling about random stuff or talking about cute boys, since Cierra loved to keep things lighthearted. And that was the bottom line, Cierra was bored, just like me and everyone else, but she wouldn't just sit there and be a willing participant, she would do something about it. Cierra also happened to be a computer science major just like me, and I recall thinking to myself just how remarkable and lucky I was to have a fellow nerd in my life who was actually really cool. I would boil down the contrast between Cierra's tech intellect and my own this way: I am a computer geek in every sense of the term, learning on my laptop since I was five years old, but Cierra truly understood the underlying science, in computer science. Sometimes, I felt like the two of us were already real-world computer engineers doing experiments on our test subjects, who happened to be our fellow students and professors. Initially, the PVSU campus served as our lab for lighthearted fun and adventure. It was only later that this place would become the crucible in which an albatross was to be hung around both of our necks.

Through fate or dumb luck, Cierra and I were able to secure rooms on the same floor of the sorority, nearly facing directly across from each other. This arrangement allowed me to get very close to my new friend. With our rooms being so close, it was easy to be there for each other and avoid growing lonely, which was amazing. Because truthfully, even being just seventeen miles away from your childhood home can feel pretty isolating for a young girl on her own for the first time. I think being this close also made us codependent on each other, but not in a bad way.

In our first two semesters on the PVSU campus, there were countless parties, boys, fun, and adventure around every corner. There was also a fair amount of actual academic activities as well, since technically both of us were in the honors program at Palo Verde, which by its very nature requires vigorous studying. Not to mention that I was on an academic scholarship, which only served to increase the expectations and pressure. I had assumed the only reason why Cierra was not on scholarship was because she came from a rich family and she probably could not be bothered to take the time to fill out any of that pesky paperwork. And besides, everybody who has attended college in the last few years knows that they do not give out scholarships to pretty little rich girls. Technically, I was on a scholarship, but it was just a reduction off of the full price of in-state tuition. I believe that discount was only in place so that PVSU could justify all of the funding they got from the State of Arizona.

Both of us being in the honors program meant that we shared several classes. I had said earlier that we were studying together, but this would have been under the special rules that Cierra would set up for herself and then force me to follow. You see, while Cierra was very smart and talented, she would get bored so easily, and would find ways to entertain herself during just about any activity. Oftentimes, this would mean cheating or skirting the rules, even when it was completely unnecessary. It could also mean Cierra found different ways to trick me using mind games, but not in a mean-spirited way. I think it was mainly focused around Cierra checking for herself to ensure she was still in control, and in those early days, the result always came back that the world around her was bending towards her will. I called it the Cierra Function Box. You would feed this box any given situation into its left side, the function would run in the middle, and the result always came out the right-hand side that Cierra was still in control.

As for the pranks Cierra pulled, some were minor, often taking just a few minutes to plan and execute. Other times, her schemes were far more elaborate, requiring days or even weeks to pull off. Around the second month of living in our dorm, I kept hearing an arbitrary tapping noise when I was trying to study alone at night and I could not figure out where it was coming from. After a couple days of hearing these noises, I went to the office down on the first floor and asked Resident Advisor Faith Carpenter about it. Faith followed me up to my room and stood there for a few minutes and of course, there was nothing but complete silence. She thought that it might be just the plumbing, and suggested I record the sound with my phone so a building engineer could identify it. While Faith was helping me inspect my room, I swear I could hear Cierra giggling ever so slightly from behind her closed dorm room door. Of course, immediately after Faith left and I went to bed, there was the sound again, the random tap, tap, tap that was starting to drive me mad. I was seriously considering going to campus health to get my ears checked, because the randomness and my inability to isolate the sound was driving me insane. I asked Cierra about it, and she turned her head down and to her right while shrugging her shoulders and said that maybe it was the hot water running through the pipes. This was clearly a lie, because unbeknownst to me, it turned out weeks earlier Cierra had ordered a tiny rechargeable Bluetooth speaker from China, and she had hidden it in my ceiling tiles. She was then using the voice app on her phone to mess with me by recording the tapping sound and then connecting to the tiny speaker to play it back, and drive me crazy. Luckily for my sanity, Cierra slipped up around the third day of her hijinks when she tried to escalate this prank and take it to the next level.

It was late, just after one in the morning and I was lying in my bed trying to doze off when I heard this faint voice whispering out my name from the darkness. "Bellllllllllaaaaaaaaaa" came this small feminine tinny whisper pouring out into the ether of my darkened room. I knew it was Cierra right away, so it didn't fool or frighten me in the least. I pulled out my phone and started thumbing through my hacker toolkit, which consisted mainly of various scanners for tracking Wi-Fi strength or other wireless signals. I tried my Wi-Fi analyzer first, but there was nothing conclusive, since there was too much interference from all the other girls' hotspots in their respective rooms. Next, I launched my Bluetooth spectrum analyzer, and I was able to find her tiny speaker using the proximity sensor tracking routine. My phone started beeping slowly at first as it locked onto Cierra's planted device, and then the pulses picked up speed until they became one solid tone. Fortunately for me and my investigation, the beds in our rooms are raised, and the ceilings are low. So, I was able to stand on my bed as I lifted up the ceiling tile, pushing it straight into the space above me, and using my phone flashlight, I reached in and grabbed this tiny contraption that had been causing me so much grief. It was a cheap piece of small flat plastic, about the size of a credit card.

While initially, I was impressed with the joke, and the tech behind this tiny device, soon the only thing I had on my mind was getting sweet revenge. So, I flipped this thin speaker over and found the Bluetooth pairing button which I used to hard reset the device and connect it to my own phone. I used my voice app and quietly recorded a special message for my jokester friend. I walked down the hall and over to Cierra's room and flicked the tiny thin speaker under the gap in the bottom of her door with as much force as I could. I opened my phone and went to the voice memos and hit play with an insane smile on my face, giddy with the tremendous satisfaction I was soon to receive.

"Bleep-bloop beeeeootch," my voice playfully whispered as the voice memo started playing back on infinite repeat.

I could hear Cierra giggling wildly while kicking her legs from under her covers.

After I got back to my room and was under my blanket, Cierra texted me and asked if I was mad. I said that I simply couldn't stand her anymore, and I was going to replace her with a cute guy and forget all about her. She told me that no boy was going to love a reject like me, and that my true home was on the Island of Misfit Toys with her. The next day I did get a little serious, and I told Cierra that I didn't appreciate practical jokes like that, and warned her to never pull something like that on me again. She did acknowledge my request solemnly, and said that she understood and gave me her word that any further practical jokes would cease. This time I believed her.

On the longer side of Cierra's pranks, for our Intro to Humanities class, around the start of the fourth week of the semester, Cierra found a tutor that had been a teacher's aide for our professor the year before. Cierra hired this guy and used her feminine wiles to woo him, even though in reality, she in no way shape, manner or form, actually needed a tutor. Somehow, after about three lessons, she had convinced this dude to hand over all his annotations on the final exam, which just happened to be almost word for word the actual test, as our professor was lazy and seldom changed it. I was not there, but I do know that she didn't even have to pay this guy for them. I don't think she paid for the actual tutoring sessions either. I can imagine that this kid just handed them over to her with a big stupid grin on his face, as I have seen Cierra use her girl powers on boys before. Later we joked that he probably thought he was going to get the hookup, which he did not, and this made us chuckle. Despite the humor in the situation, I was slightly annoyed, because I sorta had a nagging feeling about the ethics of her prank. For the first time, I felt the temperature on my Latina temper gauge rise a couple degrees in regards to Cierra's behavior.

For over two months, Cierra didn't do anything with these notes, other than keep them in her figurative back pocket.

"What are you going to do with those? Why did you even do that? Do you know how much trouble you could get in just for having those?" I asked her one time when we had been studying hard for a few hours and I had gotten bored and annoyed.

She replied that she just did it for fun, and that I should try getting out more often. "Don't be jealous because I get what I want," she said to me, with an actual tone of superiority meant to put me down, which she had never done before.

This really pissed me off so I decided to let her know my truth. "I am not jealous, I just think you're being dumb and reckless, Cierra. Grow up!" I spit back at her.

Cierra looked a little shocked that I was actually mad at her, but then she said, "Look, how many times do I have to tell you, girl, you just ain't Delta Pi Zeta material, Babe." She slinked back in the chair, and smiled at me with that muted half smile she liked to use when she said that.

And to this, we both started laughing, as this gag had aged well and was starting to become our best inside joke. Besides, it was nearly impossible to stay mad at her. I let this situation slide, and didn't think about the tutor or these notes much after this. But I was still leery about why she would go through all this trouble, and not use the notes at all, not even for homework.

It did not take long in the grand scheme of things for the answer to come out. As the semester wound down and was approaching its conclusion, Cierra had devised a plan for our upcoming final exam that I was not yet aware of.

"Professor Declan?" Cierra had raised her hand in class and said in a pretty voice, "Is there any way for the final we could make it open-notes?" She batted her eyelashes.

While Professor Declan Byrne was cool with being on a first name basis with his students, he was not cool with this idea, and his answer was no. Cierra actually seemed to anticipate this, as the rejection lit up her eyes and she leaned forward in her seat and pressed on with even more determination. "Professor Declan, please look at all these exhaustive notes I have taken from your lectures throughout the semester though. Surely there could be a reward for listening so dutifully?" Now she exaggerated the batting of her eyelashes.

She held the tutor's actual final exam notes up in front of her, and it freaked me out that she had not even retyped them.

As I fixated on the pages she held up, I felt the air conditioning hit my forehead, and the cool breeze made me realize there was a small amount of perspiration forming near my temple. She briefly looked over at me, her chin now resting in her hand, notes splayed out on her desk while she was dangling a pencil in her mouth, her right lip curling up, smiling ever so slightly at me, exposing her dimple.

Wow, *she is really getting off on this*, I thought to myself.

Again, the answer from the professor was no.

But then Cierra proposed, "Professor, ask me a question from the final right now, and I will bet my entire grade for the semester that I can retrieve it from my notes, and if I can, we will make the exam open-notes."

The entire class let out a collective "Ohhhhhhh" while they pivoted their attention from Cierra laying down the gauntlet like that, towards Professor Declan, being put under a sudden intense spotlight.

Professor Declan was a younger, and good-natured man who quickly rose to the challenge though, so he cracked a half smile and he then proceeded to ask the following question,

"Ms. Fallion, what concept, born in the mid-fifteenth century, allowed artists and architects to draw three-dimensional objects on a two-dimensional plane?"

Cierra pretended to thumb through her notes, and then responded with one finger pointing at a random note on a page that did not contain the actual answer.

"Professor Declan, Brunelleschi's Linear Perspective was invented by Italian architect Filippo Brunelleschi in approximately the year fourteen twenty."

Everything got incredibly still, and for a moment, I thought Professor Byrne was going to approach and inspect Cierra's notes for real. I think she sensed this too, and she anticipated it, so she held up the notes again, as to thrust them forward willingly for inspection. Professor Declan took a final look at Cierra, and I believe in his mind he decided that he had allowed this entire situation to linger too long, and he *blinked*. I was not expecting this to happen so easily, and some part deep down inside of me was disappointed that he did, indeed, yield to Cierra.

In my head I was fantasizing about Cierra getting caught cheating, and I envisioned her being swiftly marched out of the classroom and down to the administrative office, totally busted. But unfortunately, or fortunately, depending on how you look at it, Professor Declan folded like a cheap suit. This disappointed me in another way too, because up to this moment, I had always thought he was kinda cute for a professor, but now in this new light, I couldn't believe I ever thought that and I started feeling sorta icky. *You are supposed to be the professor, and Cierra is just a freshman student. How could you let her win, and where are your cojones,* I thought to myself angrily.

Cierra did not have a photographic memory necessarily, but it was damn near close and it was scary how much data she had at her fingertips when she was using her full brain power. I just sat there feeling inadequate, like a total imposter student when compared to the intellect and deviousness Cierra had just displayed. So once again, Cierra rolled the dice and won, as the test was indeed to be open note, and the world had yet again bent to her will.

Cierra glanced over at me proudly. But I made sure not to give her any indication as to whether I approved or not. I think this annoyed her, and it felt sort of good to push back on Cierra's extra-ness. The thing that just kills me though, is Cierra didn't even need to look at her notes for the answer she provided to Professor Declan. In fact, Cierra didn't even need a tutor because she knew all the answers already, and this whole exercise was again just unnecessary. I know this, because anytime when we were studying for this class, or any class for that matter, Cierra would always give me answers to homework while patting my head and saying, "There you go, Bink-Bink."

Now typically, if any girl even tried to patronize me, (or heaven forbid, insult me), I wouldn't tolerate her behavior for even a moment. But there was something about Cierra, and her soul, and her heart, and her slightly sad gaze that made me feel, just the tiniest bit, sorry for her. Allowing her to pat me on the head was just my way of letting her have her moment, and so that she could have something of her own to be proud of, as silly as that explanation sounds. We were two counterparts that became something greater when together.

Now as for myself, I knew better than to ever even try to cheat. I am the type of person that gets caught immediately trying to do anything that is not completely above board. I know my limitations, and I have lived most of my life on the straight and narrow. This approach had been very beneficial to me and my personality and in fact, my disciplined approach to academics won me the Delta Pi Zeta Sorority "Smarty Pants" award our first semester at PVSU. This award was given to the girl with the highest GPA out of sixty-five girls. I was pretty proud of myself for this achievement, but deep down, I wondered if it was possible that Cierra could have won that award over me, if she really had wanted to? I was not entirely sure, but there would be no way we would ever find out because Cierra just didn't give a rip about things like that. Yes, Cierra was smart, but she did not have the tenacity and the stamina to do the actual work, not the way that I do.

Anyhow, the "Smarty Pants" award was given to me one night at chapter when we were gathered down in the first-floor grand room of our building with our fellow sisters all dutifully in attendance. The award itself was a painted plaque in the shape of a boat oar, and it came with a sash, like those that beauty pageant contestants wear, and it had my name emblazoned across the front of it.

"You're pretty smart for a binky girl," Cierra whispered to me as I sat back down after they had draped my sash over my head and across my right shoulder.

I kindly whispered back in her ear that if there was a prize for chugging Fireball whiskey, she would have won the lifetime achievement award. We giggled quietly. On our way back up to our floor that night, we first stopped at my room. I recall carefully placing the plaque on my makeup table, and hanging the accompanying sash on the corner post of my bed. I had briefly run to the community bathroom, and when I came back, there was Cierra in the center of my room, doing the floss dance with my sash between her legs. Not a huge surprise, and I told her that she could have it after she had contaminated it with her cooties because "My sash touched your butt."

We giggled again.

Truthfully, I was slightly annoyed by this situation, but at the same time, Cierra was having an honest laugh, and so I just let her have this moment. I could tell that she was really proud of me after all, in spite of her best efforts not to make a big fake display of it. Most girls that I have known throughout my brief history on Earth would have probably turned this situation into a contest. They likely would have said something passive aggressive about it, like a backhanded compliment, but not Cierra, she was just using this opportunity to joke around and blow off steam, and I loved that about her. I think Cierra being on the opposite end of that spectrum from me is one of the reasons why we bonded so easily and never really argued. In fact, Cierra relished seeing me sweat with discomfort anytime she was pushing the boundaries of the envelope, like she did with Professor Declan.

Chapter 6

Pookie's Organic Hard Seltzer

It was now October of our freshman year. On the first Sunday night after midterms were over, I was laying on my bed trying to relax by playing a pay to win game on my tablet. The game was called Fruitman Fruit and it was a generic clone of just about every other match three game out there on the app store. I am not even sure why I waste my time on some of these mindless games, but they do help alleviate boredom and this one lets you grind your way to victory without spending any actual real-world money. I furrowed my brow and focused on clearing the current level when Cierra barged into my room with a plastic Red Devil bag filled with ice-cold cans of some kind of booze in her left hand. This was the beginning of October in Phoenix, and the high temperature was still reaching over one hundred degrees daily. So, the heat caused the cans to sweat through the plastic with beads of watery condensation, sorta like red meat under shrink wrap at the grocery store deli counter. I was not certain, but I think I could make out the labels and they said "Pookie's Organic Hard Seltzer." There was no mistaking that whatever was in the bag, it came from the Red Devil convenience store, as I knew what that store's logo looked like by heart, from any distance.

Red Devil was the local convenience store within walking distance of the Greek Leadership Village. Having Red Devil nearby was great, because the male cashiers would rarely card pretty underage girls like us, so it was a frequent stop on just about any given night to pick up party supplies. Typically, we would not drink on Sundays though, as this was our day to rest, reset and recover from a long weekend of partying. Personally, I found it too difficult to show up to classes on a Monday morning with a hangover. So I gave Cierra a WTF look, but she completely ignored me. One thing I had come to know about Cierra is that she would get what she wanted and couldn't be bothered with any weak protests from me to stand in the way of her having a good time. Lately though, her behavior was starting to get just a tiny bit played out and annoying. My dad would often tell me that familiarity breeds contempt, and this made me feel a little strange inside as in that moment, I was really starting to understand what he meant by it. I found myself agreeing with him and for some reason that made me feel old.

"Shotgun this right now comp-u-dork, and don't question my orders, Babe!" Cierra shouted while throwing a sixteen ounce can of "organic" fortified alcohol at me.

I caught the can and just kinda held onto it, and my body language immediately relayed to her that I didn't know what she meant by the term shotgun.

Our roles in this little diorama of two bored college girls quickly shifted, as she rolled her eyes and got a little annoyed at me, but then she quickly pivoted into her, *"teaching Bella to be a degenerate mode."* In my own defense, I am not innocent or naive, but I was also most certainly not as experienced with partying as Cierra was. Also, while I enjoyed the social aspects of drinking, I did not have the blood, meaning typically I was not looking to get drunk. The blood is what my dad would often warn me about when it came to drinking alcohol. He taught me that people that have the blood, when they have even a tiny sip of booze, they would step over their own mother's dead body to get another one and they would not stop until they had their fill. And that certainly was not me. I didn't enjoy the taste of alcohol, and I liked getting only buzzed enough to alter the mood. I was starting to wonder if Cierra had the blood? I was beginning to believe that to be the case, since her behavior lately when it came to partying was starting to come undone. She was no longer hiding it from me, and was now exerting just the tiniest amount of peer pressure on me to take things further.

People can be like inhabitable planets to each other, drifting in their orbit relative to your own celestial body, exerting the force of their gravity over you. While they pass by you, typically any activity that is occurring on the surface of their planet is obscured by a cloudy atmosphere. And while you cannot resolve and see what is going on with them in any meaningful detail as they hover by, you are certainly influenced by their planetary mass regardless. Their gravity pulls and tugs at you, and conversely, you pull and twist on them as well, and most of the time this is just fine, until it is not. Because sometimes the people in your orbit are not planets. They can be stars or even black holes, and most of the time the mystery of who they actually are will not be known until it is too late. You might get burned or you could get sucked in, and that was Cierra for sure, some of it good, some of it bad, all of it tragic.

Cierra dropped the Red Devil bag on my bed, while she reached over the top of her head with crossed arms, and ripped off her shirt, revealing a black Nike sports bra underneath. Cierra's skin on her arms had a tanned, golden color to them, but her torso was definitely more of a pale, milky white hue, not that I was checking her out, because I wasn't, *bleep-bloop*. Although I couldn't help but notice that her breasts were rather large for her small frame, even bigger than mine, and this was slightly annoying to me, even though I am honestly not even sure why it bugged me. Bug me it did though, and I was offended by Cierra barging into my room, undressing, and using terms I did not understand, and I decided I would react in a way that would convey that I simply wasn't having it. The final straw was Cierra throwing her shirt in my general direction.

"Whoa, take it easy MS. BIG BOOBS!" I said emphatically, while dramatically twisting my body away from her, feigning over-the-top theatrical disgust in an attempt to hide my slight discomfort and annoyance with this current situation.

Cierra completely ignored me as she then reached over to me and started pulling off my top, which shocked me and my body language pushed back with all the *what the hell girl* force I could muster.

"What the actual F Cierra?" I had reached my peak annoyed state of being.

She told me to relax, and that she just wanted to show me something, and that she wasn't intending to do anything indecent to me, but she indicated that things might get messy. I sensed that fighting her was futile, so I complied with her wishes yet again, and pulled off my own top and put on an old sports bra from high school cheer. She then grabbed two cans of the ice-cold alcoholic drinks and ran down the hall to the common area showers laughing and telling me to "Hurry the F up, Binky."

I knew right away to bring the can of booze she threw at me, because whatever we were doing, the two cans she was holding were all for her.

When I caught up with her a few moments later, Cierra had stepped into one of the common area showers. She had drawn the curtain back and had placed the cans of seltzer on the pony wall that took up the first quarter of the shower from the left by the shower head. She reached in her back pocket and pulled out a rather large knife. This was no normal Swiss Army style knife, like the innocent red handle one your grandpa carries around. This was a big black tactical knife, incredibly razor sharp on one side of the blade, and jagged and serrated on the other. It reminded me of the one my dad has in his home office that has USMC emblazoned on one side. *What kind of a girl carries a knife like this and is that thing even legal,* I thought to myself. Cierra, of course, was the answer that immediately snapped back at me.

Cierra picked up one of the cans and she pierced the outside bottom edge of it with her knife and twisted the blade so that it made a pea sized hole in it. She then quickly pivoted her entire body underneath the can with the hole in her mouth, so she looked like the Statue of Liberty, but with a can of Pookie's Organic Hard Seltzer in her hand, instead of a torch. With the base of the can firmly seated in her mouth, she popped the top and the booze quickly flowed out until it was empty, in an event that seemed to take less than ten seconds.

She did not spill a drop of those sixteen ounces and at the end, she wiped her mouth and she let out a burp that was so loud, it felt like the walls shook and the paint was going to chip off the ceiling.

"Your turn!" she bellowed her devious instruction at me with a sparkle of danger in her glassy eyes.

Inside, my bravery kicked in and I said F it to myself and I hopped in the small shower stall. And as I did, I quickly realized why Cierra had pulled off our tops and ran down to the showers in the first place. Before we even got started, she knew that I was not really up for this challenge, and most likely I would make a big old mess. She knew me very well, and at that moment, I wasn't sure if that was a good thing or a bad thing.

The only thing I knew for sure is that this evening, a Sunday night, represented a shifting of the paradigm of our relationship. For the first time it made me seriously question if Cierra had a problem that she was hiding from me. For the record, I did not ponder it too much right then, as Cierra and I ended up getting smashed. Over the next hour and a half, we finished all the booze we had in the bag, as well as the booze we had hidden under our bed, and even in the closet, until every container was bone dry. Then once the two of us were all sorted and setting sail properly drunk, we wandered downstairs and over to the frat together to flirt with the cute boys that were always hanging around in front watching TikTok videos on their phones and drinking beer.

Chapter 7

The Warning

I WOKE UP THE next morning with a splitting headache. I was still drunk, which was both a new experience and a new low for me, *yay*. I didn't really want to face the reality that my best friend in the whole world might have a problem, but there it was in the back of my mind first thing when I woke up, cutting through the alcoholic fog from the night before like an uninvited guest. I am not the kind of person that would typically get black out drunk, like I said. This level of intoxication was a first for me, and I was so freaked out by this whole situation that my heart was beating fast, making a headache throb near my temples. In our dorm rooms we have these rack type beds that are raised about four feet off the floor, so that a roller chest of drawers can slide underneath. I opened my eyes fully and laid halfway up in my elevated bed and felt a sort of dread start to bubble up from the pit of my stomach. It was not nausea from too much drinking, but something else, like I had a bad dream and it was creeping in from the corners of my psyche. I decided to take a deep breath, and lay back down and get my bearings.

As I lay still for a moment, a series of memories, like a set of grainy photographs, started to slowly play back in my mind, like a slideshow. The first mental snapshot rippling in my mind's eye was of me and Cierra stumbling over to the frat across the way from our building in the dimly lit GLV courtyard. Next, I could see the two of us pounding some alcoholic drinks, but in my mind, I could not make out the labels, so I had no clue what we were drinking. The only thing I knew about what we had consumed was that the word "strong" kept ringing in my ears. Like I was hearing an echo of someone repeating that word over and over again.

Then, another burst of light in my head as I saw some unfamiliar girls walking up to the front frat courtyard where we were hanging out. All I knew about them was that they were not our sisters, and the impression I got was that they went there bored and looking for trouble. The next memory to light up in my head like a flash from an instant camera, was Cierra extremely drunk. She was forcefully pushing one of the girls, and this girl tripped and hit her head on a low cinderblock wall, cutting her forehead. I said ouch to myself under my breath while wondering, *How bad was that injury? How serious was this?*

Before I could contemplate further, the final memory came roaring into focus. It was the last virtual photograph, and it was of the PVSU campus police walking up to us with their ultra-bright flashlights on, shining them in our faces. Then it came roaring towards me in no uncertain terms, the stinging reality that yes indeed, this was serious. I had enough of this mental photo show, so I decided to get up and start a fishing expedition to see what kind of trouble the two of us were actually in. *Get up, get dressed, get a drink of water, and walk down the hall to Cierra's room,* I told myself as I was gathering up the courage to actually do so.

When I sat up in bed this time, something caught my eye and I looked down on the floor. To my surprise, there was Cierra, rolled up in a ball, using one of my towels as a blanket, laying directly on the hard floor.

"Oh my gosh, can we not do this right now, Binky?" Cierra groaned after sensing that I was now awake, and that I had concern for her on my mind.

This remark made me want to giggle, but it also annoyed me, because we were definitely in some kind of trouble that I had not fully ascertained yet. It made me nauseous to even contemplate laughing when I was so nervous and feeling like hell warmed over. Quite simply, I was not in the mood.

"Hey Cierra, hey Babe, are you ok?" I asked, and then continued with, "I'm worried," in a timid voice. "I can't believe what happened last night, we were lucky to come away from that unscathed." I continued with a sigh of relief that conveyed the fact we were in my dorm room, and not in a campus police holding cell.

"*Did we,* though?" Cierra asked in a voice that signaled that something was definitely wrong.

And this was annoying to me too, because she knew whatever it was, but was trying to tease me by withholding it from me. This time, I didn't play along with her, and instead I sat up in my bed, leaning on my left elbow and I furrowed my brow so that she could see that I was getting angry. Cierra knew better and was an expert at playing games, so she wouldn't look at me and she ignored me. I did my best to project my angry stare in her direction, focusing incredibly hard, attempting to burn an imaginary hole in the left side of her head.

Cierra had rolled over onto her back, and her hands were clasped in front of her stomach tightly. Initially I thought she was just trying to keep her stomach calm, but then, she thrust her hands straight up in the air, revealing two pieces of paper, one in each hand, and I demanded that she hand them over to me for review. The pieces of paper were sorta smoothly crumpled, like they had been in her jean shorts back pocket for some time, and there was also a slight moisture to them, most likely Cierra's nervous palm sweat. Exhibit A, that she had concealed in her left hand, was a yellow carbon copy citation from the PVSU police. It had that funny chemical smell from being fresh, and it was emblazoned with the PVSU Police letterhead across the top, making it look very official and intimidating. Luckily, underneath the letterhead, it had a WARNING checkbox crossed off near the top, directly above where the campus officer had handwritten, Cierra Fallion as the Subject next to Non-Traffic Infraction. There was a notes box below, and inside the box the officer had written in two statute code infractions and spelled out Public Intoxication with Underage Drinking, followed by a blurb that saying she was being released on her own recognizance from being detained, provided she went straight to her dorm room. It closed with language to the effect of as long as there were no further infractions for the next seven days, she was free and clear from any further action on the part of the PVSU Police.

That simple piece of paper really made me feel like crap. Much worse than being hung over. And I was scared too. I have this image in my head of what I am supposed to be, and I thought of my father, and I was immediately worried that even though my mom would understand and comfort me, I would bring shame on him. *Ewww, ick,* I had to stop this feeling, but unfortunately, Cierra was only halfway done with what she had to show me.

Exhibit B, was definitely more problematic, and it was not a carbon copy paper, it was a printed out 8.5 x 11-inch piece of solid white paper that was neatly folded and smelled like a copier machine. This piece of paper had the official letterhead of the Delta Pi Zeta Sorority across the top, and it was labeled an official Misconduct Report that was signed by the DPZ Resident Advisor, Faith Carpenter. It had the word Intoxication circled near the header. I nervously scanned it, hoping somehow the word Warning would be listed somewhere, but it was not, and this gave my stomach that awful sinking feeling one gets when things get real. This report listed Cierra's name, her Student ID, her room number and it said that the sorority had a zero-tolerance policy for drugs and alcohol abuse, and that this served as Cierra's only warning and the next incident would be expulsion from the chapter and her dorm room. *Phew!* A warning was there after all. This made me feel a little relieved as out of the two pieces of paper, this one certainly had more gravity to it. Not that I think Cierra gave a rat's ass about being in trouble with the sorority, but I did get the feeling that the idea of being kicked out of her dorm room definitely had her paying attention in a way I hadn't seen from her before. The report made a point to solidify and expand upon the earlier warning, saying the next violation, no time period specified, would result in her being called before the Delta Pi Zeta Disciplinary Committee, and that she would be removed from the sorority and evicted from the dormitory altogether. Not could be. Would be.

I started to feel sick to my stomach, and then I worried that perhaps somewhere on my person was my own set of white and yellow chemically smelling carbon copy papers ruining my life. I was thinking about my parents and the excuses for my poor behavior that I could use with them as I started to pat myself down and look around the room.

"Relax Babe, you didn't get in trouble, and your powers of persuasion are the only reason I was not actually arrested," she reassured me.

I squinted my eyes and thought, How does she remember all this so clearly, and I cannot, even though she is the one that got in trouble? That makes zero sense. Clearly Cierra's alcohol tolerance had to have something to do with this, which made me worry about my friend even more. Cierra elaborated further, telling me that after the police had arrived, I had launched into a sort of mini public defender mode, letting everyone know that Cierra was such a good person and how this had never happened before and to please show mercy for what was really just a big misunderstanding. She said that at first my pleas had fallen on deaf ears, until I broke out my hidden secret weapon, the water works. She was laughing quietly while relaying that my tears were so genuine and heartfelt, that it made the whole situation last night embarrassing, and everyone got uncomfortable and then just tried to disperse as quickly as possible.

Almost everyone, with the exception of RA Faith Carpenter, had been moved by my theatrical tears. In fact, she did not have to file a report on this situation at all, but she did it anyway, just to mess with us.

"But you did save me from imprisonment Babe, and for that I am grateful," she said in a somber voice. "I shouldn't have pushed that girl, I stepped over the line, and now I have to deal with that." A moment of honest clarity and reflection.

To which, we both laid there halfway upright on our elbows quietly contemplating everything that had just transpired. I think Cierra grew tired feeling the lingering tension in the room, because she then stood straight up, let out a loud burp that was not ladylike in the least, and then yelled as loudly as she could, "F you Faith Carpenter, ya stupid bitch!"

I began to feel energized and hopeful from having my earlier heroics brought to my attention. It occurred to me that perhaps it was time to clean up our act, and that I was going to drag my friend along with me for the ride. So I gathered my courage and said, "Rather than drinking tonight, like I know you are going to want to, how about we go to the gym instead? Right after I said that, I kinda wished I hadn't, as my suggestion drew an immediate response that caught me off guard, even by my crazy friend's standards.

"Bye Binky!" Cierra said in equal parts mocking and jovial, as she quickly pivoted 180 degrees from me, and then motioned that she would be traipsing off to her own room. Her face had a look of literal disgust that I cannot even properly articulate, it was that bad and she was that mad.

She made a point to forcefully slam my door on her way out and then seconds later, slam her own door even harder.

I thought about this whole ordeal for a few moments and then decided that I was not going to let this one slide, and I quietly snuck down the hallway to her room. I was going to gently knock on the door and call out her name, but then for some unknown reason, I instead pressed my ear against her door and what I heard shocked me and made me sad. Even though I could tell she was doing her best to be discreet, I heard Cierra retching into her dorm room trash can. I felt a deep foreboding. It shouldn't have had this impact on me though, because what, some young college kid being sick from a night of partying, no big deal, right? But there was something more serious, something ominous about this whole situation, that made me feel like I might throw up as well.

I sat down on the floor there in front of her room, with my back against her door. I closed my eyes and started to try to come up with a way to get my friend to reconsider her risky behavior. But all I could envision was Cierra as a little girl, and how the little girl version of my friend might have behaved in this situation. Something told me that she had most likely been a smaller, slightly more innocent version of how she acts today, but in many ways, probably exactly the same. I shook my head in frustration as I quickly realized that it was to be no easy task to get Cierra to alter her behavior in any meaningful way. *She was just born like this,* my inner voice conceded.

"We come into the world who we are, our personalities are already fully formed, even when we are only an hour old," my dad would often tell me.

I did not want to believe that, but then the other thing my dad would always say came into my mind, "People rarely change unless it is for the worse." He loves to say that to me any chance he gets because he knows we share the same sarcastic and morose sense of humor.

I shook those images from my mind and tried to focus on the issue at hand. *People can change for the better,* I told myself, I just had to believe that, and I was not going to allow my friend to get worse. I swore to myself that I would get a handle on this drinking situation, her BS behavior, and get things to improve. Then I got up and went back to my room without saying anything to Cierra.

Chapter 8

Student Bodies in Motion Move in Weekend!

I LAID DOWN ON my bed and closed my eyes, trying to focus on everything that had happened with the alcohol incident. More importantly, I wanted to piece together how I'd ended up in this unfamiliar territory in the first place. I grew up surrounded by all kinds of structure, but when I arrived at PVSU, I got a small taste of freedom. But now, it felt like I was getting simply too much freedom. *Is that even a thing?*

Strangely enough, when I concentrated, I found my focus centered on Faith Carpenter, like I had no choice in the matter. I guess I thought of her now because I remembered that things were not always contentious between the three of us like the way things were now.

It was move-in weekend at the sororities in late August, earlier this semester. There was a long-established move in procedure that PVSU followed to the letter. There is no street access leading up to the Greek Leadership Village, however, there is a very wide sidewalk that stretches out to a spillway about a quarter of a mile away from the buildings to the west. This gap can serve as a driveway that cars can pull up onto and get close to the buildings. In the packet of information Cierra and I received after being accepted to

DPZ, there was a yellow information sheet that had all of these instructions on how to move into the dorms, and what to expect on, "Student Bodies in Motion Move in Weekend." We were instructed to drive our loaded-up vehicles, along College Avenue to the spillway driveway, and form a line on the western side of the Greek Leadership Village courtyard. The iron gates to the GLV courtyard were propped open, and there were large pieces of felt-covered plywood with interlocked hinges that were placed over the stairs. This was done so that carts could easily and safely be rolled across them. Then several 2nd and 3rd year students would come up and down those makeshift ramps with big yellow canvas lined carts to grab your stuff, while they wrote your names and room numbers on clipboards that were attached to the cart on a pole like a flag. You were to unload belongings into these carts, and the upperclassmen would then haul the items up to your respective rooms. I say upperclassmen specifically, because interestingly enough, most of the volunteer "*helpers*" happened to be buff burly boys that seemed awfully interested in helping the pretty girls exclusively.

Early morning move in weekend was on a Saturday, and miraculously my parents and I managed to fit almost everything that I was planning on taking to the dorms into our oversized Lexus SUV. My dad had to squish himself behind the steering wheel, because his seat had to be moved all the way forward, but from what I could tell, he was happy to do this, if it meant less trips. Part of me was slightly offended as I pondered for a minute that perhaps my father was a little too happy about this and was excited to be getting rid of me. I put this thought to the side as my mother and I got into my Honda, and we formed a tiny convoy, trailing my father in the Lexus as we drove towards campus. As we pulled up to the PVSU campus spillway and my dad got in line, my mother dropped me off while she went to find a place to park my Honda. So, I walked along the outside of my parents' SUV as we waited for our turn to unload, which did not take too long as things were moving surprisingly fast.

Out of nowhere, a young muscle-bound boy with shoulder length brown hair, tan skin and hazel eyes bounded up the ramp headed in our general direction. Before I even got a really good look at him, I already knew who it was. It was the boy from the PVSU Library, the kid holding the programming book. He came in hot, his skin flush and shimmering, and made a straight line towards me like a laser. I took one look at him and our eyes briefly locked and it seemed like that moment had lasted much longer than the actual two seconds that it was. I was sorta flattered, because the look in his eyes said that he recognized me too, and was all perky and suddenly attentive towards me. I am not usually overly impressed by good looks or muscles, but this boy had it all together, that was for sure. He was like a complete unit, he had a perfect body, hair, beautiful eyes and his aura had a naturally kind disposition.

I was standing there thinking about this boy, and nothing else but him, when it felt like someone was looking at me, like my left ear was burning from someone else's stare. I turned my head and realized that it was my dad. He had taken one look at this boy, one look at me, and was now standing there with a sort of half grimace. His mouth was slightly ajar, and his face carried the tired look of cynical disapproval common among fifty-year-old men. For a moment I tried to picture what my good old Dad would have been like as a young man. Even though I tried as hard as I could, I just could not resolve it in my mind's eye. The image remains as he is now: a tough as hell, slightly jaded, but sweet mountain of a man, towering over me, grounding me to reality, and keeping all the cute boys at bay.

I didn't want to let this moment pass me by, so I ignored my dad and quickly said, "Hi" to the boy. In one fluid motion, he shook his hair back, wiped the sweat from his palm on the side of his purple PVSU tank top and then he daintily grasped and kissed the top of my hand, just like a gentleman would do in the very old black and white movies my parents like to watch. My jaded attitude towards boys told me that this suave masculine display was just a tad too rehearsed and slick for my liking if I am being honest, but I was bored and feeling brave, so I just decided to play along.

"Hi there, my name is Bryce Hemmet," the tan boy (*that I had already nicknamed Gunther in my mind*) said to me earnestly as he was still holding my hand gently.

He was slowly folding my hand into his, like he wasn't going to let go and maybe pull me in a little closer. At this point I had enough, like a cat that was petted the same direction one too many times, so I shook my hand forcefully back and forth and then pulled it away. I flashed a furrowed brow at Bryce, but he didn't even notice my look of slightly miffed disapproval.

As I was standing there pondering my next move, I then felt another set of eyes looking at me, or at least towards my general direction. I peered off to my left expecting to see my dad again, but instead there was a plain but pretty slender girl standing by the GLV courtyard gateway about thirty feet away from me. She had straight long brown hair with bangs, slightly narrow pretty blue eyes and an intense focus on her face. I thought I had cornered the market on nerdy-pretty girls, but this chick had me beat, hands down, though she tilted more towards the nerd side of the equation honestly. For a moment I thought she might be a professor or some other administrative staff member, but then I saw she had a student ID on a lanyard around her neck. She stood with half her body obscured behind a red cinder block pillar that was part of the GLV gates, leaning into it to support her body, and her eyes were fixated on something in my general area. Her hands were clasped in front of her, with her right thumb caressing her left thumb, in a gently rocking self-soothing motion that looked like a long-established habit. She managed to do this, even though she was holding a clipboard and a large oversized metal ring of keys that looked heavier than a boat anchor in one of her hands.

I made a point to stamp my foot on the ground to see if I could get her attention, but she was too far away from me and even if she had heard the noise I made, she was oblivious to me. Then I looked over at Bryce, and put two and two together, and I figured out that clearly this girl knew who he was and she was enthralled by him. I did not care about this sudden competition, because at that moment, I was honestly just amused by this whole situation.

My father, Bryce, and I quickly completed the process of loading up my cart, and Bryce went tearing off up and then back down the ramps. It was like he was taking advantage of this situation to get a workout in, or maybe he liked to be glistening with sweat when he would come back down the plywood covered stairs to greet new pretty girls. Regardless, at this point my mother had just walked up and rejoined us, but I was eager to get to the bottom of this new situation. So, I quickly turned around and said goodbye to my parents with reassurances that I would "be safe" and "call them later" as I firmly pressed them into the direction of getting back into their SUV and driving away, quickly.

As I walked up to the GLV courtyard gates with my parents disappearing into the horizon, the slender, nerdy but pretty girl had rotated her body ninety degrees, in Bryce's direction, and now faced away from me.

I made a point to approach her with a stealthy intention, and as I got within five feet of her I tersely and loudly blurted out a "Hey" as I extended my hand towards her.

This time she heard me, and quickly came back down to Earth with her mouth slightly ajar. Her eyes were off in outer space, and she looked equal parts happy, confused and annoyed.

"Hi, my name is Bella," I said in a jovial tone that was laced with manufactured cheer.

This girl jutted out her hand clumsily with a stiff motion and somehow our two hands awkwardly met. Once they were in union, she seemed super relieved, while inside I was put off as her hand was warm but kinda moist with nervous perspiration.

"Hi, I'm Faith," she said while fiercely shaking my hand in hers. Her voice had cracked slightly when she introduced herself, so she took a second stab at it, this time with an even more official tenor. "I am the Resident Advisor for Delta Pi Zeta, Faith Carpenter," she told me awkwardly, in a manner that sounded like what I imagine a first-year elementary school librarian would sound like. I got a good look at her ID on her lanyard, and it said that she was a Graduate Student. This struck me as odd, as I felt she looked younger than me.

"Why were you staring at Bryce?" I asked her in a playful but matter of fact tone.

Faith got incredibly serious, furrowing her brow with her lower lip jutting out while nervously wagging her head like the way a puppy wags its tail. She denied even knowing who he was, but she wasn't fooling me. I could sense from her body language, her jealousy over me simply uttering his name. This let me know that she clearly knew who Bryce was and she obviously liked him because when I said his name, her chest caved inwards ever so slightly, like she was trying to protect or keep something hidden from me.

"I was merely observing the move in process to ensure there were no issues. It's part of my duties as Resident Advisor for Delta Pi Zeta." Her tone was a little too serious while she jutted her chin up and to the right in a sign that she had regained her composure. Then rather suddenly and robotically, her arms dropped completely limp to her sides, and there was her thumb again, but this time it was gently caressing the seam on the right leg of her denim jeans.

I made a point to look down at her thumb, and then our eyes met, and she said, "You are up on the third floor, right this way." She quickly turned about in a fashion that let me know she expected me to follow her without any questions or delays.

"How do you know I am on the third floor?"

"Because I assigned your room to you, and we put all the newbies up on that floor, dear."

She had briefly put me in my place and I decided to just let this slide.

Faith showed me up to my room while pointing out all of the features of the dorm building on our way up like what one might expect from a seasoned New York City tour guide. It was actually pretty cool to get all this inside information from Faith, and clearly, she loved her job and she was quite good at it too. I can recognize skill and talent, and Faith was obviously knowledgeable about rules, policies and procedures and letting you know all about them. She turned out to be bright and friendly with a nearly bubbly personality and she did make me feel comfortable, like I could trust her, but not quite. There was something holding me back from going all the way to that place with her.

We got up to the third floor via the elevator, and we went down the hall towards the rooms, when I noticed something slightly out of place. There, parked astray in the hallway, was the yellow canvas cart with my name on it, but Bryce was nowhere to be found. Faith and I made our way around the cart, and she reached towards her master key ring, and she counted them out until she got the key for my room. She made a motion like she was going to hand me the key, but then she straightened her arm fully, put the key into the lock and opened my room door while beckoning like a proud hotel bellboy that this was the spot. We were moving forward like we were going to step into the room, but then we simultaneously heard some muffled laughter and then a deep cute boy voice saying something I couldn't quite make out coming from down the hall. In my mind's eye, I could see what was about to happen. Clearly Cierra had arrived before us and was already in her room with an uninvited guest of the male persuasion that would soon be revealed. Judging by my unattended cart, I knew exactly which boy was about to make an appearance.

As Faith and I stood out there in the hallway trying to figure out where the commotion was coming from, the door to Cierra's room in the middle of the hallway suddenly burst open. She exited her room all flush with laughter, dragging Bryce out the door with her. Surely not too much had happened in such a short amount of time between them, but enough did happen that when I turned to look at Faith, she had gone flush too, but her face quickly turned sickly with anger.

Faith pursed her lips as her arms went limp yet again down to her sides. This time though, when I looked, Faith was not caressing anything with her thumb like before, and instead her whole right hand was balled up tight, in a proper boxing fist. I sensed this undertow of aggression, and clearly Cierra did too, because Cierra pushed Bryce forcefully towards the elevator, motioning for him to leave. Bryce started pointing at my yellow moving cart and was about to say something in protest, but Cierra covered his mouth with her hand and gave him a friendly but firm shove. She tilted her head slightly to the left as Bryce complied and started slinking away, giving her ample opportunity to look at his cute posterior.

Cierra turned around and walked right over to Faith and started stroking her shoulder gently, getting all up in her personal space. "Hey Faith, I think that boy is into you," Cierra whispered to her in her left ear, so that only the three of us would hear it as Bryce was already disappearing from view.

I wasn't sure if Cierra was being genuine, but I couldn't tell otherwise either.

I was somewhat offended that Bryce left, and I was annoyed with Cierra too as I looked at my full yellow moving cart that was still by my door, overflowing with my unloaded personal items. I quickly got over it though, as Cierra said something that fully diverted my attention.

"Bryce is going to help us get fake IDs!" Cierra exclaimed proudly with a matter-of-fact tone, like all of us had already agreed to this.

My mind was racing at this taboo thought that was so wrong and so right at the same time to the point that I was nearly drooling.

"Oh, hell to the naw!" Faith immediately protested, completely dropping the prim and proper routine she had perfected that had been on display previously.

"Oh yeah?" Cierra pressed up against Faith. "Bryce says that he will take us to all the bars out on College Avenue once we have them, and by us, I think he means you, Faith." She crinkled up her nose playfully while she poked Faith firmly in the center of her chest.

I saw the look on Faith's face as the gears in her head were now turning. I knew that look, because I had recently made it myself. Faith was acquiescing, letting Cierra's good luck rub off on her. Again, I looked at her lanyard, and somehow, Faith was a graduate student here that had not yet turned twenty-one. I did find out later that Faith showed up to PVSU with 120 credits of AP classwork and was already classified a Junior at age seventeen.

This entire turn of events hung in the air briefly as we all stood there in silence looking at one another to get clues for how we should react. Then, out of nowhere the three of us all locked arms, while we jumped up and down chanting "BRYCE! BRYCE! BRYCE!" as loud as we could. This moment was similar to other earlier events with Cierra in that I felt like I didn't even have a say in what was happening. I was more watching us jump up and down rather than the one actually doing the jumping.

Briefly frozen in time, standing in that hallway, I pictured the three of us girls becoming the best of friends. But again, something crept into the corners of my mind, not allowing me to trust Faith one hundred percent. I found it strange that she was a graduate student, a resident advisor, and yet she was all too eager to make friends with us. Not to mention, there was now cute stud boy Bryce, and in the back of my mind I was already plotting to trap him and keep him all to myself, away from these other girls whom I hardly knew.

A few weeks after the fake ID proposition from Bryce, we did follow through with our part, providing our headshot pictures and money to him. It did not take all that long for him to produce the fake IDs, and we used them extensively over the next couple of weeks to hit all of the bars on College Avenue on a nearly nightly basis. At first, we went to the bars exclusively with Bryce, and it was interesting to me that even though he enabled our delinquency, he was always there to keep a watchful eye on us. Like he was a good guy, but for real. In time, we got braver and started going without Bryce.

It would just be the three of us, me and Cierra with Faith tagging along as a third wheel. No matter how many times I whipped out that fake ID, each time it provided me with such a rush of adrenalin that never grew old.

Things were going great until one night when we decided to go to a pool hall just off of Miller Street, one block west of our normal hang out spots on College Avenue.

It started earlier when Faith popped into my room with an announcement. "Hey babes, Cinder Moon is playing at Pinkie's tonight."

"What is a Cinder Moon?" Cierra asked genuinely.

Faith seemed a little bummed that we did not know what she was talking about, but she then shifted gears to giddy excitement as she explained that Cinder Moon was an indie band from Mesa, Arizona, that she was absolutely shook with. Secretly inside, I was sorta impressed to see this other side of Faith. She was turning out to be slightly more interesting than initially met the eye.

"Check out Tom, I have been following him on Insta since day dot." Faith unlocked her phone, pulled up Insta, and held it out for inspection. She then leaned back and gave herself a semi-self-hug.

"Day what?" I asked genuinely.

"Since the beginning when I first heard him play a guitar solo, I knew he was my number one!" She uncurled her arms so she could point at Tom.

Cierra had enough of this entire conversation, and she reached over and yanked Faith's phone out of her hand, causing Faith to raise her eyebrows as high as they could go to show her extreme annoyance.

"Wait, 'ArizonaFireFly480,' Who the hell is that, is that *you* Faith?" Cierra's lips twitched as she fought to keep a straight face, the amusement in her voice barely concealed.

"Well, I do like his long brown hair and blue eyes," I said after catching Faith's phone, which Cierra had chucked at me while playing hot potato. I thought he looked a little like Bryce, but less jock and more rocker. I kept that thought to myself.

"Yeah, he is a'ight, but I have seen much better," Cierra joked.

Once this excitement had passed, Faith absolutely insisted that we all go to see them play and so we reluctantly agreed so she would quit bugging.

I knew right away when we entered the Pinkie's Poolhall entryway, that this was a completely different scene. This place was not like the modern, fresh, hip and fun bars on College Avenue. It reeked of sweat and pee and felt all dark, dusty and run down. I spun 180 degrees in reverse as if to make my exit, but when I turned around, there was Faith looking up at me so pathetic, with big sad doe eyes and a pouting lip. I thought to myself, *if this is so important to you, why are you hiding behind my skirt?* But I turned back around again, swallowed hard, and faced the bouncer at the door who was fat, bald and looked like a wannabe biker. Maybe he was a for real biker, because upon closer inspection, he looked like a real hothead dick, and when he took my ID, he grabbed it forcefully, not to just go through the motions, but to actually inspect it.

I swallowed hard again, and put my hand on the front of my chest to brace myself because my woman's intuition immediately told me by the way he grabbed my fake ID that something bad was about to happen. A small part of me also started to wonder if this was somehow racially motivated. It did not happen often to me in Arizona, but every once in a while I would find myself in situations where I was the only minority and I felt like I was sticking out like a sore thumb. I try to ignore it when it happens, but honestly, it can feel lonely and isolating.I convinced myself that his motivations for a closer inspection didn't matter—I was stuck now. My inner voice gave me some courage, reminding me how my dad always says that the quickest way through any tough situation is straight through it.

The bouncer started his examination by flashing a blacklight flashlight over the surface of my fake driver's license, which revealed a holographic seal, making it look super official and authentic. I thought this might do the trick, but instead, biker dick bouncer man just pursed his lips and let out a dissatisfied "Humph." He moved on to the next step of his inspection and folded my fake ID slightly between his thumb and index finger. "This cardstock is too thin to be a real New Mexico Driver's License, *Shannon Hilliard.*"

The way my brain works, I was quickly offended by his actions. Yes, my ID was indeed fake, but how dare he do this to me. To me? Really? Being offended distracted me slightly from my earlier feelings of fear. I felt brave, and all of a sudden I was not intimidated by him, so I told him bluntly to give me back my ID.

"Yeah, give her back her ID dude!" Cierra spit at him, and when I looked in her direction, I noticed her right cheek dimple was popping out next to her slightly curled lip.

I had gone from initially being really nervous, to now being fully emboldened and enjoying myself, rebelling and telling this big jerk to shove it. Being backed up by my sister Cierra I felt like my presence had been puffed up to three or four times my actual physical size. However, in our overenthusiastic confrontation with bald fake biker bouncer man, neither of us had noticed that Faith had gone into a full-blown panic attack right next to us. She dropped her fake California ID on the ground and ran like a crazy person out the door with her arms flailing all over the place. All of the air completely escaped our balloon, and he seized this moment to reach down and pick up Faith's fake driver's license. He then sneered at us, "Well, your friend's reaction there tells the truth, the whole truth, and nothing but the truth, now don't it, ladies?" as he smugly folded his arms, thoroughly happy with himself for a job well done.

He looked at Cierra. "Hand over your fakey too blondie, and both of you leave peacefully like your psycho friend earlier, or else I am calling the cops."

Cierra looked enraged, but she had no choice but to comply, and we suddenly realized that perhaps the good times had come to an end. As she was handing over her fake ID, the door to Pinkie's suddenly swung open quite dramatically, as some sort of entourage was making its presence known in an over-the-top grand entrance into the building. At first, before I figured out what was going on, I thought it was Faith coming to her senses and quickly making her way back to help her sisters out with this jerk of a bouncer, after realizing that she had been a coward by running away. Then, I slowly realized who was walking through the door, and I looked over at Cierra to gauge her reaction, but she was already making a beeline for the people who had just entered. She was always at least one step ahead of me, like playing chess against a computer.

"Tom, hey it's me, ArizonaFireFly!" Cierra yelled at the handsome slender man in all black with long brown hair and piercing blue eyes.

He looked equally surprised and pleased at the same time, as Cierra wrapped her arms around him. It was Tom, the guitarist for Cinder Moon, the band that Faith had dragged us over here to see. Clearly, he did not know who Cierra was, and she realized this, so she continued pressing her body on him in a slightly suggestive way to keep this ruse going.

"It's me, Faith, I follow you on Insta, and I can't wait to watch you play and party with you after." Now she really pressed up against Tom, going for broke.

And believe me, Tom was now all but too receptive to this new situation, since Cierra had gotten all dolled up, and she looked so cute and dangerous. Of course, Cierra looked nothing like Faith Carpenter, and you would think that would matter, but for Tom, he either hadn't ever looked at Faith's profile, he didn't remember, or he did not care. He was grinning from ear to ear and his eyes were bright and open.

"These girls are with you Tom?" the hothead wannabe biker bouncer asked with extreme annoyance, but also with a hint of subservience, like an employee talking with their boss.

"Yes, they are, *Cookies*. Is that going to be an issue?"

"Why didn't you guys say that in the first place?" he asked, as he looked first at Cierra, then me, and finished by looking all around for Faith, who had never come back.

"Just because, *Cookies*," Cierra slinked up to the bouncer, emphasizing his nickname, while she plucked all three of our fake IDs out of his hand.

Because of Cierra's amazing luck, quick thinking and our steady perseverance, we were then able to make our way into the club without any further hindrance. We didn't even pay the cover charge. Cierra and I looked at each other, and there was an unspoken understanding. This whole chain of events, while very cool and amazing, still left one major issue that was unresolved. Faith had bailed on us, and that just was not going to be allowed to stand. In the end, we made it through two songs by Cinder Moon, and then we had had enough. We walked back to the dorms, talking about how bad this band was, and how pissed we were with Faith Carpenter.

And with that, our friendship with Resident Advisor, Faith Carpenter, ended that night. Sure, we could have called her and beckoned her back, but that was not the point. This was a test of her friendship, and Faith had failed us miserably. It has been my experience that unfortunately, once girls disappoint one another, the resentment is baked right in, and it is oh so difficult to come back from that place. Sorry Faith, but it is an unwritten rule of the oft-times-petty-bitches: one strike and you are out. In an act of mercy, we did not mention this chance encounter with Tom and the band to Faith, but that meant that we also could not give her back her fake ID either.

Chapter 9

Jump Town

THAT NIGHT, WHEN I got back to my room I laid down on my bed and threw on my headphones so I could unwind with some familiar and calming music. To my surprise, the first song in the mix however, was "How Soon Is Now" by The Smiths. Sometimes my dad likes to log into my music over the Internet and plant random songs that he finds relevant in my playlists, which I appreciate, but can find annoying. It wasn't a bad song I guess, but it definitely wasn't my style and it sounded so old to me. However, the words to the song did strike a chord in my mind that night, no pun intended.

At first, the lyrics Morrissey sang reminded me of the situation caused by the hot head bouncer we ran into at the club a few hours earlier who had the audacity to try and confiscate my fake ID. But no, that wasn't what I was thinking of. I pushed my head back into my pillow and really forced myself to think, to recall and remember. Then it hit me and suddenly my entire brain was filled with a memory from when I was eleven years old.

In sixth grade, my homeroom teacher was Mrs. Pugh, a kind older woman who was beginning to lose her hearing. She was too proud to admit it, though, and did quirky things to cover it up. Sometimes, she'd have us bring in books—even comic books—and let us read them quietly for the whole period while she "graded papers." Mrs. Pugh had a warm, pleasant personality, and I really enjoyed her class. She made things fun, partly because she couldn't always hear what us young troublemakers were up to during study time. I also suspect she might have been a bit burned out and sometimes used her hearing loss to her advantage, creating a relaxed, free-spirited atmosphere we all loved. I was at just the right age to appreciate that little bit of freedom. Sitting across from me was a boy from my neighborhood named Ian Harris. He was slightly taller than me and had blonde hair and blue eyes. I'd seen him around before, but something about being in Mrs. Pugh's class together made me notice him differently—or maybe I just hadn't been ready to see him that way before. And even though he sat next to me in class, I still didn't pay much attention to him until one day, during D.E.A.R. hour (Drop Everything and Read), he leaned over his desk toward me and broke the ice.

"Hey, Bella. Do you like video games?" he asked.

"Yeah, sure. I like Mario. I play Wii with my dad all the time," I replied.

"Well, do you like Pokémon?" he asked again, suddenly excited, encouraged by my answer.

"Yeah, sure I do," I said, smiling.

He squinted at me suspiciously, his tone growing slightly testy. "Oh really? What is your favorite water type?"

"I love un-evolved Totodile," I responded proudly, because it was true.

Ian got so excited by my responses that he asked me if I wanted to walk home with him so I could see his collection, and maybe we could find things to trade. In truth, I think he was starting to get interested in girls and he devised a strategy to get to know one he liked, namely me. I did end up walking home with him after school that day, and over time we began trading more than just Pokémon. We exchanged phone numbers and we started off a friendship that would last exactly until the first semester of my freshman year of high school. We were more than friends over those three or so years, we kissed several times and held hands walking home from school fairly consistently. He never asked me to be his girlfriend, and that was just fine with me. We just had a cool little kinship going on that was fun and interesting for both of us. I did find it interesting that any time Ian would try to express his feelings towards me physically, if I would resist, even a tiny bit, he would back off, a little too quickly. Something did seem a little off about this, as I recall the way other boys I interacted with had more of a hunter or predator nature about them, that was lacking in Ian.

About a month before the end of 8th grade, shortly before my first panic attack, I walked to the Circle K with Ian. We got sodas and candy, then sat out there on the curb talking and drinking and eating sugar and having a grand old time. We had done this several times, nothing out of the ordinary and quite common for us. However, this day was different, and it would represent my first taste of the petty bitchiness and mean spiritedness that some girls like to dispense for no apparent reason. As we were laughing about something random, I suddenly felt a burning sensation, like someone was staring at me from a distance. I looked over at the gas pumps ten feet to the east of where we were sitting on the curb, and there was Samantha Elsher, in the front seat of her mother's oversized black Mercedes SUV. This wasn't the low-end model, believe me, and there was her dad pumping gas while everyone else in the SUV was surfing on their phones. But not Samantha, oh no, she was staring right at me and Ian with a scowl on her face. Just the meanest, stuck-up little bitch face you could imagine. I am pretty certain she even took a picture of us on her phone, and she gave me a devious little smile as they drove off. I tried not to dwell on the situation, but whenever I did, my stomach would drop, leaving me with the unsettling feeling of hanging out there in the wind—unresolved and twisting. That's how intimidated and nervous she made me feel.

By the time my freshman year of high school started a couple months later, Ian and I had already started drifting apart. I think some of it was due to word of my panic disorder spreading like wildfire, tainting everything around me, but some of it was also purely organic. Perhaps out of desperation, and because I valued our friendship, one day I determined that I would salvage what I could of my relationship with Ian. I was not going to go down without a fight, so I decided to force the issue. Out of the blue, and with nerves of steel that I didn't even know I had, I bluntly asked Ian if he wanted to be my boyfriend, to which he said that he definitely did. After we made it official, there were a few weeks where we were kissing and heavy petting and holding hands and it was really enjoyable. We never said, "I love you" to each other or had sex or anything like that, but it certainly was serious, and looking back, I think Ian was the first boy that I ever loved. Again, we would push things physically, but Ian was always just reacting to my actions, not the other way around, which again struck me as off.

At the same time that Ian and I were heating up, out of nowhere, Samantha reintroduced herself into my life and feigned being my friend. I knew it wasn't real, but I had no choice in the matter, since she was just forcing the situation and all I could do was react. At this point I won't even mention Megan, although she was directly involved. She was just a high-strung little lapdog for Samantha and of no real consequence. The three of us started hanging out more frequently, particularly after school. At that point in my life, I was all too willing to lie to myself and be their friend, because damn, being a freshman was hard enough and it was just easier to adjust to having them in my life than to fight with them.

A few miles from our school, there was this trampoline center called Jump Town where we all used to hang out after classes. On one Friday in particular, Samantha, Megan and I ended up at Jump Town, and I recall that Samantha kept looking all around her. I asked her what was up and she told me she kept thinking she had misplaced her phone or some BS like that. I definitely knew something was going on beyond us just hanging out, but I was stuck there wondering what to do about it. As I was gathering the courage to make up an excuse and leave, out of nowhere, in came Ian. I knew right away that this entire event had been premeditated, as Ian looked at me with a quizzical look on his face when our eyes met. I looked over at Samantha, and there she was looking like a starving and rabid coyote about to score a meal.

Just like that, Samantha jumped up, ran towards Ian where there were also several other teenagers standing around, and she loudly announced, "Hello everyone! This is Ian. And see that freak over there? That's Bella! She's Ian's beard!"

I had no clue what any of that meant, outside of her calling me a freak, which did piss me off. But everyone else clearly knew exactly what Samantha meant, and they all started laughing hysterically while pointing at Ian and me. Ian apparently knew what Samantha meant too, and he looked over at me with a deeply hurt expression. All I could do was stare at him helplessly as I had zero clue as to what was happening. Ian turned his gaze towards Samantha and roundly told her to F off, to which she started laughing even more hysterically while he turned around and left the building.

I stood up quickly to chase after him, but right then, Samantha and Megan grabbed me and held me back. They pretended that they were going to tickle me, but they were both strong and had no intention of letting me catch Ian. By the time I did manage to escape them and give chase out into the parking lot, Ian was already long gone. Thinking back, I am not entirely sure if Ian was gay, and I was certainly no one's beard, and none of that matters even if it were true. But the damage was done, and it was devastating for him and me, and those two bitches had harmed us both equally, effectively ending my friendship with Ian.

Ian never gave me the opportunity to explain. He blamed me directly for that day, as Samantha and Megan had made it look like I had asked him to come to Jump Town by texting him from my spoofed email address. Honestly though, I think Ian was probably done with me anyway and it was an easy way to get rid of me and my panic disorder in one clean sweep. Ultimately, none of this mattered, since Ian and his entire family ended up moving to Wyoming later that year and I never saw him again.

That day after the situation at Jump Town, I swore to myself that I would eventually get even with these two mean girls. I imagined ripping them limb from limb or running over them with my car, that's how deeply hurt and angry I was. The thing is, I did not know at that moment, but those two were not even close to being done, and they continuously found ways to mess with me throughout the start of my freshman year. Months of this abuse went on, with little comments, laughing, nasty text messages and weird social media posts aimed at ridiculing me and my panic disorder.

That winter, over Christmas break, Megan had a bad accident while skiing in Colorado with her family that left her with a broken leg and six months of long recovery. This event was fortunate timing for me, as the three of us naturally all sort of drifted apart and we forgot about one another. By the time that Megan reappeared at the start of our sophomore year, it was clear that her skiing accident had changed her somewhat. She was never the instigator that Samantha was anyway, but the accident did clearly soften her, at least enough for her to ignore me. This ended up giving all of us some much needed space.

Through the grace of God, I was able to avoid contact with Samantha and Megan for the rest of my high school years. Sure, I did not get my revenge on them back then, but I was able to survive and move on, which I was grateful for. Though I didn't know it back then, one day these two jokers would meet Cierra face to face. And on that day, they were going to wish they had never even met me.

Chapter 10

Pillarfall

FALL SEMESTER SEEMED TO rush by in a blur of classes, late nights studying, and Greek life events. Oh, and partying, *lots* of partying. Each serving to bring me and Cierra closer in ways I'd never experienced with anyone.

Looking back, winter break had felt like a rare breath of fresh air, a chance to recharge and reflect on the whirlwind of experiences we'd shared. I returned home grateful for the chance for some downtime, but the solitude also gave me space to replay some of those moments. There were times when Cierra had seemed very reckless in her choices, pushing limits I wouldn't have dared to test on my own. This worried me a bit. What concerned me the most, was that Cierra did not return home over the break, and she refused my invitation to come home with me. She said she was staying in her room and that was that. I know that one of the perks of joining the sorority is that they let you stay, even over long breaks. However, thinking back, I am not sure where or what Cierra did over winter holiday. Whatever it was, she kept it to herself, *super secretly*.

As January turned into February and then March, the campus felt slightly warmer. I had to admit that I felt different too, but maybe slightly colder. I'd come to PVSU for new experiences, but I hadn't expected the edges between fun and consequence to blur so quickly. That was not all that was bothering me.

I remember one day I was lying there thinking about how Cierra and I had been through a lot together in the eight months since our GLV courtyard introduction. Up to this point, everything had seemed like harmless fun and of no real consequence other than lessons learned. However, the incident with the PVSU Campus Police literally swirled all around me, and it kept caressing my thoughts, like cold winter air rushing out from the gap on the bottom of an ill-fitting door, chilling one's bare feet to the bone. I think this unease was my subconscious mind reaching out to grab my attention, making me realize that Cierra was slowly becoming my best friend and that her risky behavior might possibly put us both in danger. It was kind of like that feeling you get when you have a nightmare and it sticks in your head for the rest of the day, even when you are not thinking about it directly.

Then it dawned on me fully and my stomach dropped, as I sadly realized that I never even had a best friend before. That was definitely what was bugging me. Now that I had a best friend, and our current situation was not perfect, as I had imagined my experiences would be, it made my stomach churn. I knew that I had decided to join a sorority at PVSU for new life experiences, but these feelings were tugging at my heart with a definite sense of jeopardy, like I could get hurt now. Not only that, but I got the sense that with my inexperience, I could hurt my friend as well, and this whole thing felt like a big jumbled spaghetti mess in front of me. I was conflicted, because while I was excited and happy to have Cierra in my life, I hated this feeling of knowing now that I had a responsibility to someone else on this level. I did not feel like I had the courage necessary. Sure, I'd had friends before, close ones in fact, but those were mere playdates compared to the gravity of this situation that I found myself in.

Something was serious. Something was off. I stirred in my bed spinning around trying to get comfortable. But this feeling of sickly cold dread refused to leave my presence. These realizations were also scaring me, because they were making me feel like I really didn't know my best friend at all, and that felt terrible. It was making me question my own self-worth. Was I a horrible best friend? I tried my best to be like my father and rationalize and categorize these feelings logically, but I am emotional as hell, and I am a Latina that feeds off vibes. I just couldn't shake this ominous presence. I was deeply disturbed.

Like I said earlier in regards to interpersonal relationships, I like to envision that we are like celestial bodies in orbit to one another, and while you may have a friendly planet in orbit next to you, will you ever truly know what that celestial body is made out of? What does the other planet even know of itself? Even at my young age, I think it is safe to say, not much, given the way I have seen most people live their lives. The only thing I knew for sure about my own solar system here at PVSU was that I was a planet from Arizona, and Cierra was a planet from Florida.

I knew her family lived in Apopka, near Orlando, but she rarely talked about them. It was as though her past was locked in her brain, and she had thrown away the key. This was in sharp contrast to me and my family. Our lives were an open book. I rarely could go a day without mentioning my dad's sarcastic remarks or my mom's relentless affection. Cierra didn't seem to mind my endless stories though. If anything, she seemed to enjoy and take comfort in them. However, while I wore my family history like a badge of honor, Cierra's silence about her own family loomed large in my mind. I didn't know if her reluctance to share with me was out of pain, or indifference. Whatever the reason, it left me both curious and cautious. Her past was a puzzle, and I wasn't sure if I was meant to solve it or whether to even try.

My mother has often told me that the only person capable of truly knowing who a person really is deep down inside, is that person's mother. I do think there is a ton of wisdom in that, and I would wager that nearly every single person in the world would agree that their own mother knows exactly who they are, even more than they know themselves. From my experience, what a mother chooses to do with the knowledge of who their own children are, varies wildly from case to case. Take my own mother, for example. She is truly the kindest person you could ever meet. However, she is also as hard as nails, and she takes zero BS from anyone, especially me. She calls me out whenever I color outside the lines, and she says it is not tough love, but the honest truth.

From my earliest memories, I can recall that my parents were always on my ass. They would constantly tell me that it was for my own good, because when there is an issue, it is easier to be proactive and pay now to get it over with and solve it, rather than to have to pay later when it is out of control.

"The quickest way through any problem, is straight through it," my dad would say, when I complained about long homework assignments back in high school.

So, our family worked together to keep each other honest and this foundation provided me with confidence, strength and a deep sense of right and wrong. From what I can tell, the committee approach to growing up properly that I was born into, is not anything close to the experience that Cierra had.

Piecing everything back together of what I know now, versus that which I did not know back then, I am certain that Cierra had decided from the time she was a little girl that she was not going to allow anyone in. She shut everyone in her family out from being a part of her life. This exclusionary doctrine of Cierra's own doing seemed especially aimed towards her mother. I feel as though Cierra channeled the negative energy she harbored toward her mother, wielding it like a baton to beat her down. On the surface, it seemed as if Cierra was simply being nasty to her mother. However, I don't believe her actions were driven by meanness. Rather, they felt like a twisted self-defense mechanism, a way to shield herself from a deep, inner pain. I worried that her choice to withdraw into isolation would eventually have serious consequences—not just for Cierra, but for everyone close to her.

The whole point that I am trying to make is that there was one giant issue that I did not know about my best friend in spite of my efforts to get to know her. I only found out this information much later after the fact when it was too late to do anything about it. And that absolutely haunts me. It turns out that Cierra had bipolar disorder, and she would use booze, and other items (drugs both legal and illicit), to cope with her emotional turmoil. I knew about the booze obviously, but I had no clue about the drugs and her mental struggles. You may call me naïve, but I just never put all the pieces together as my information was incomplete. At that time, I couldn't see just how messed up Cierra truly was, as she kept all her secrets carefully tucked away. And knowing Cierra, there was probably nothing I could have done to change her behavior even if I had confronted her directly. I think she would have punched me straight in the face if I had tried to insert myself too much into her private life. I mean, how do you help someone who doesn't want any help? People do what they want to do and that's just reality.

Up until this point in our friendship, I had mostly experienced the "up" or manic side of Cierra's personality—the vibrant, fun side radiating with incredible positive energy, with only a few exceptions. The incident with the PVSU police and the Delta Pi Zeta leadership was just a small taste of the trouble to come from her manic side. Because it turned out that there was the "down" or depressive side of Cierra's personality as well. I only saw this one time over the span of the final five weeks that I knew her. Even then, I did not get to see how deep this downside went until it was much too late and things had slipped through my hands like water. Cierra's deepest depths of despair came on fast, and it was literally over in less than thirty-six hours. When Cierra had fully descended into this low place deep inside herself, she became unrecognizable to me and to others around us.

Our sorority, Delta Pi Zeta, has a schedule of countless social events, such as Family Volunteer Weekend. Anyone could tell from outward appearances that Cierra's family had money. It was evident from the clothes she wore and the way she would always pay for everyone's food and drinks with her black credit card. However, not once did Cierra attend any of these social gatherings geared towards families. Definitely the most prominent example of this was Cierra not inviting her mother to the official DPZ Mother's Weekend. It was shocking that she chose to abstain from this event, as I had been looking forward to it since I first saw it on the event calendar at the beginning of spring semester. I had asked her about it then, when I first circled that date in my personal planner, but she made it crystal clear that this topic was off limits. It was about two weeks out and after noticing that Cierra's name was missing on the electronic reservation sheet for Mother's Weekend, I saw her in the hall. Our eyes met briefly and she somehow immediately knew what was on my mind. "Just don't, Babe," she said in a firm tone of voice with one finger up in the air in front of her, but in my general direction. She was pushing back against me with all her might, as if she was driving a vampire back with a crucifix. I did not want to make things worse than they already were, so I decided to let it go, to her face anyway.

One Friday around dinner time, I walked over to Cierra's room to see what she was up to. I also wanted to see if an opportunity to intervene positively in this matter might present itself. As I quietly crept up to her closed door, I heard her talking on the phone to someone in a weird, cold tone of voice that I had not witnessed from her before.

"You are definitely not a Delta Pi Zeta mom," Cierra said in that very cold voice.

At first, I thought she might be being silly and teasing her mom, like when we met and she told me that I was not Delta Pi Zeta material. But this was no laughing matter. Cierra sounded like she was seething and ranting at someone that she clearly did not respect.

"You don't dress like one, you don't have the looks and you certainly do not talk like one, so I really do not want you here," was the last thing I heard Cierra say before I recoiled and ran back to my room.

As I later sat there thinking about it in my room, my blood began boiling as I could not believe she had the audacity to dare speak to her mother like this with such disrespect. I clenched my fists, stood up and began pacing back and forth. As a surge of anger washed over me and gradually began to subside, I sat on my bed with my knees pulled close, my arms wrapped tightly around them, curling into a ball as I tried to calm myself. I was seriously pondering marching back down the hallway to her room and beating Cierra's ass, I was so mad. As my anger waned further though, I started to think about our relationship over the previous eight months, and about how Cierra had never disrespected me, and we hadn't ever gotten overly angry with each other. I convinced myself that if she had an issue with her mom, there must be some deep-rooted reason—something beyond my understanding and something she would never let me explore. With that, I realized I was at a stalemate. After careful consideration I decided to tuck this information away inside the back of my mind as something I didn't understand and didn't respect, but something I was going to have to accept if I wanted to remain friends. I consoled myself with the idea that perhaps I would be able to invite Cierra to hang out with me and my mother during the upcoming Mother's Day Weekend.

Chapter 11

Palm Walk

A FEW WEEKS WENT by and somehow April arrived almost without warning. The last cool breezes of March slipped away, leaving the campus covered in sunlight, with bright green leaves and desert flowers springing up everywhere. But while things around me seemed to be lightening, a small weight still pressed on my mind: Cierra and her mother. I tried to talk to her about it, but she brushed it off with a laugh, totally dismissing my concerns. I didn't want things to grow contentious between us, so I decided to set the issue to the side. I instead focused on balancing classes, studying, and small moments of fun with Cierra. But inside, I didn't let go of my worry for my friend.

One early afternoon, I was sitting on my bed doing homework when I suddenly realized I was hungry. I had missed lunch and my stomach was growling to let me know I had made a mistake by ignoring it. I got up to walk downstairs to the community kitchen, but I did it too quickly and got an immediate head rush and became dizzy as I was heading out my door. I closed my eyes as I braced myself against the door frame. When I opened them again I was given a slight jump scare. It was Bryce, and he was reflexively grasping my upper shoulders firmly to brace me from falling backwards. Bryce is at least a foot taller than I am, and he slouched down so that we were almost at eye level as he was checking to make sure I was ok. I briefly stared into his hazel eyes, and they were so beautiful that I wanted to fall into them and simply disappear. But then, I quickly caught myself and stood upright and brushed his hands off, even though his embrace was sweet and it was the last thing in the world that I actually wanted to do.

"What are you doing sniffing around my door, Bryce?" I asked with a hint of playfulness. I didn't pour it on too much, though—it's better for a young woman to keep a little mystery. In my experience, boys enjoy the chase, and girls who make things too easy often don't get what they truly want. Of course, I might be a bit out of practice. I hadn't really dated anyone since my junior year of high school.

"I just came to check up on you, see how you are doing," Bryce said with an earnest voice that made me halfway believe him.

"Is that right?" I asked incredulously, pointing my words at him like a small dagger. "Nice try, buckaroo," I continued in a tone that let him know his opportunity to impress me was slipping away.

Bryce did not fold though, he doubled down, and this manly confidence and courage bubbled up from deep within, in a way that really made my heart melt a little. He stood there, with his feet shoulder width apart, like a towering monolith that was not going to go away, in spite of anything I would say or do. I could not believe I was letting this vulnerability in my armor be exposed, but Bryce had seen right through my defenses like they did not exist. Then I thought about Cierra and all the other pretty girls swirling around me, and I decided to be selfish and unafraid and just go for it with Bryce.

"Come with me my lady, I want to show you something," he said in a tone that let me know that he was not going to take no for an answer.

I took a look at Bryce again, to seriously gauge what was going on, and he flipped his shoulder length brown hair back, and when he did, I took another deep look into his beautiful hazel eyes that were set like heirloom quality gemstones in his perfectly tanned skin. It was pointless to resist him any longer, so I agreed and we were on our way.

Bryce and I walked down the stairs of the sorority building, crossed the GLV courtyard, and made our way onto the main campus. In the warm breeze, I'd occasionally catch Bryce's scent drifting through the air—a pleasant mix of fresh cologne with a subtle hint of something sweet and slightly musky. The smell reminded me of my dad's home office, where he'd sit listening to old Rush records, puffing on an unlit cigar filled with sweet aromatic tobacco. Whatever this was, I wanted to swim in it, completely hypnotized. I didn't want this moment to end.

Bryce made some witty comments and small jokes as we walked, but more importantly, he asked me some serious questions about myself, revealing more about who he was as a man. The first thing I learned was that he seemed to genuinely be interested in getting to know me. And the second thing I learned was that Bryce was really a nice guy, a gentleman, kind and confident, a real throwback. And this is rare in life now, as most boys are only interested in hookups, or else they have no clue what being a man really means.

I was wooed, so I decided to let my guard down and give him a break, a real shot.

"So, Bryce, do you do this to all the new pretty girls, come by their room to swoop them up and take them for a walk?" I asked him playfully, but also to test for his reaction and answer.

Bryce was unfazed and told me to just hold on, and that he really had something to show me. He assured me that this was no routine, this was something special. Now my curiosity had totally taken over me and I was starting to grow slightly impatient in anticipation. I told my inner dialogue to put a sock in it, and to let myself just enjoy the moment.

We continued walking down to Old Main, which is a collection of the first buildings ever constructed on the Palo Verde State University campus back in the early 1920s. We then turned onto what is referred to as The Palm Walk which is a straight footpath that runs the entire length of the campus and is lined by palm trees every thirty feet, two on each side, like a series of gateways. We got halfway across campus, right before the massive Palm Walk footbridge that goes across University Avenue, when we finally arrived at our apparent destination.

Bryce grabbed my hand and we walked off the main sidewalk path and onto the grass towards this old brick building. It had a sun-faded sign which spelled "Humanities" in an old-looking font. In one corner of the exterior wall of the building, there were these hanging vines that were sorta out of control and other various plants forming a kind of wild garden. Bryce told me to close my eyes or I would ruin the surprise. Now he swung around me, and his hands were on my waist near my hips, as he guided me. It was too much and I started to giggle and slightly protest, but he was having none of it.

"Just hold on, it's worth it," he said.

Finally, we stopped and Bryce told me to lean forward as I felt his hand go in front of me to grab something. I felt a small tickle to my nose of velvety smooth material and then a glorious perfume smell filled the air all around me.

"Ok, open your eyes."

In front of me was a solitary large sterling rose bush, in full bloom. It was the largest rose bush I had ever seen, yet it remained completely hidden from sight just off the main path. This was one of the single most beautiful things I had ever seen, and was truly a magnificent discovery that Bryce had made.

My heart raced and my voice quivered slightly as I asked, "How did you find this?"

Bryce didn't respond, and when I looked in his direction, he was reaching in his back pocket for a small tool that had a little pair of clippers that folded out. He deftly reached down one of the long rose stems, towards the bottom that had five leaves on it, and he snipped it and then handed it over to me. It was a grand gesture that was so sweet, genuine and maybe a little over the top. It was all too much for a girl honestly. I stood there totally captivated by what was happening. I clasped the rose in my hands and noticed that somehow Bryce had also clipped off the little thorns from the stem. How I missed that was beyond me, but it was a nice touch. I held it up to my nose and deeply inhaled its beautiful aroma.

"Thank you, Bryce, you are one of the good ones," I said sweetly.

I was definitely caught up in the moment, enjoying myself, but then, much like a cat that has been stroked the same way one too many times, a different emotion crept in. A faint twinge of guilt washed over me for feeling this way, considering that earlier that day, I had been deeply worried about my friend Cierra and the unsettling dynamic I had uncovered between her and her mother.

That slight twinge of guilt turned into a full-on outburst, and suddenly I decided that I did not believe or trust Bryce. My inner voice reassured me that this was all a ploy to get what he wanted. So, I pushed the rose back into Bryce's chest, forcefully returning it to him.

"I appreciate it, Bryce, but I have to go," I said flatly, ready to storm back toward the Greek Leadership Village.

"But wait, Bella, what's going on? Did I do something?" he called after me, his voice fading as I quickly walked away.

In my peripheral vision, I saw his silhouette standing there, arms wide, with the rose in one hand and the clippers in the other. *Why am I like this?* I asked myself. I stopped to ponder that thought, and as I did, I caught another whiff of Bryce's scent. It made me pause, reconsidering. I turned back, walked over to him, and gently took the rose from his hand. Standing on my tiptoes, I kissed him softly on the lips—not a full-on kiss, but definitely more than a peck. It was a genuine show of affection.

"I'm not quite ready for you, Bryce," I said, meeting his gaze. "I just need a little time to work through a few things. Then you'll have my undivided attention."

He smiled wryly but said nothing. I turned to leave, and this time, I didn't look back.

As I finally hit the GLV courtyard, my emotion turned yet again, this time from guilt to regret. Bryce had tried to do something nice for me and worse than blowing him off, I felt like maybe I dissed him. *He is just trying to sleep with you,* my inner dialogue scolded me, as I bounded up the staircase to my room. I opened my door, rushed to my bed and lay down, with sweat running down my forehead, joining the mist of tears rolling down my cheeks. I made up my mind that I would help Cierra with her relationship with her mother and that I would make it up to Bryce after I figured out the first part.

Cierra obviously didn't have a close relationship with her mother, and that absence was a serious loss by my estimation. This kind of disconnect can lead a person to unravel in our unforgiving world. Most young girls have complicated relationships with their mothers—sometimes you argue, sometimes you resent them, but you still love them deeply and can't imagine life without their presence. That's the part that often goes unnoticed: young girls need their mothers. Navigating that relationship helps them stay grounded, preventing them from falling apart.

When I was trying to find my way, I'd often ask myself, *What would my mom think? What would my mom do?* Having her perspective was a kind of compass in my life, especially when she wasn't there with me. Sure, I needed my dad, too—to help me understand my worth and set healthy boundaries—but my mom took care of all the messy, complicated stuff that dads often struggle with.

After sophomore year in high school, I got pulled over by the police one summer for texting and driving. It was a serious offense and I remember just how sad and disappointed my parents were. My mother grabbed me firmly by the shoulders, and she said to me "Izzy, if anything ever happened to you, it would completely destroy me." That stuck with me from that point forward in my life. I made a determination: I was going to talk to Cierra's mom and make sure that she said something similar to Cierra. I felt that this would be the catalyst towards those two having a better relationship. Delta Pi Zeta Mother's Weekend was in a few weeks. I was going to strike at that moment on behalf of my friend who didn't even ask for my help.

As I was going to get up to hit the shower, Cierra showed up in my doorway.

"Hey Babe, did I just see Bryce up here?" she asked, her tone a little too perky.

"Spy much?" I responded, trying to use my voice as a shield.

"Do you *like* him?" Cierra asked me, or more like, teased me, by drawing out, and emphasizing the word like.

"Define like," I responded evasively, trying to get Cierra to back off, even just a little bit. I was trying not to reveal too much, because at this point, even I was not sure exactly how I felt.

This only encouraged Cierra to dig harder. "So, when are you gonna make his dreams come true and invite him to study biology in your bedroom, babe?"

She wasn't meaning to be funny, I don't think, but it didn't matter, because it came out so comical that we both started laughing, hiding our faces in our own hands.

"Come with me." She ran up to my bed, grabbing my hand and then tugging me to get up.

"Where are we going? And what's with the sudden handsy vibes, babe?" I asked, half-joking, half-serious.

Cierra completely ignored me.

We ended up down the hall in Cierra's room, and she gestured towards the whiteboard hanging from the wall. Each room had a whiteboard, and I imagine that the administration had intended that we use these to help us keep organized, or to brainstorm ideas. However, I would say they were used for academic purposes around zero percent of the time. Cierra had drawn all these cute doodles of hearts and roses on her board, but I only saw them briefly, as she quickly reached out and erased them with the dry board eraser.

"Should Bella sleep with Bryce?" She quickly jotted it out with a black dry erase marker across the top of the board as she spoke.

"Damn, Cierra, really?" I found myself a little insulted by her brash behavior and I was seriously wondering where her decency had gone.

"Quiet Binky, or else I will list the pros and cons of me sleeping with Bryce."

I wanted to get this over with quickly, so I picked up a marker and divided the board into two sections, which I labeled Pros and Cons.

Cierra perked right up, and she said,

"That's the spirit Babe, maybe we can finally get somewhere and diagnose your condition, to see how bad you got it. Pro, Bryce is hot AF. Con, you are a bit on the nerdy side." She jotted down a summary of her initial thoughts.

Playfully, I grabbed the marker from her hand while pointing at her and said,

"Pro, I do not have any competition from any sister living on this floor." I then pointed at myself and said, "Con, I don't sleep around."

Cierra then thought of a good one. "Pro, Bella has not gotten any Vitamin P in a long ass time." She jotted it down.

To which, I kinda slipped and accidentally admitted, "Con, Bella has never had any-" Then I caught myself, but it was too late.

Cierra understood what I was about to say. She dropped her hands down to her sides, and just stared at me, with no expression on her face.

"Are you messing with me Binky?" She wanted the answer, while simultaneously trying to lighten the suddenly tense mood.

I know that Cierra was just trying to have fun with this whiteboard discussion, but for some reason, my earlier interaction with Bryce suddenly popped into my head and all this combined made me sad and angry at the same time. I slammed the marker down on the floor with all my might, making the cap fly off, and it bounced up and hit Cierra in the face. This caught me off guard, and I slowly started moving backwards as I was trying to figure out what to do next. I guess I went backwards too much however, because I ended up hitting the back of my head against Cierra's door, which was still slightly ajar. Somehow it ended up hurting me, even though it was only a slight bump.

"F this." I turned, opened the door all the way and left, slamming the door shut behind me.

Why am I like this? I thought to myself as I ran down the hallway towards my room. I am like a cat that gets pissed off looking at its own reflection in the mirror. Just as I was about to enter my room and close the door to make my escape, Cierra swung her own door open and yelled out for me to stop. I felt like things were getting out of control, so I hesitated, taking a moment to decide what to do next. After a brief pause, I spun around, marched down the hall, and took her hand.

"Now you're coming with me," I said, leading her toward the staircase at the southern end of our building. We dashed down the hallway, hand in hand with huge smiles on our faces.

"Ooh-la-la! Where are you taking me, we on a hot date now, Babe?"

We both started laughing and were off down the stairs and out of the building.

I thought I knew what destination I had in mind when I grabbed Cierra's hand, but I was not entirely sure, because I was ad-libbing and making this adventure up as we went along. I ended up retracing the steps I had taken earlier with Bryce. In my head it was fully my intention to go and show Cierra the hidden rose bush. But, before I could do that, something stopped me. As we were cresting the Palm Walk footbridge, the sun was setting, and it was suddenly illuminating the entire Arizona sky with the deepest iridescent reds and purples that I had ever seen. Both of us saw it at the same time and we stopped and turned to face this perfect display of the beauty of mother nature. There were some high cumulus clouds in the eastern horizon, and they were chased across the rest of the sky by super high cirrus clouds. Each one of them was soaking up the bright red and magenta rays from the west. The entire thing was a true spectacle, everything was illuminated, and seemed to dance as one living organism. This was a moment that made you want to slow down, just so you could take it all in.

"Damn, sometimes Arizona can just be so freaking beautiful," Cierra remarked.

There was a four-foot-high pony wall on the Palm Walk Bridge that ran the entire length that served as a barrier to keep people from walking over the edge. Cierra jumped on top of it and then sat down, kicking her feet out in front of her. I joined and we just sat there, taking in this incredible view.

"Whether you have had sex or not, is none of my business, Bella. And if you are saving yourself for someone special, I think that is very cool. I am proud of you in any case."

"I have never felt ready, I have never trusted a boy or wanted them badly enough, I guess. So, what about you?"

"My body count is fairly low I guess you could say." She turned and looked at me, and we could both tell that this conversation had run its course.

"Boys are dumb," she said as we continued to look out into the sunset.

Suddenly, a rhyme I hadn't thought about since I was a little girl popped into my head. I stood up and shouted at the top of my lungs,

"Girls go to college, to get more knowledge! Boys go to Jupiter, to get more stupider!"

Cierra smirked as we both jumped off of the wall and back onto the bridge and started walking again with big smiles on our faces.

"You hungry, Fireball?" I asked, as my stomach started growling.

"Yeah, let's roll to the Outback, Binky."

The Outback was what we began calling the mediocre little PVSU cafeteria that is east of the Greek Leadership Village within walking distance. Girls on scholarship get to eat for free, so even if it isn't the greatest, I found myself here quite often. Cierra wasn't on scholarship, but she ate there probably just as much as I did. We walked over to the cafeteria, sat down and ate some fairly pedestrian American fare and talked about boys some more. However, this time it was certainly a little more superficial, as I think the two of us had tired each other out from sharing too many personal details earlier. We ate our *linner*, which is what we decided to call a late lunch that also serves as dinner and went back to our rooms and said goodnight. I laid down in bed and thought about that day and everything that had happened. I felt really lucky to have Cierra in my life.

Now at this point, I imagine most girls would have started texting Bryce right at that very moment. Well, I am here to tell you that I am not most girls. I am old school, and besides, I realized that I didn't even have Bryce's phone number.

Chapter 12

Cruel Slummer

IT WAS THE END of May, a couple of weeks into summer break. I wasn't taking any classes, which was a relief. Despite all the partying, Cierra and I had managed to pass all our classes once again. We were officially sophomores with a respectable amount of credits under our belts.

I think I mentioned this before, but first and second year PVSU students are expected to leave campus housing during extended breaks. However, one of the perks of Greek life is the option to pay a bit extra to stay year round. It made sense, and I'd estimate about half of us took advantage of that option. Cierra was sleeping all day and there were no official Delta Pi Zeta sorority functions, so I found myself actually getting bored for the first time in *like forever*. It occurred to me that I had gotten spoiled from all the action of the first two semesters, so not having something to do was a major let down.

On top of everything, DPZ Mother's Weekend had come and gone, and Cierra's mom was a no-show. It left me feeling disappointed as that wasn't at all what I had expected. I thought I was going to be the hero, but instead, I felt like a failure, and that made me sad.

I tried my best to make a connection happen, but Cierra didn't make it easy for me—neither did her mom.

A few weeks before Mom's Weekend, I managed to hack Cierra's cloud password and access her contact list. It was surprisingly easy. I gave Cassiopeia some demographic details and other information about Cierra, and it generated a list of keywords and terms. Using those, I built a dictionary of possible passwords and wrote a simple program to test them all at lightning speed. Either I guessed correctly, or I overflowed the buffer—but either way, I got in. Genius move, right?

I got the number, and one day during lunch, I worked up the courage to give her mom a call.

I gripped the phone tightly as it rang.

"Hi, Mrs. Fallion. This is Isabella Amescua. I'm Cierra's best friend at Palo Verde," I said.

"Right, I know who you are," Mrs. Fallion replied—not unfriendly, but not exactly warm either. Her unexpectedly defensive tone caught me off guard. Swallowing my surprise, I steadied myself and asked,

"I wanted to see if you were planning to come to Mother's Day Weekend?"

"I doubt it," Mrs. Fallion said. "*She* doesn't exactly want me there."

"I get that. But I think it'd mean a lot to her," I said carefully. "She's been having a hard time lately."

I heard Mrs. Fallion sigh quietly. "Right. When isn't she? What is it now? Grades? Boys?"

"It's more serious. She's been drinking... a lot... and other stuff. I'm really worried."

"Right, sweetheart, look I've been through this countless times before. Rehab, therapy—she always ends up back where she started. She has to want to change. We thought sending her to Arizona was the answer."

Rehab. Wow. New information that had me completely shook. And scared. But I had no time to dwell on it.

"But she could hurt herself. She needs to hear from you," I continued. I wanted to say more, but she cut me off.

"Look, *she's* an adult," Mrs. Fallion said bluntly. "I can't fix this anymore. She barely talks to me now."

I realized I wasn't getting anywhere. Pushing was only going to make things worse.

I adjusted my tone and swallowed my frustration. "Okay. Well, I hope you can come. I'll help. I'll be the bridge," I offered.

"We'll see," she replied.

The call disconnected, and I sat there with a nervous pit in my stomach, searching my soul for what to do next. I told myself I wouldn't give up.

I tried calling again the next day between classes, but it went straight to voicemail. Then I used the only trick I knew to check if I'd been blocked—I called from the office phone at the GLV headquarters instead of my number. She answered, but I chickened out and hung up.

I decided to reach out to Cierra's dad to try an end-around. However, I think my original phone call must have gotten back to Cierra because when I tried to access her cloud contact list again, the password had changed, and she had enabled multi-factor authentication.

I knew I could have overcome this obstacle by hijacking her phone's SIM, but when I ran into Cierra before dinner, she looked at me and didn't say a word—just slowly shook her head: *Don't*. Then she turned her back, and walked away, in an incredibly forceful unspoken display of, *back off*.

That scared me, so I went back to just doing my best to keep a close eye on her and reassuring myself that her mother would show up for Mom's Day Weekend.

On a Tuesday morning, I got up especially early for me, just before eleven. I slept like crap the night before, so I decided I would go out and get a strong coffee to burn out the cobwebs inside and wake my ass up. There was a strip mall with a JavaMan Coffee inside it just down the street from the GLV. Ever since my Freshman year of high school I have been addicted to JavaMan Coffee. I figured I would go there and get something sweet and strong to drink and then spend the rest of my day shopping for clothes and exploring, as I hadn't done much of that since setting foot on campus nine months ago.

I sat down in front of my mirror and decided that instead of getting dolled up to go out, I was just going to say hell with it and go out like a bum. I put on some shorts and a baggy t-shirt and headed out my door and down the stairs. I was able to walk to Rural Boulevard fairly quickly and into the coffeeshop in just under ten minutes. It was so unbelievably hot that day and I was sweating profusely just from walking. I checked the weather app on my phone and it said it was 106 degrees. There was also an alert on my screen that read that Sky Harbor airport was on emergency standby, because if it hit 118 degrees, they would close the runways following the FAA safety protocols. *Wow, now that is hot,* I thought to myself.

I opened the door to the coffee shop and it was amazingly refreshing to be hit simultaneously with the ice-cold air and smell of finely ground, perfectly brewed coffee. I placed my order (which has remained exactly the same for the past five years): A large Stop-Sign Mocha with the Works. The Works meant for them to put boba in the bottom and whip cream and caramel over the top.

As I was waiting, this well-dressed lady in business attire walked in and stood there, carefully studying the order menu that was hanging from the ceiling. She was in deep concentration, and she asked the dopey looking barista behind the counter, how many servings of coffee were in the large to-go container that they sold for twenty-two dollars.

The poor guy looked incredibly exasperated and put out by the question, which made me smirk with amusement. He sighed before responding,

"I don't know ma'am; it is hard to say without knowing what kind of coffee drinkers we are talking about."

I thought the lady's question was a little odd, to be honest, but the dopey kid's answer completely threw me for a loop. Then, as if determined to top his response, she followed up with something even more bizarre. In a serious tone, she said,

"Well, the people in my office are about medium-type coffee drinkers."

I craned my head from the business lady back to the barista, my eyebrows raised in disbelief. Then the barista took this ridiculous discussion to its final dopey conclusion by saying,

"Ma'am, it's entirely variable you see, so it's hard to say how many servings it contains, it just depends."

I'd had enough of this conversation. I furrowed my brow in concentration as I looked up at the order menu board to study it for myself. It said in bold white font: Large JavaMan Coffee Jug to go (1 Gallon!) - $22.00. I knew from elementary school that there are 128 ounces in a gallon, so next I picked up one of the small paper cups next to the counter and on the bottom of the outside edge, it said ten ounces. However, if you think about it, you have to leave room for creamer and sugar, so that means there would be approximately just over six ounces of coffee per cup. After doing the math in my head, I proudly gave them the answer.

"There would be approximately twenty-one servings in a to go container," I announced triumphantly, waiting for their accolades to come pouring in, no pun intended.

Instead of praising me, the business lady looked at me blankly, only to jut out her lower right lip slightly like, *who asked you.* She then looked down at her phone, ignoring me completely. Thrown by her reaction, I turned and looked at the barista for some backup, but he had a dismissive, *I doubt it,* look on his face. Then like an automaton that had suddenly switched on, he completed my order and robotically plopped it on the counter.

I am medium-type done with both of you right about now, I said under my breath as I grabbed my drink and headed out the door, stomping along the way.

I turned the corner and started walking towards some of the clothing shops near the end of the strip mall. The one thing I knew for certain about this retail plaza was that my favorite used clothing shop named Midtown Tightwad had a store in this location, and that was my destination. I was really starting to enjoy myself, as this coffee tasted amazing and was doing its job. All I could think about was super cute clothes I just knew I would soon discover. I started to pick up my pace in anticipation. However, as I got closer, the door opened at the little video game store fifty feet in front of me, and out came Bryce, with about four athletic looking meatheads pouring out behind as he held the door for them.

"No way," I muttered to myself. I was so embarrassed by my appearance, so seeing Bryce and his friends was about the last thing I wanted to be doing that morning. Thinking quickly, I opened the only door I could see between us and walked immediately towards the back of this unknown establishment I had just entered for the first time in my life.

Phew, I don't think he saw me, I reassured myself.

"Applications on top of the counter young lady," a voice called out to me.

I turned and looked, and there was this pretty black woman looking at me, but she was speaking with a thick Vietnamese accent. She had beautiful long hair in a braid, and she looked to be in her thirties. After my earlier confusing conversation in the coffee shop, this new dialog had me a little perplexed. I hadn't come in to apply for a job, and I don't recall ever meeting a black person with a Vietnamese accent. This new twist of events was not annoying to me like my experience earlier at the coffee shop, and in fact it was just the opposite, I was completely intrigued by what was unfolding. Seeing her made me think about my own situation, my jaded attitude, my nervous energy, my struggle with panic disorder, all of it.

I approached the counter, and the woman said stiffly, "Hello my name is Natalie Nguyen. My father was black and my mother was Vietnamese. Welcome to my cosmetics shop. You are definitely looking for job."

Is she on the autism spectrum? I thought to myself. I said hello back to Natalie, and I was about to tell her that I was not interested in a job. But then I thought about how bored I was and how immediately comfortable this place felt to me. Then I started envisioning having something to do while earning money. Not to mention I am an expert with cosmetics, or at least I was convinced I was. I picked up the application, which said Golden Dragon

Fine Cosmetics across the top in a beautiful tribal font. After studying this and taking everything in, I told Natalie that yes, I was definitely interested in working at the Golden Dragon cosmetics shop.

She cut right through my dreams though when she said, "You are a pretty girl, but you are very plain and you dress like crap."

Normally candor like this would have been very offensive to me, but it was so damn true and her delivery was perfect.

"I will get all dolled up and come in tomorrow to fill this application out and you will see that I know how to dazzle," I told her as sincerely as I possibly could.

"No! You will come in tomorrow morning at five am to start work!"

Awesome, I thought to myself, even though I was not sure how in the world I could make myself get up that early. There was a little break room in the back of the shop where I spent the next thirty minutes filling out the employment application. Once it was complete, I handed it to Natalie, and I have to say that it felt good to be doing something instead of wandering around aimlessly, both physically and mentally.

She told me "Bye now," as she pointed me towards the door to leave, and told me to not be late, and I assured her I would, in fact, be early.

I spent the next seven weeks working at the Golden Dragon. It turned out that Natalie and her small Golden Dragon Cosmetics shop needed a lot more help than I could have ever imagined. Over that time I would discover that Natalie had a way of just cutting through all the BS and striking a chord. There was nothing I could really say to dispute the pronouncements she would make, and I loved every minute of it. The remainder of that summer I worked seven days a week, from the early morning, until well past six. Natalie knew that she was asking for a big commitment from me, so she was paying me five dollars over minimum wage. She let me take home a ton of samples from vendors, as well as items from the floor that were getting close to their expiration dates.

It was a sweet deal. I got to know Natalie well, and I ended up having fun working there. Natalie told me stories about being smuggled into the United States. She said that it was scary, and that she wore three pairs of underwear during most of her journey in an attempt to feel safer around a bunch of smugglers. She said that she had been married and had one child since migrating to this country, but that her husband had been abusive. So they separated and she moved to Arizona, while they remained in California. Despite all her hardships, Natalie was grateful to live here, and she was not bitter about her past. Her only regret was not having a good relationship with her daughter. With her condition, whatever that was, she lacked almost any kind of empathy, but I could tell that she had a good heart.

Natalie's observations on life were truly something to behold as well. The running commentary she had on customers, on current events, and even my makeup and clothes were spectacular. Oftentimes her quips were humorous because she did not even realize how funny she was being, but most of the time, it was just special to hear things being broken down into their base components so perfectly. After meeting Natalie, I read quite extensively about autism spectrum disorder and other related conditions. What I can say is that either Natalie only had a slight case of it, or she'd had years of behavioral therapy, or both. Either case, I can truly say that I felt lucky to work there and to get to spend time with someone like her as she was just so different. I valued our time together. Sometimes we would stay late in the evenings to do inventory and receive new shipments. Natalie would allow me to bring Cierra in, so she could help and earn some cash under the table and some free samples and expiring lipsticks for herself, just like she did with me. I noticed that Natalie would always keep a close eye on Cierra whenever she was in the shop, although Cierra didn't seem to notice. I didn't really appreciate the extra scrutiny being applied to my friend, when she was just there trying to help. One time, Natalie watched Cierra like a hawk from the time she said she needed to use the bathroom to the time she came out. I pulled Natalie to the side and just bluntly asked her what her problem was.

"Your friend, she is adrift. She has no anchor. I am afraid she is going to easily float away. I am trying to figure her out, but so far, I have nothing, Bella. I know she is sad. I know she is in pain. She is all alone."

Those words hit me hard. Natalie and I glanced over at Cierra, but she seemed oblivious to being the focus of our conversation. I felt a wave of nausea. Somehow, Natalie had picked up on my worries about Cierra and shared the same deep concern. The thought of losing Cierra was unbearable, and Natalie's words felt like a weight settling heavily on my shoulders, making me feel even worse.

Chapter 13

Cody

I SPENT THE SUMMER working at the Golden Dragon cosmetics shop for Natalie, and those hot months passed by in a blur of routine. As the fall semester of my sophomore year began, the first two months felt just as uneventful bordering on the mundane. My days were filled with lectures, homework assignments, and the usual rhythm of campus life. There was nothing out of the ordinary or worth remembering, yawn. Then, on a seemingly quiet September night, something notable finally happened. I was lying in bed, struggling to fall asleep, when a loud and deliberate knock shattered the stillness, jolting me wide awake. I stood upright quickly, and stomped over to my door. I was planning to tell whomever it was to go away. But then I opened the door and was greeted by Bryce. I was shocked to see him, since I had avoided him all summer while hiding out at the Golden Dragon Cosmetics Shop. I had also managed to not lay eyes on him at the beginning of the fall semester as well, yet there he was, with such perfect timing. I stuck my head out my door slightly and saw nobody else out there in the hallway. I was impressed that Bryce had managed to sneak all the way up here to my door undetected, which is quite the feat with all these nosey girls around here. Boys were not specifically forbidden to be on our floor, but it was definitely frowned upon. Perhaps it was pure instinct that made me check to ensure no one else was around, because even before I finished, I knew I was making the right decision.

I cannot tell you how Bryce was just such a welcome sight for my weary eyes. I wasted no time. I immediately reached up to him and threw my arms around his neck, pulled him down to my open mouth and started kissing him passionately. I grabbed his arms and carefully walked him into my room. As we passed the door frame, Bryce gently closed the door behind him. I didn't care if I wasn't being ladylike by throwing myself at him, I wanted to drown my sorrows in the essence of his being and burn my reality down to the ground until only embers remained. I longed to draw him so close that our souls intertwined, merging on a molecular level, until he was a part of me and I was a part of him. That is how badly I wanted him. And I can tell you, Bryce was certainly up for this moment. He came down to meet my kiss and grabbed my hips and pulled me close to him, grinding up against me. He was wearing a black Hugo Boss button-down dress shirt with the top two buttons undone, and I could see just a tiny tuft of fine brown chest hair peeking out across the tops of his bulging tanned pecs. Bryce and his hair and his muscles and his eyes and his scent were not too little, not too much, they were all just perfectly beautiful to me. He was wearing some oversized Joe jeans and a big black belt with a heavy buckle. I wasn't too crazy about his dark cowboy boots, but at that point, I really didn't care. I pulled him over to my bed, then pulled him down on top of me. I didn't even realize it, but some hot passionate tears threatened to escape my eyelids. I said that I was sorry for my rude behavior with the rose a few months back as all my tears came streaming out.

"Don't worry Bella, all is forgiven, you are forgiven," he said, with a reassurance that resonated deeply within me, within my very being, while he was wiping away my tears. Bryce was there to rescue me, to reassure me, to protect me, he was to be mine.

I grabbed Bryce by his shirt, and I looked right into his eyes with my mouth slightly agape.

"Are you into me, Bryce?" I asked him honestly and with passionate intent, staring directly into his eyes, *into his soul.*

He looked at me, his eyes scanned my whole face and then they met my intense gaze again, and he nodded slowly in a way that verified his truth.

"Are you going to hurt me?" I whispered in his left ear, with my fingers clasped behind the back of his neck.

This time he did not look away and he shook his head slowly while staring into my eyes, our gaze never breaking.

"Let's have some fun," I said to him while smiling, invitingly.

Bryce spent the entire night with me. We got oh so very close to going all the way, but right as things were getting overly serious heading towards the point of no return, Bryce abruptly stopped. He laid on his side and turned towards me, propped up on his right elbow. "What's going on with you Bella? Something just doesn't feel right."

I pulled a blanket over my nearly naked body, suddenly embarrassed. I didn't say anything, because I did not want him to leave.

"Look, I like you and I don't want to force anything. I am not a f-boy and I want more from you."

I stared into his perfectly beautiful hazel eyes.

"I'm being serious, Bella."

So, I was trying to run away from my feelings, and just throw everything to the wind and fall into Bryce and forget all this BS around me. But instead, I opened up completely, and I spent the next couple of hours confessing everything to him. I told him about how Cierra scared me with her behavior and that I felt that things were beginning to unravel. I suddenly realized that I had gotten so caught up in telling Bryce all about Cierra that I suddenly felt silly, like I was being a little goody two shoes.

Then Bryce stopped me, took my hands in his, and looked at me very seriously. "You're right to be concerned, Bella. I ignored my older brother Cody's behavior and chalked it up to boys being boys until it was too late. He was three years older than me and I looked up to him." He continued, telling me that Cody was an alcoholic who would drink at every single opportunity that presented itself, but that he did a pretty good job at hiding it. "Everyone knew though, at the end of the day, we all knew."

Bryce told me that there was a Halloween party that Cody had attended in Prescott a couple years ago. Prescott is a small city about two hours to the north of Phoenix, and it is very much a high desert town, with a national forest and mountains surrounding the area. Cody had gotten black out drunk, and passed out in the back of his best friend's pickup truck bed, under a picnic blanket, as it was cold. In the cab, his buddy was making out with some girl and they had the heater going, so the truck was idling. After a couple hours, the people in the cab realized that Cody wasn't moving around anymore, so they got out to look. They found Cody had died from carbon monoxide poisoning. The truck had a leaky exhaust and the bed of the pickup was partially rusted through. The combination of breathing the carbon dioxide fumes, and being covered under the blanket for a few hours killed him. Not exactly Cody's fault, but the alcohol was definitely a contributing factor. The look that Bryce had on his face was of total resignation and heartbreak from the loss of his brother. That made me feel so incredibly gloomy and sad.

I understood that maybe the situation that Bryce had described wasn't exactly what I was going through with Cierra, but damn, the randomness of all this seemed to have swallowed his brother whole, in one gulp, and that scared me. Bryce said he deeply regretted that he hadn't tried to intervene earlier and to convince Cody to get help with kicking his addiction, and if he had, maybe he would still be alive. Suddenly, everything that Bryce had said to help me was too much for me emotionally, and once more, I had the feeling of a cat that had been petted one too many times. I thought I might bolt, but then I looked at Bryce, and I sensed that he was waiting for me to comfort him back. His large eyes were filled with so much sadness, and I melted.

"Bella, do not let Cierra's self-destructive behavior just slide. Do not lose her to this disease. Do everything in your power to stop her."

I reached out and caressed Bryce near his temple, stroking his hair. I agreed that I would heed his advice, and that I was so sorry for what he experienced. And I also thanked him for telling me that deeply painful story. We fell asleep in each other's arms. I had a restless sleep that consisted mainly of waking up every few minutes, looking at Bryce sleeping peacefully like an angel, looking at the clock on my phone, and then closing my eyes again without actually ever sleeping.

He had school club lacrosse practice, so around four thirty in the morning, he had to leave. Before he did, he gently shook me, gave me a big hug and softly kissed my forehead. He told me he would come back later that afternoon to hang out and talk some more, which I made him promise to do.

Chapter 14

Tortilla Flat

AFTER BRYCE LEFT, I was laying there tossing and turning, still unable to fall asleep. I tried a trick my dad had taught me, where I think about happy thoughts and physically force myself to yawn. This trick really works when I am restless, and I can usually fall asleep in a few minutes. After closing my eyes, the first memory that flashed into my head was the night that Cierra, Faith and I almost had our fake IDs confiscated at Pinkie's Pool Hall. I shook my head and decided that while I would not call that a bad memory, it was not exactly falling asleep happy place material. Then I remembered the impromptu road trip that Cierra and I took not long after our run in with that hot head bouncer in Fall of our freshman year.

"Hey Binky, what is there to do in this town? In Florida, when there was nothing to do, we could go to the beach or the lake, but Arizona is so boring, yuck."

We sat in the first-floor kitchen of the sorority drinking our morning coffee and nursing our hangovers. I was slightly embarrassed by her question as I literally could not think of one fun thing we could do. I thought about the medium size amusement park near downtown Phoenix that my dad used to take me to when I was little, but then I pictured Cierra with a snow cone in her hand looking at me with miffed disapproval and quickly decided to nix that idea. Then I remembered a field trip my senior high school class took to Canyon Lake, which is only fifty miles to the east of the PVSU campus. I thought about how perfect this place is, nestled right up by the Superstition Mountains. Since it's one of the smallest lakes in Arizona, it's often an overlooked destination, usually not overcrowded like most places are during this hot time of year.

"I know a place that will knock your socks off, Fireball," I said as I poked Cierra in the side, motioning her to get up and get ready.

"What? Where are we going Binky?"

"Relax babe, I am going to show you a good time. Just meet me back here in fifteen and bring your swimsuit."

Cierra and I got ready in about an hour, we gathered up our stuff, headed downstairs and started walking over to the parking garage where my Honda was waiting. Cierra had christened the Honda with the nickname Hailey, so we jumped into Hailey and started heading down the US-60 freeway on the way to our destination. As we rode along, we played all our favorite songs and sang at the top of our lungs, completely enveloped in pure joy. Cierra played me a song she used to love back in elementary school, and I shared some of my childhood favorites with her. When I played her "Tom Sawyer" by Rush—a song my dad used to force me to listen to on long road trips—she didn't say much beyond, "It's got a good beat."

To make it up to her, I blasted a real classic oldie banger that still slaps: "Fancy" by Iggy. We rocked out hard, singing the lyrics we knew by heart like we were headlining a concert. As the song was ending, Cierra turned down the radio and asked,

"Hey Binky, you ever kissed a girl?" She began leaning over to the left, slowly inching closer to me.

I was taken aback by this question as it was so random.

"No, can't say that I ever did that, Fireball."

"I did one time. I had this friend in seventh grade, we were sitting there listening to music just like we are now and I guess she got really comfortable around me and she went in for the dagger and kissed me passionately." She leaned over even closer from the passenger seat, motioning like she was going to try to kiss me.

"Pucker up buttercup," she said with a giggle as she started leaning ever so closer to me, grabbing my right shoulder and pulling me towards her.

Cierra pulled me with surprising strength, and it made me jerk the wheel and almost lose control of Hailey, which would have spelled disaster as I looked down at the speedometer, which registered 87 mph. I used the force of the car jerking to push Cierra away from me, sweeping my hands off the steering wheel, and forcing Cierra back into her seat with the same force she had grabbed me with.

I was visibly shaken, and Cierra laughed and then sighed as she sat back and said jokingly,

"Relax, you prude, I'm just messing with you. You're not my type anyways. Besides, your lips look like they are chapped and I only like white girls anyways, you chola."

"I am glad you do not have a thing for Latinas, and you really need to bathe and brush your teeth, you goof." I playfully poked her in her side and turned the radio back up.

To this we both started laughing hysterically.

Just then Post Malone's "Wow" came on the mix and we both started dancing and gyrating in our seats with our hands up in the air. Hailey is a very sleek and powerful car and my dad says it has a turbo, which means she is fast, and that day we were absolutely tearing up the road. We drove through the Lost Dutchman State Park on our way to the lake, but instead of stopping there, we kept on driving to the small ghost town called Tortilla Flat, which was about fifteen minutes past our initial destination. I wanted to surprise Cierra by taking her to lunch, as I knew of a cool tiny western bar right there on the strip. We pulled into Tortilla Flat, and it was surprisingly empty, not overrun with tourists and others trying to escape the mundane routine of living on the surface of the Sun known as Phoenix, Arizona. There was a parking spot right in front of the strip of buildings, so I parked Hailey, and we walked inside and over to the bar. The door to this place was modern steel and glass, but it was recessed and pushed back into the walls of the front of the building. An old time wooden double door swung out in its place to give it that real old western ghost town feel. Although it was the lunch rush, it was early fall, so the foot traffic here was what I would consider fairly light. So we were seated immediately and our waiter came over right away and put down some menus on the table in front of us. I could see Cierra eying the drink menu, but I kicked her under the table and gave her a look that screamed, *not today, Babe.*

The waiter gave us some time before returning and we studied the menu. I ordered a cheeseburger in a lettuce wrap with a side salad, while Cierra got a strawberry salad with grilled salmon. While we were waiting for our food, we ended up mainly talking about what a dummy Faith was for abandoning us and nearly getting our fake IDs taken away. It didn't take long for our food to arrive, and it was surprisingly delicious. We sat there talking and eating and truly enjoying ourselves. It was really relaxing and fun.

Then Cierra changed the subject to something she had obviously been waiting to talk about.

"What is going on with you and Bryce?" Her right lip curled up, revealing her dimple.

"Nothing really, or nothing yet I should say. I am interested in him," I admitted.

"Oh, my, he is so hot with three t's, h-o-t-t-t! His beautiful eyes and perfect hair and he has a cute butt too."

To this, I felt the ever so slight twinge of jealousy rear up inside me, even though I tried my hardest to not let it show.

Cierra sensed this and decided to let me off the hook. "Relax Babe, I don't want him, you can have first shot, I will give you that, Binky."

"That's cool Fireball, I don't think he likes buck teeth anyway, but he might be tempted by your ginormous boobs."

That made Cierra laugh, and for a moment, we were both simply happy, enjoying each other's company while finishing our meal.

Out of nowhere, I felt an unwelcome burning sensation on the top of my left ear, like someone was staring at me with ill intent. This feeling was truly annoying as I was having such a good time, just chilling with my friend. I turned and scanned the dining room to see who was looking at me, and my goodness, in this small town, miles away from everything, there was Samantha Elsher sitting across the room having lunch with her best friend Megan Sommerset. I had not seen these two snobs since my early high school days, and to see them then, when I was having such a good time, was a major bummer. I pushed back in my seat as I pursed my lips and furrowed my brow in disbelief. I was actually a little scared and intimidated just looking at them. *What in the hell are they doing here,* I thought to myself.

Cierra looked at me, then over at them, and she could see that I was upset so she asked me who they were.

"When I was in high school my freshman year, I had this point in my life where I was really struggling mentally, and that eventually manifested physically into full blown panic disorder. And those two girls were supposed to be my best friends, and I confided in them. Instead of helping me out, they told the entire school that I was a freak and really made my life a living hell. Especially the one on the left, Samantha, she is evil incarnate. She is the reason my middle school sweetheart broke up with me."

"Is that so?" Cierra asked as she took one final sip of her ice tea. She pulled out fifty dollars cash from her wallet and plopped it on the table.

She did it with precision and flair, and I was reminded of the first day I met her when she did the same type of maneuver pulling out a mini shot bottle of Fireball whiskey from the same tiny purse.

Before I could say or do anything, Cierra bolted, tearing off in the direction of Samantha and Megan, the two bitches I could not stand. I was powerless to stop her as she was already gone and all I could do was trail behind her with a deep foreboding feeling in the pit of my stomach.

"Hey Samantha, how are you?" Cierra called out, with fake enthusiasm, as she made a beeline towards their table.

Samantha and Megan looked up in Cierra's direction with perplexed expressions on their faces. Cierra then leaned down incredibly sloppily, and motioned to shake Samantha's hand, but instead she used her momentum, knocking Samantha's soda into her lap. As Samantha was signaling that she intended to stand up, all in a tiff to make a dramatic scene, Cierra reached down and put her hands firmly on Samantha's shoulders, forcing her to remain seated with tremendous physical strength, effectively squelching any intentions Samantha may have had. Just then, Megan indicated with her body language that she was going to stand up and do something about all this disrespect.

Cierra kept her left hand on Samantha's shoulder with an incredible grip and she snapped her fingers with her free hand in Megan's face without looking at her. "Keep your seat bitch."

Samantha was wincing in pain under Cierra's uncomfortable grip, and Megan quickly recognized how serious this situation was becoming, so she slowly sunk back in her seat, putting her hands up in the air, to indicate that she was done.

Cierra then used her right hand to grab Samantha by her jaw and guided her face in my direction, squeezing hard, until Samantha's cheeks and mouth were pressed into a pout. Cierra then looked directly into Samantha's eyes and gave her the following ultimatum, "Take a look over there Samantha. See my girl, Bella? At one point in time, you were supposed to be her friend when she confided in you about her medical condition, and instead, you were a giant bitch to her. Even now, just earlier, you were staring at her, trying to mess with her. But guess what bitch, I have good news. This is your moment of redemption. I want you to look at Bella, and truly apologize for ever hurting her. Do that, and we will leave and you can put this all behind you. Choose not to, and I am literally going to beat the ever-loving F out of you, right here and right now. Look at me. I am prepared to go to jail. Do I look like I'm joking, bitch?"

At first, I was scared by what Cierra had just done. I even started to feel a tiny bit bad for Samantha, because this was probably the last thing in the world she had been expecting. But then, like a film playing back slowly in my mind, I remembered that my freshman year Samantha Elsher used gossip and lies about my mental condition to break up me and my boyfriend Ian Harris. I cocked my head back slightly and my eyes were cool and I let all the emotion drain from my face and body. I stood there as a witness to this situation, and I judged that Samantha deserved all the smoke she was receiving and then some. Cierra lifted her hand off of Samantha's shoulder, and gave her mouth a final wag as she let go. Cierra then leaned back while she crossed her arms, waiting to see what Samantha would do, ready for either outcome. I now noticed that there were red and white finger marks left on Samantha's shoulders between the spaghetti straps on her top and her mouth and cheeks were all red as well.

Samantha took a final look up at Cierra and then she looked over at me. Her mouth was quivering and her deep blue eyes were pooling up with tears of fear, pain and regret. "I am sorry for ever hurting you, Bella. I really am. I was going to go over to your table and say as much anyway."

Megan quickly piped in like a good little lap dog and said, "It's true."

Cierra snapped her fingers at Megan again. "*Shut...the...f...up...bitch!*" She emphasized every single word.

In the middle of Samantha's apology, Cierra turned her back to both of them, and she was now looking directly at me, smiling, with her dimple popping out like never before. I was scared by Cierra's sudden display of malevolence and violence coupled with a complete disregard for kindness and orderly conduct. However, I knew in my heart that no other girl I had ever known or would know in my entire life would stick up for me and defend me like this. This was a display of complete loyalty, fearlessness and love. It was beautiful, just like that first time I met Cierra in the GLV courtyard. So, I nodded my head in unison with Cierra, who was already doing so.

I then looked at Samantha and said, "You are forgiven, honey child." Then I spun on my heel and left, joining Cierra who was already headed out the door. As I was leaving, I turned to look at Samantha and Megan one final time.

They were still in their seats, frozen in time, trying to assess where exactly they messed up in life. I knew that would be the last time I would ever have to see their ugly faces. Even if I ran into them again, they would surely turn to run away from me. I looked around the restaurant, and for a brief moment, it was like the entire place had turned into an oil painting, and time had stood still for everyone. How did this entire spectacle not cause a ruckus, I thought to myself. Not a single person had noticed this crazy ass incident, which felt nearly impossible to me. Yes, the place was fairly empty, and though there were people around us, they were apparently too distracted to witness what happened.

"*Honey child*," Cierra jokingly said in the car on our way out of Tortilla Flat. "I have said and done some crazy twisted things in my life, but that is some otherworldly creepy next level horror movie nightmare fuel language stuff right there! You are deranged, girl!"

We both had a good laugh at that, and if I am being honest, it did feel good to put Samantha and Megan in their place remembering all the torment they put me through back in high school. Yes, I am fully aware that revenge is wrong, and it is not good to seek it out. However, sometimes the brutal truth of retribution needs to be delivered and there is nothing wrong with witnessing someone who truly deserves it, facing the consequences of their actions.

"You didn't have to do all that, Cierra."

"Do what? That was all you Babe, I was merely tapping into the stream of consciousness and reacting to the energy you were putting out into the universe."

"Thanks, Fireball. I love you."

I was driving, but I looked over to Cierra, who had suddenly grown quiet.

"I love you too, Binky. Forever." She said it, without a wink, without a sly half smile, without her dimple popping out. She meant it.

After all that commotion, we didn't even end up going to the lake, because by that point we were exhausted and we just wanted to go back to the dorm and drown ourselves in alcohol. As we drove back in silence, I thought about how Cierra was so fearless, loyal and willing to literally put it all out on the line for me like that. I swore to myself that I would do the same for her. I prayed that I could live up to the standard displayed by my friend, because I was uncertain if I possessed the strength to take our friendship to the levels that Cierra was obviously willing to.

Lying there in my bed remembering our trip to Tortilla Flat made me even more restless than before. There was obviously no way I was ever going to fall asleep, as I was literally burning with passion and emotion. Plus, I was full of excitement thinking about Bryce returning later that day. It was too much for me.

Chapter 15

Pivot and Strut

"BELLA, COME QUICK!" FAITH yelled at me, while barging into my room.

My door wasn't locked, granted, but I was a little miffed that she came in uninvited. Besides, my relationship with Faith was not in a good place at all. It was late Saturday morning towards the end of November, right before lunchtime, and I suddenly remembered that there was a *dayger* being thrown at the frat across the courtyard. A dayger is a concatenation of the words day and rager, and it is exactly the type of party it sounds like: an excuse for a bunch of college kids to get hammered during the day, drinking excessive amounts of cheap alcohol. The boys at the frat had even gotten clever and named it the "Thanksgiving Turks Dayger." Nervously, I remembered that last night, just around twelve hours earlier, Cierra came bursting into my room super excited about it. I could tell that she had barely slept the night before and she must have spent the previous several hours drinking. She looked like a mess. I just knew that whatever was upsetting Faith enough to come in my room uninvited had to be concerning Cierra.

I was right to be nervous, because this day was going to be the end of Cierra's academic career, and would set in motion what was going to be the end of her life. A deep sense of guilt and worry overtook me as I looked at Faith's super-concerned and troubled face. The previous night, after Cierra had left my room, I closed and locked the door. This may sound bad to say, but I had my fill of everyone around me and all their issues. The noise inside my head was becoming unbearable. I have my own problems too, I said to myself. And it is true, I can't save everyone and I have wants and needs of my own. Looking back, I should have made some kind of effort to stop Cierra, even if it hadn't made a difference.

As I was sitting there lost in thought and feeling guilty, Faith reached down and grabbed my hand, and yanked me out of my room and down the stairs. With a deep sense of foreboding, I realized that she was dragging me to the dayger that was in full swing, and that obviously something concerning Cierra had happened. We ran down the stairs to our building and came out the front and across the grassy GLV courtyard, headed to the back of the boy's frat.

It was only one in the afternoon, but I could literally smell beer in the air and I heard the sounds of loud music pouring from behind the boy's fraternity building. This was a full rave. When we turned the corner there was already a large circle of people that had formed, and they were watching something. Faith and I pressed forward and forced a hole in the middle of the crowd to see what was going on. When I saw what was happening, I was shocked and horrified at the sight before my eyes.

It was Cierra all right, and her hair and clothes were soaked in something, maybe sweat or maybe beer, or maybe both. Whatever it was she definitely appeared like she was black out drunk. She was yelling something angrily at the crowd and looked frantic. I was reaching forward to grab her and take her back to her room, but before I could, I saw something else. Cierra was not yelling randomly, she was shouting at our chapter president, Stacey Williamson, with her finger wagging in her face. In general, Stacey was nice enough, I guess. But above all else, I think Stacey envisioned herself as a future high-level executive, so I guess you could say that her entire demeanor was all business. She was standing there looking at Cierra with a smug look of disapproval, arms crossed, contemplating her next move.

It appeared that she had finally had enough, as she uncrossed her arms, leaned in closer to Cierra and began telling her off by yelling sternly, "This is not an authorized event, and we do not allow drinking on campus anyway, and you're done." Stacey then turned and spotted me and Faith, her face red and burning with anger. Quickly she recognized and assessed that we were sober and not partaking in that day's activities, so she trained her attention towards us looking for backup. "You two, sisters, get her ass outta here before I have her arrested."

With Stacey's head turned like this, she could not see what was going to happen next. However, I could see perfectly what was about to unfold. It was all unwinding right in front of me in slow motion, and I was powerless to stop it. Cierra reached out and grabbed Stacey with her left hand, reeled back with her right fist, and punched Stacey straight in her jaw in a beautifully fluid demonstration of muscle control, finesse and power. Drunk or not, this display was quite impressive and if I was not feeling like my entire world was crumbling around me, I would have taken a moment to sit back and admire this show of physical prowess. This right hook caught our chapter president square in the jaw, a perfectly connected strike. I was impressed that Stacey did not bleed from the hit, because she certainly got knocked on her ass, and she sat there for a moment, holding her injured chin, fuming with anger and disbelief.

"Faith, call the campus police." She caressed her jaw, feeling for damage and assessing what just happened, trying to shake it off.

Knowing Faith as well as I do, I thought she would simply follow Stacey's order without hesitation. However, Faith shook her head while furrowing her brow in contemplative thought, then knelt down and started whispering something in Stacey's ear. Stacey pressed her lips together firmly while she listened to Faith, and her eyes were vacant.

"Fine, get her ass outta here now! Cierra Fallion you're are done! You NEVER put your hands on me, girl! YOU ARE DONE!" Stacey yelled in an authoritative voice.

Cierra was too out of it to even hear Stacey's words, let alone realize what she had just done: she had just thrown away the remaining pieces of her sisterhood at the Delta Pi Zeta sorority.

Eventually things settled down and we were able to drag Cierra back to her room to sleep it off.

Two days later, first thing Monday morning, there was a white piece of paper taped up on Cierra's door. It was a letter informing her that she had violated the substance abuse and the acts of physical violence clauses of the Delta Pi Zeta code of conduct. She was to appear before the Delta Pi Zeta Disciplinary Committee in one week for an expulsion hearing. It was so serious that the notice said that the chapter attorney would be there and that Cierra had the right to legal representation as well. I didn't even have to ask, because I already knew that Cierra would be representing herself in this hearing. This turned out to be another one of Cierra's mistakes, as the universe was starting to turn on her, and it was not to bend to her will any longer. Cierra just was not aware of it yet. None of us were.

The notice had a profound impact on all of us, but Cierra seemed to spiral the most. She stopped caring about outward appearances and began openly drinking every day, as if trying to escape reality—or maybe it was just an excuse to get drunk, abandoning any concern for the consequences. Despite being familiar with her heavy drinking, it still shocked me how effortlessly she could consume alcohol like it was water, with seemingly little effect compared to the sheer volume she drank. What I didn't realize at the time, though, was that she had started mixing drugs with alcohol. Looking back, it's clear how her behavior was unraveling, each day marked by increasingly reckless and erratic choices.

Cierra's disciplinary hearing ended up not being much of a hearing at all—it was more like a ceremonial defeat. The fact is that she had already sealed her fate the moment she laid her hands on our chapter president. The committee's decision was swift and final. Still, as harsh as the outcome was, it didn't shock anyone who understood the gravity of what Cierra had done. The thing that was shocking, at least to me, was that Cierra wasn't able to get herself out of it.

Time marched on, even as Cierra seemed to disappear from the world around her. It was December in Arizona and that meant Christmas was fast approaching. I do not know if you are familiar with Arizona, but with the desert climate, it is just about the least "Christmassy" part of the country that you could ever imagine. While most Americans are dreaming of a white Christmas, walking on frozen ground that crunches underneath their feet, in Arizona we typically spend our Christmas Eve barbecuing in the backyard next to our swimming pools in shorts, flip flops and tank tops. The beautiful weather in Phoenix makes getting in the mood for celebrating a winter holiday challenging; however, other things that frequently come with winter, like depression and feelings of isolation, certainly are there.

For Cierra, that weight became unbearable. Losing the disciplinary hearing, coupled with the seasonal melancholy, left her completely shattered. She wasn't just crestfallen—she seemed like a shadow of herself, stripped of the spark that had once made her so magnetic. Her superpowers, as I had always thought of them—her charisma, her charm, her ability to light up any room—had vanished. It was like the decision from Delta Pi Zeta had drained the life out of her.

Looking back, I can see all the signs of the danger we were walking into. But at the time, it was just a blur of chaos and confusion. It's easy to say now what I should have done differently, but in the moment, we're all just trying to keep up. We don't connect the dots until the dust has settled, and by then, the picture is already complete.

I think that Cierra had imagined that she was going to be able to go into the DPZ hearing and use some trick, some technicality to get out of trouble as she had so many other times. However, she had failed, and she received a lifetime suspension from Delta Pi Zeta, and she was given thirty days to move out of our building.

I recall telling Cierra that she should be grateful, since there had been the possibility of being kicked out of PVSU altogether, which they certainly could have done. The chapter had shown her mercy, in that they did not report this to the school administration, and I told her to please consider that before she made any rash decisions. Honestly though, part of me wonders how purely merciful this was on the part of DPZ. I think they did not want the visibility of an alcohol related incident being raised with the school administration. Perhaps we could have leveraged that for a better outcome. Whatever the reasons, I didn't really have time to consider it, as we had thirty days to find Cierra a new living situation. The three of us, Faith, Cierra and me, got together and set to work. Cierra made it clear that moving back home to Florida was not to be considered, even though that option was probably the most realistic. Luckily, Faith had a friend who had a two-bedroom apart-ment off campus nearby, and we were going to move Cierra out of the dorm after Christmas and into this friend's apartment, allowing her to sublease it and in that way, she could remain in school. We all agreed on this, or at least I thought we did. But Cierra never planned to move out of the dorm. She was making her own plans. I think she just planned to die.

The sorority used a group chat app on our phones called DPZ-BabeNet so we could quickly communicate broad ideas and updates to all members. It was our go-to virtual bulletin board. Typically, we would not use the app for trivial matters, as this was viewed as spam and the girls would let you know if you were abusing it. However, in the last month of Cierra's life, starting in late December after her expulsion, she had started using this app as her personal sounding board. It started with a simple message on a Tuesday morning stating: Hey girl, quit knocking on my door and running away, just come in, it's unlocked. This was an unusual message, so much so that nobody really said anything. I think everyone was mainly curious what this message meant and were waiting for more information before saying anything one way or another. This was especially true for me, and I recall sitting in my room just staring at the screen worriedly. I popped my head out my door several times, and I even sat in the hallway on the floor waiting around to see if I could get more meaning to this message, but nothing ever happened. I would go over to Cierra's door and knock hard several times, but she would not answer. I even tried the door knob, but it was locked. Other girls were in the area too, and they made up excuses to come around our rooms, hoping to catch a peek or a clue as to what was going on with Cierra. Eventually, after about the fifth time I tried knocking on Cierra's door with zero response, it dawned on me. Cierra was sending that message on DPZ-BabeNet in response to me rapping on her door over and over again. *Is she that far gone?* I thought to myself, completely disturbed at my realization. Again, it may seem like I was stupid to let this slide, but I was doing my best to balance helping my friend while simultaneously not making things worse.

On the north side of our building, a staircase abutted directly to the outside of my dorm room door. I believe this was there to keep the building in compliance with local fire ordinances. Every once and a while you would hear girls using the stairs, but for the most part, everyone would use the elevators in the middle of the building, as it was much more convenient. Much like the DPZ-BabeNet messaging app, in the last month of her life, Cierra started using the stairs as her own personal area of activity. Like I mean she really started using the stairs. She would send a message on the group messaging app, and then *boom, boom, boom* I would hear her little feet stomping down those stairs, and then bounding back up a few minutes later. I decided I had enough, so after I had heard her go down, I opened my door and stood waiting for her return.

When she came back up, I stopped her and I said, "What the F girl, what are you doing?"

I looked into her eyes while grabbing her shoulders. I noticed that she had sweat on her forehead, and that she appeared like she had not taken a shower in at least two days.

She seemed exasperated, and she used her arms like a fulcrum inside of mine and brushed me off. "Not now, Babe." She wouldn't even look at me when I was inches away from her face, and she stormed off to her room without another word.

I don't know what to do, I said to myself, but unlike Cierra who always knew how to handle me, and despite how I swore that I would do so, I had no clue how to help her. *I am not built for this, I cannot handle this, and I am scared,* I said to myself. I let out a resolute sigh, and decided that I was going to call my parents and confide in them for advice. Just then, Faith appeared at my open door.

"Bella," Faith gently called out. "We need to talk."

Faith and I sat across from each other on my bed, as we pieced together everything we'd noticed about Cierra over the past few months. She shifted restlessly, and I could see her rubbing the fabric seam of my blanket between her thumb and finger nervously. Faith swallowed hard and said,

"You won't believe this, but on top of everything else, Cierra's been skipping classes. I saw her sneaking back to the dorms. She was stumbling too."

I raised my eyebrows, but then quickly furrowed them, as I did not like Faith knowing more about my best friend than me. That quickly passed, and I decided to throw in my own confidential info by saying,

"Well, she turned down my offer to come home with me for Christmas. She's staying here over the break."

Faith's eyes widened, but it seemed a little theatrical to me. She might have just been jealous I never invited her. Faith continued,

"Really? I would say that is weird, but Cierra's behavior has been pretty unpredictable lately." She glanced away for a second, rubbing my blanket even harder. "I'll be staying here too though—working, mostly. I'll keep an eye on her and make sure she's okay."

I hesitated, a nagging doubt lingering at the back of my mind. Something about leaving Cierra behind didn't sit right with me, but I was so ready to escape.

"Thanks," I said plainly, shaking off the feeling of unease and letting myself off the hook eagerly. I wanted to get the hell outta there, and who could blame me? I mean looking back now, I could have never imagined then that my friend was going to die. I was laser focused on myself and what I wanted to do. This turned out to be a mistake I deeply regret, as over the next few weeks, Faith and Cierra grew closer than ever, spiraling further together into deadly chaos.

Chapter 16
X Hours 'til 5:14AM

THE FIRST DAY OF sophomore winter break, nothing happened. The second day, same thing, yawn. But on the third day, around 10 in the morning, something *finally* happened.

"Bell, someone's here! Bell! **BELL!**" my dad yelled, followed by an impatient, "Will somebody wake this kid up already?"

Half awake and still in my PJs, I stumbled out of my room and down the long hallway to the front foyer, where my dad was yelling. What I saw stopped me right in my tracks—our front door was wide open, and there was my dad, shaking hands *rather firmly* with Bryce.

He patted Bryce's right shoulder with emphasis, pulled him inside, and shut the door forcefully. I felt like I was watching two bears on a nature show, one younger and one older, locked in a primal display of unspoken manliness. *Yes, we get it guys, you're both great champion warriors,* I thought to myself with a smirk. Still, I had to give Bryce credit for holding his own against my dad's overbearing presence, meeting him as an equal but with just the right touch of deference. Not gonna lie, seeing him handle this situation with my dad like that was definitely earning him points.

With one final firm pat on Bryce's back and a muted smile, Dad pivoted sharply, like a Marine late for inspection, and disappeared into his home office, leaving us standing there alone.

"What are you doing here?" I asked him warmly, but with genuine curiosity.

"Well, I did not end up going home for break, and then I came around looking for you. I ran into Faith, and she gave me your address, so here I am," Bryce replied all matter of factly.

At this point, Bryce and I were definitely seeing each other, but not officially dating. So, him showing up unannounced at my house made the situation a little bit jarring. For some reason, it brought to mind the first time I met Cierra and our crazy encounter with Fireball whiskey at the GLV courtyard. Instead of letting it upset me, I chose to just go with the flow.

"So, what is up," I asked him sweetly, *invitingly*.

"Get dressed and put on some tennis shoes. I have a coffee for you in my truck. I want to take you somewhere," he replied excitedly.

I quickly got ready and said goodbye to my parents. We got into his dark gray lifted Ford F150 pickup truck and started driving. It was exhilarating to be going somewhere and doing something. We drove about five miles from my house, to the base of a small foothills trail system called Tapestry Pass. Bryce put the truck in park and motioned for me to, *wait one minute.* He quickly got out, came around to my side, and held my hand as he helped me get down from the truck. He put on a small backpack, and then started bounding up the trail, without even waiting for me. I called out his name, but he just turned around and playfully said to *hurry up.*

We hiked about less than a half mile up the trail, and then Bryce stepped off and started walking into what looked like the middle of nowhere. This new adventure reminded me of the sterling rose bush near the PVSU Palm Walk that Bryce had shown me. So, I knew I could trust him and I did not protest. About maybe a tenth of a mile off the main trail, the desert opened up into a giant slab boulder that hung off of a cliff. There was about a hundred foot drop at the end of it. It provided a beautiful view of Calebrea Canyon. Bryce opened his backpack and pulled out a comfy picnic blanket. He skillfully unfolded it and carefully spread it out onto the surface of the boulder. He then reached into his pack and produced a small brown paper bag, which contained a toasted asiago cheese bagel with cream cheese, my favorite.

We had carried our coffees with us, so we each crossed our legs and then sat there next to each other and shared that bagel. This was December in Arizona, so the temperature was a balmy 55 degrees and sitting in the sun was absolutely perfect. I have to admit, I felt warm, protected and appreciated being there in his presence.

"So I heard about the trouble that Cierra got into. How is that going? Is there anything I can do," he asked earnestly.

"That is super sweet of you *babe*," I said, which was a slight slip up. I mean, I called Cierra babe all the time, but that was a sorority thing. However, when I said it to Bryce, I certainly meant it in a different connotation. I didn't even have to play it off, because when I called him babe, Bryce pulled me in close and gave me a warm passionate kiss. After, we sat there and stared into each other's eyes. I did look away, playing shy. Bryce stroked my hair back and rubbed my shoulders. We spent another hour just talking about things.

After our date, we drove back to my house. Bryce gently stopped the truck and put it in park. Once again, he got out, and carefully lifted me down from the cab of the truck in his gentlemanly manner.

"I will be back around 5pm. There is a new movie I want to go see," Bryce said, again matter of factly.

During winter break, we spent as much time together as we could. Bryce had a knack for planning something new to do every time he saw me. Though there were two occasions where I turned the tables and planned our date.

The first time, I took him to a local archery range. As I steadied my compound bow and hit several bullseye shots, I couldn't help but notice the surprise in his eyes at my display of physical prowess. The second time, I ended up snagging tickets for his favorite hockey team. He seemed a little shocked at the face value on the tickets, as his mouth opened to protest, but I was able to quickly assure him it was my Christmas gift to him.

At the game, during intermission, Bryce slipped his hand into his pocket. He pulled out a small red velvety box and handed it to me, a warm smile in his eyes. Inside was a delicate gold necklace, spelling "Isabella" in an elegant cursive. Somehow he knew my love for anything with my name emblazoned on it. Goal.

It was getting late on the last day of my Christmas break at home, and the sun was going down as I backed my car out of my parents' driveway. Our house is located in the foothills on the southern edge of Phoenix. It is a huge single story split floor plan, with incredibly high ceilings, painted deep dark brown on the outside and solid white on the inside. As I was pulling away, I took a moment to take in the perfectly hung multi-colored icicle Christmas lights that my dad had hung along each line of the roof. My parents have a routine every year on the day before Thanksgiving where my mom does the inside of the house with the tree, and my father hangs lights on every eave and overhang of our home. They work together in harmony to accomplish such amazing and beautiful things.

As the lights twinkled, I focused in on a strand right above the third garage bay door, where I had parked my car earlier. I suddenly felt a twinge of pain deep near the center of my torso, right around the top of my stomach. This sensation was coupled with a dash of panic and guilt for having taken this break away from Cierra, who was most likely alone at this very moment. I felt like such a terrible friend. I put the car in drive and started moving towards the PVSU campus. I drove slowly at first as I gathered my thoughts, but I increased my speed in ever more frequent intervals as the tension inside me started to build. I was worried about the myriad of possible situations that awaited my return at the dorm, because I knew there were several bad and not too many good ones.

Cierra and I had texted during the time I was at home on break, and I saw her update her social media profiles with random posts during that time frame. However, on this last day of winter break, Cierra had posted a picture of her sitting in the GLV courtyard in a tiny string bikini. It wasn't too revealing or over-sexualized, and this being Arizona, girls post pics of themselves in bikinis year-round, so that in itself was not unusual. The thing that scared me was that Cierra looked like she hadn't washed her hair in days, and she was so super skinny. Her skin also had lost its natural milky white hue, and it was replaced with a waxy gray tone that felt to me like it was her body's natural way of crying out for help. I hadn't seen her since the beginning of break, and seeing how much she had changed in such a short time really struck me. That image of her provided me with extra motivation as I sped towards campus. I just did not realize how little time I actually had left with my friend. Deep regret filled my entire mind, body and soul for going home and enjoying myself.

Phoenix, Arizona is a huge spread out metropolitan area, surrounded by several adjoining cities, like Glendale, Tempe and Mesa, and it sprawls out upwards of sixty miles across in all directions from end to end. Even going twenty miles an hour over the posted speed limit all the way, the drive back to the PVSU campus took me a full thirty minutes. Parking my car and walking back to the dorm took another ten. There was an eerie emptiness on the streets on the drive back and it seemed to have oozed itself onto the PVSU campus as well. There was nobody around, and it felt deserted. *Everyone must have still been on break,* I thought to myself, trying to self-soothe my feelings of dread away. I finally reached the front of our building, scanned my ID on the RFID card reader, and swung open the door hard. I was preparing to bound up the stairs. I didn't even want to wait for the elevator as that would have been even slower.

"Bella."

I immediately heard a timid and nervous voice reaching out to me in the stillness of our mostly abandoned building. I knew it was Faith without even turning around, and for some reason, this annoyed me greatly.

My shoulders bunched up, like an angry cat that is about to let out a mighty hiss. "What is it, Faith?"

"Cierra isn't doing so well," she told me, with her eyes down, looking at her flip flops while her thumb was gently caressing the seam on her jean shorts. She asked me to sit, so that she could explain the situation of what unfolded after my winter break absence.

I didn't want to do that. I wanted to blow Faith off and run up to Cierra's room, but she grabbed me and persuaded me that what she was going to tell me was really important—like she was preparing me for something. Immediately, I felt suspicious about Faith's motivations, but at the same time, I didn't feel like I really had a choice. I slowed my pace, took a deep breath and decided to acquiesce.

We sat together in the sorority's front lounge, Faith's voice started breaking as she revealed a secret she and Cierra had kept hidden for months. They had reconciled after their falling out over the fake IDs, rekindling their friendship and keeping it from everyone—including me. The words were painful to hear, and they hit me almost like a betrayal. My defense mechanisms wanted to dismiss it as a lie, but deep down, I knew Faith had no reason to make all this up. Still, it didn't add up.

Why would they hide this from me? I thought to myself.

Determined to uncover the full story, I pressed Faith for the entire truth. Though I couldn't match Cierra's cunning in situations like this, I kept pressing, and eventually, Faith cracked. She admitted that their secrecy went beyond friendship. They'd been entangled in a lifestyle of illicit drug use, something that had spiraled out of control in the past two months.

Faith looked down, rubbing her index finger and thumb together as she talked. "I've been on Adderall since I was a kid," she said quietly. "But here at PVSU, things got more complicated." Her voice began trailing off, and

I could almost see her retreating into her memories. "At first, it was just minor stimulants, nothing crazy. But then Cierra and I..." She swallowed hard, glancing up at me to gauge my reaction.

I felt the weight of her words hit me before she even finished, it was getting that serious. They had dabbled in everything you could imagine: antidepressants, narcotics, even sprinkling in some cocaine. She described it like a game, each of them daring the other to take things further. As I listened, I felt anger building up inside me, but beneath that anger, a twinge of guilt began to take root. *How had I missed this? The secret friendship, the reckless spiral, how had I been so blind? Cierra was my best friend. You think I of all people would have noticed,* my inner voice scolded me.

My fists clenched as Faith spoke, my anger waned and a surge of determination took over. This was going to end. I would make sure of it.

"Where are the drugs coming from, Faith?"

"There is this Asian guy in the frat, we call him Buck. He is our normal go to supplier. But lately the stuff that we were looking for, Oxy, that was not something that he could get. So, he turned us on to this old lady we call Dixie, who lives in a high rise in Scottsdale. It is weird, she is this totally professional looking woman, with pretty blonde hair and glasses and in her forties maybe. If I did not know any better, I would say she is a doctor."

"I want to know who they are, Faith, their real names, now," I demanded, pointing my finger firmly towards her.

"It doesn't matter. We are big girls, and we knew the risks, we are not innocent."

That last part pissed me off. Even in her expanded confession, I knew in my heart that Faith was still not telling me everything. I decided that I'd had enough of her BS. I stood up and walked away from her.

"Don't follow me, Faith, you got it?" I turned briefly to make sure she heard me.

I started to walk up the stairs, but for a brief moment standing there in the stairwell, I felt my knees buckle, and I had to brace myself on the banister to keep myself from falling. I took a deep breath and managed to hold steady. *Come on Bella, your friend needs you, shake it off*, I told myself. I made it up the stairs, and started walking down the third-floor hallway as I had so many times in the past. Except this time, I was filled with so much dread that it was palpable, and it made this familiar place feel foreign to me, like I was out of place. I shook my head to regain my nerve, and I continued walking towards Cierra's room.

I breathed in and out slowly several times, then knocked gently on her door. There was no answer. I twisted the knob, and this time, to my surprise, it opened. Immediately it was obvious that something was not right. Cierra's room was rank with this bizarre unknown chemical smell mixed with dirty laundry and a few days of living in filth. I scanned the room and I saw Cierra there laying on her bed. She was completely blitzed, intoxicated out of her mind, in a near comatose state. I did not think she was drunk because I could not sense the telltale signs of alcohol, so I surmised that she was totally drugged out. I said,

"F— this," and pulled out my phone to dial 911. Just then, as I was motioning to make that call, I felt a clammy hand reach out to stop me.

"Wait, don't call 911, we can handle this," Faith said pleadingly.

"Forget that noise," I said.

I paused and looked at Faith, and she started to explain that calling 911 was going to mean getting sorority leadership involved, and making things even worse for all of us, especially Cierra. She suggested that we should call an Uber and take Cierra to the hospital ourselves because there was one so close to campus. This time I looked at Cierra, and I had to do something, so I caved and put my phone away.

It took us about forty minutes to wake Cierra up enough to stand on her own. I did not know this, but found out later, that someone who is drinking or on drugs is most intoxicated about an hour after their last drink or pill. I could not understand how Cierra was even more out of it than when we first started, but that is the reason, and it made things worse for all of us.

At first, while trying to get Cierra to move, she told us to F off and that she wasn't going anywhere. Then I gave her an ultimatum, that either she went with us willingly or I was calling 911. Cierra looked right into my eyes, and even though her own were barely open, she smiled, patted my head, and slurred, "Whatever you say *Blinky*." Cierra had slurred my nickname. That moment is forever locked into my head and it tortures me to this day. *Blinky*... I certainly had no clue, but did Cierra understand at that moment, just how close she was to dying, I still ask myself. And if she was aware, how could she just be so nonchalant about it like that?

Why I let Faith talk me out of calling 911, I will never know, but I agreed and we called an Uber instead of the EMTs. We had great difficulty, but we loaded Cierra into our ride when it arrived on College Avenue and we were dropped off at the hospital a few minutes later.

In hindsight, not calling 911 was the biggest mistake we made. I feed off of vibes, and I knew right away when we walked in that place that we had messed up bringing Cierra there. Nobody looked willing nor capable of helping. With a sinking feeling in the pit of my stomach it dawned on me that perhaps if we would have called 911, the paramedics would have avoided that place and taken my friend to one of the better facilities in the area. Either in our haste to help our friend, or our sheer ignorance, we chose wrong. More likely, Cierra and our collective luck had finally run out.

For years, my parents and I used our phone location app to track one another for reasons of safety and convenience. Most of the time this tracking was beneficial, but sometimes, like at that moment, it could serve to alarm or potentially scare the hell out of someone. I decided, after dealing with this all on my own, to call my parents and confess. However, when I dialed my Mom, it was my Dad who answered, and I chickened out.

"I am calling because I am at the hospital. Cierra is sick and we don't know what is wrong with her," I advised my parents. "I don't want you guys to freak out if you see my location, ok?"

I mean I had a pretty good idea what was going on with Cierra, but I was not ready to tell my parents specifics about it, so I told a small white lie. This was a near scripted, very contrived phone call obviously and I feel guilty for having lied to my parents. I wish I had told them the truth so they could have helped me by intervening, and I believe they feel the same way to this day. At that moment in time, I felt that I was still in control and I was trying to salvage this situation and not make it any worse. For a moment, I fooled myself into feeling like I had the Cierra superpowers, being in command of an out-of-control situation. My intentions were good in spite of the eventual outcome.

A mere fourteen hours later that following morning, I made a much different call to my parents. This next call that I placed was completely unscripted, and it was chaotic, and the pain of it has scarred me, and my parents, for the rest of our lives. To this day I think my dad has some PTSD from the sheer shock of my voice and the message that I delivered to him and my mother that morning. It was one of the last things they ever wanted to hear and it shook them to their core to the point that they have still not fully recovered. None of us have. Nobody ever truly does.

"Cierra is dead," I said through streams of hot burning tears. It sounded surreal to me as I said those words. It was as if I wasn't even saying them.

It hit my parents like a ton of bricks and all I heard on the other end of the line was their shallow breathing. I could picture them looking at the phone and each other as I could tell I was on speaker when I announced Cierra's death. My parents for all their wisdom and guidance had nothing of substance to say to me, outside of checking that I was all right, and their empty platitudes of, *everything is going to be ok.*

No, it is not going to be ok, I thought to myself, *nothing will ever be ok, ever again.*

I could tell that even my normally confident and upbeat parents were full of nothing but doubt and dread at this revelation. How could my dad, who was Superman to me, suddenly be out of things to say or have no guidance to give. But there he was mostly silent and buried in the sheer shock and desperation of this situation. It was sad that this announcement had reduced the pillars of my life to ash, and all we could do was sit there in silence while we grasped at what to say or do next. It pains me to admit, but all I knew, was even through my tears of grief and disbelief, I was extremely angry at the world. I was pissed at my parents for not knowing what to say and do. I was pissed at myself for allowing my best friend to die. But most of all, I was pissed at Cierra for doing this to me.

I still have not gotten to the worst part of what was to follow, explaining to my parents how my best friend died exactly, with specificity.

I don't want to talk about the final twenty-four hours of Cierra's life. Especially the part you have not heard, about how she died in the hospital from a drug overdose. In fact, I just flat out refuse to do so. I know I have to tell you the story though.

After Faith's deceit, I felt like she owed me and I was able to get her to ask her dad (who is connected to the PVSU Police Department) to get me a copy of the transcript for the official witness statement that I gave them in regards to Cierra's death. That transcript is presented un-redacted in its entirety so that I do not have to talk about this any longer.

PALO VERDE STATE UNIVERSITY
CAMPUS POLICE DEPARTMENT
OFFICE OF STUDENT INTERACTIONS
TRANSCRIPT

Interview Time: January 8th, 1:35PM to 1:57PM
Case Number: PV0000098721
Offense: N/A

Interviewer: Thad Johnson (TJ)

Interview Of: Isabella Maria Amescua (IMA)

On January 8th at 1:35PM, Detective Thad Johnson interviewed Isabella Maria Amescua at the campus field office on 26 W. College Avenue in Phoenix, Arizona. Also in the room were her parents, Michael and Bonnie Amescua of Phoenix.

- **TJ**: It is presently 1335 hours on January 8th. I am Detective Thad Johnson of the Palo Verde State University Campus Police Department. I just want to collect some basic information from you Isabella to start so we can nail down some information, ok? First of all, I want to let you know that you are not in any sort of trouble whatsoever. We are only trying to figure out what happened with your friend. And again, nobody is in any trouble ok, we just want to figure out what happened, bottom line, ok? Can I please get a copy of your student ID?

- **IMA**: Yes. Let me grab it ***inaudible*** in my purse.

- **TJ**: Ok thank you, got it. Your name is spelled I-S-A-B-E-L-L-A M-A-R-I-A A-M-E-S-C-U-A correct? And your student ID is ************?

- **IMA**: Yes.

- **TJ**: And you live on campus at the Delta Pi Zeta Sorority in room 301, correct?

- **IMA**: Yes.

- **TJ**: Who are the two people in the room with us?

- **IMA**: (Starts crying). ***inaudible*** My parents.

- **TJ**: (Stands and retrieves box of tissue and hands to IMA). Ok look you are not in trouble. I know you are sad. This is a tragedy and we are all sad but it is important that we take a report and get everything into a statement, ok? Please be strong for your friend, ok?

- **IMA**: Ok.

- **TJ**: What year student are you?

- **IMA**: I am a sophomore.

- **TJ**: Ok, what is your major?

- **IMA**: Computer Science.

- **TJ**: Ok, that's cool those computer things confuse the hell out of me. I am pretty dumb when it comes to technology. I still have a VCR if you can believe that. You probably do not even know what a VCR is, am I right?

- **IMA**: (Slight laughter).

- **TJ**: How long did you know Cierra Fallion?

- **IMA**: (Starts crying). ***inaudible***

- **TJ**: Look Isabella, I need you to get it together and shake this off. We need to get a report for your friend, ok?

- **IMA**: (Coughing / Clearing throat). Ok ok sorry. I, uh, knew her for just over a year.

- **TJ**: Were you guys close?

- **IMA**: Yes absolutely. She is... was... my best friend.

- **TJ**: Can you tell me about what happened to her yesterday?

- **IMA**: She died.

- **TJ**: Yes, I understand that. Can you please tell me what happened last night in detail and also tell me about the circumstances leading up to last night please? It is important.

- **IMA**: I noticed a few weeks ago that Cierra started acting strange. She started to act like, like she did not know me and she just did not give a rip any longer. She was in trouble with our sorority. And she thought she was going to get herself out of it. Out of trouble I mean. But she didn't oh goodness no she didn't and they were going to kick her out of our building and she could not escape this fate and it was too much for her. Cierra always got her way but, in the end, everything caught up with her, and her powers to bend people to her will were all gone. And I was not there. I went home on Christmas break and left her alone.

- **TJ**: Powers? Bend to her will? Wait, tell me more about this past week and specifically, the trouble she was in with Delta Pi Zeta.

- **IMA**: Cierra got really wasted drunk a while back and she punched our chapter president in the face. There was a disciplinary hearing and they just railroaded her. They wanted her gone.

- **TJ**: Who wanted her gone? You mean gone from the sorority?

- **IMA**: Our chapter president. They would not even let me or Faith speak on Cierra's behalf. They let her plead her case for all of five minutes, they adjourned for 15 and then they came back and said she had 30 days to leave the building.

- **TJ**: Faith Carpenter? We talked to her and took her statement. What do you think Faith would have to say about your friend?

- **IMA**: I am not sure? I imagine she talked about how we took her to the hospital, but it was too late.

- **TJ**: Yes, she did talk at length about that situation. Can you tell me more about that please?

- **IMA**: We went up to her room. We knocked but she would not answer so Faith and I just turned the knob and walked right in her room. And she was in really bad shape. She did not look like she had eaten or taken a shower for a few days. She was so skinny and she just looked gray and dead. She looked like she was already dead!

- **TJ**: What happened next?

- **IMA**: I don't think she was drunk, but she was clearly on something. I asked Faith if she had taken anything, but she played dumb and said she did not know. But she did know. I was going to call 911, but Faith would not let me. She said we could take her to the hospital in an Uber.

- **TJ**: The hospital on Miller Avenue next to campus?

- **IMA**: Yes, we took her there and they let us into the emergency room. We were sitting in the waiting room actually, waiting for a doctor or something to happen or for them to take Cierra back. It was all a big joke to Cierra. She sat there making jokes that made no sense. She even made me pose for a selfie with her on her phone, which was really annoying. Then they did admit her and took her to the back, but the staff there would not let any of us go back with her because they said it was a family only policy in place.

- **TJ**: So, what happened next?

- **IMA**: Faith and I sat in the waiting room for the next, lets see ***counting on hands*** 13 hours texting with Cierra. The cell tower reception back there was not good, so we could not do video calls and pictures were not going through, so all we could do was text.

- **TJ**: How long did that go on for again?

- **IMA**: 12 or 13 Hours. And then the last message I sent to Cierra at 5:14 AM, she left me unread. And then she was gone. That is the time the nurses said her little heart gave out and she died! ***inaudible*** (starts crying).

- **TJ**: Why do you think she died?

- **IMA**: She was doing drugs. She did too many. On purpose. I think.

- **TJ**: What kind of drugs?

- **IMA**: I think she had some Oxy pills hidden in her pocket when we took her there. I don't know how she was sneaking them, but she definitely got even higher once we got there.

- **TJ**: You never did drugs with her?

- **IMA**: No never. I never do drugs!

- **TJ**: How do you know it was drugs?

- **IMA**: You would have to ask Cierra about that, but she is dead. I don't know! You should ask Faith F'ing Carpenter!

- **TJ**: Ok ok, look sorry, remember you are not in trouble here, we just want to know what happened.

- **IMA**: I don't know much about the drugs she was on. I just know that obviously she was doing them. And it cost her big time.

- **TJ**: So, you believe that Cierra died from secretly taking too many drugs and that she did that on purpose?

- **IMA**: Yes. Absolutely. I know this.

- **TJ**: Ok I understand. Look Isabella, I am really sorry about your friend. You look like a good kid. Go home, get some rest and try to put this behind you. ***Motions to parents*** Your parents will take care of you. Get some rest please and put this behind you. You didn't do anything wrong.

- **IMA**: Thank you.

END TRANSCRIPT

Reading that back now, it is so obvious to me that the PVSU Police just wanted to get my statement to show that they, and the University, did nothing wrong. And I guess it is true, the only person to blame for what happened to Cierra, is Cierra. End of.

Chapter 17

Demilune

Two months had slipped by since Cierra chose to end her life. It was now March of my sophomore year, and if the plants outside were blooming or it was turning to spring, I wouldn't be able to tell you. Everything seemed hazy and distant. I was doing all the things I was expected to, but it felt robotic, like I was just going through the motions.

People who knew Cierra were still reeling from the shock, especially in the days immediately following her death. My parents were absolutely devastated, which, honestly, I found a bit annoying. Cierra was my best friend and they barely knew her. I guess they were just scared though, as Cierra's death forced them to confront their own daughter's mortality. So, they made it a habit of checking in on me constantly. They texted me over and over again every single day. Sometimes they'd call out of the blue, which was bad enough, but there were times they actually showed up on campus. I love them, and I know they were trying to help, but deep down, I hated it. It just made me even madder at Cierra, even as I mourned her loss.

That wasn't the only thing I found incredibly frustrating during this time. Everyone who heard about Cierra was saddened, naturally, but they were all too eager to let me know. The worst offenders were people on the very periphery of our social circle. I even saw a couple of girls who had never met Cierra post heartfelt *'rest in peace'* messages on their timelines. It felt shallow and maybe even rude, given the gravity of the situation when coupled with the truth. Still, I guess I forgive them as it's just so hard to process when a young college student, with her whole life ahead of her, chooses to end it all. I get it, but damn, *she was my best friend.* Cierra ripped my heart out and stomped on it. This was my grief to bear, not theirs. My heart lay shattered under the weight of what felt like the ultimate betrayal from my best friend. She had her reasons, I will give her that, but she's gone, and I was left to pick up the pieces. What hurts the most was knowing she didn't give herself, nor me, the chance to find another way. I may be young, but I know there is always another way, regardless of the situation.

Bryce was my absolute rock through this difficult time, thank goodness. He gave me just the right amount of support and space. Which made sense being he was an astrophysics major, no pun. I knew that from earlier conversations, but it was something I didn't truly appreciate until one late afternoon about five weeks after Cierra's death.

There was a knock at my door, and when I opened it, he was standing there with a muted smile, hands tucked deep in his pockets.

"I know it's been a rough patch," he said softly, looking pensive up towards the ceiling. "So, I thought it might be healthy if we could get away from here for a bit. Just the two of us, under the stars. No expectations, just a quiet night."

He paused, meeting my gaze. "Sometimes, the universe has a way of reminding us of things. Things we don't even know we need. Besides, it is going to be an extremely clear night."

I looked at him, and I found myself unsure. But in that moment, something tugged at me inside, telling me to listen to him. I was filled with a hope that maybe a night away could help me find my way through all that I had lost.

"Okay," I said, and grabbed my purse as we headed out the door.

We walked to the parking garage and found Bryce's truck. He opened the door for me. As I climbed into the passenger seat, the smell of Bryce's cologne, pine air freshener and worn leather filled the cabin. He quickly climbed in and smiled at me as he started and put it in gear.

"You're not hungry are you," he jokingly teased me, but I already knew—he was taking me to my favorite pizza joint.

The drive was quiet and filled with a comfortable silence coupled with the low growl of the powerful engine. When we arrived, the warm, savory aroma of coal oven pizza met us as we stepped inside the door. Bryce confidently took charge of ordering, and he nailed it. We got a Caprese salad and a large pepperoni pizza, my absolute faves.

As we waited for our order, we talked about everything and nothing. It wasn't deep or profound, but it was easy and natural. Somehow, Bryce knew exactly how to steer and navigate our conversation keeping me engaged and entertained.

When the pizza came out, Bryce slid a plate toward me and served me a slice of the pizza like a perfect gentleman. In that moment, with the hum of the restaurant around us and his relaxed presence beside me, I felt something I hadn't in ages: normal.

After dinner, we got back into his F150 and started driving again. We drove for about an hour east towards the Superstition Mountains, where Bryce told me we could escape all the light pollution of the city. He said that he wanted to try and catch a glimpse of the rarely visible Trifid Nebula (M20), which sounded so mysterious and exciting to me. In the bed of his truck underneath a tarp, Bryce had a huge telescope and tripod in a black heavy duty cargo container. It was securely cinched down with blue nylon straps.

Bryce glanced over at me, one hand on the steering wheel, and said softly,

"This will be good to get away from Palo Verde for a bit. Just you, me, and the stars."

"It doesn't feel the same without her here." I didn't look at him as I spoke. I was worried that seeing him might make me cry. So, I continued gazing out the passenger side window.

"I understand." Bryce paused, watching me. I think he was trying to choose his words carefully. "But maybe there's a way to feel close to her out there. Stars in a clear night sky can have a way of holding things close for us. Like memories or precious moments. Maybe you'll see something tonight that feels... familiar. Something that can help you heal."

I finally looked at him and gave him a gentle nod. "Well, Cierra loved looking out at the sunset. Said it reminded her of the true beauty of nature."

Bryce smiled and squeezed my hand gently in his, pulling his truck to a stop in a secluded spot on an access road a couple miles off the main highway.

"Let's see if the sky has anything to tell us tonight," he said with an upbeat tone.

We got out of the truck, and Bryce began quickly setting everything up on a giant tripod. He had a small table that held a MacBook and a lantern that emitted red light. While he was working diligently he told me some light astronomy facts that were interesting and thoughtful.

"Technically, it's a waxing crescent tonight," he said, catching me staring up at the beautiful moon. He smiled and added, "But I prefer calling it a demilune—it just sounds more romantic, doesn't it?" He glanced back at the telescope and continued, "It's actually perfect for stargazing—the dim light won't wash out the stars."

Bryce then told me about how he wanted to be an astronaut ever since he was a little boy. I found him opening up to me in this way to be incredibly romantic. Then after one final adjustment and an excited look from Bryce in my direction, it was ready.

"Bella, take a look," he said.

I peered into the eyepiece of this rather large scope. At first I couldn't see anything but my eyelashes, except they were all giant for some reason. Bryce recognized my difficulty, and he patiently told me to open my one eye wide and really press it into the lens. Then it resolved, and I saw the nebula filled with brilliant deep hazy blues and purple clouds surrounded by some absolutely dazzling white stars. This telescope must have been extremely powerful, because it was like seeing photos of space that NASA publishes on their website. As I was appreciating this spectacle, something else happened. For just the briefest moment, I swear, that the nebula, which looked like an eye anyway, was looking back at me. But more specifically, I felt like I was sensing Cierra's presence coming from the great unknown out there and back at me through the telescope.

I thought I was going to get upset or sad once I felt this haunting and disturbing sensation. However, I did not let my emotions get the best of me. Something in my inner voice or spirit told me that what I saw or felt was real, and that I needed to use my computer skills to figure it out. I put this all in the back of my mind, determined to return to this idea, when the timing was right.

After we were done studying the nebula, I pulled Bryce down next to me on the blanket. The spot he picked was a grassy field, and the blanket that he brought was very thick and comfortable. We were laying there feeling the warmth of each other. As we talked softly, I rolled over and laid on top of him. He reached up and brushed a strand of hair from my face, but his touch was lingering just a little longer than before. Our conversation trailed off and it was replaced by a deep, meaningful silence. When our eyes met, they locked long enough for both of us to sense an unspoken understanding passing between us. He cupped my face gently, our foreheads touching, and it was like we were breathing in each other's essence. That night, on our warm blanket bathed in starlight, we found a new depth to our relationship in each other's arms.

As we were lying there together in the quiet moments after, I leaned over and pressed my ear against his chest. I was listening to the steady rhythm of his breathing, feeling a warmth that was reaching beyond the physical. We were out in the middle of nowhere in near complete darkness, yet I felt a deep sense of calm and safety being with him. It was a certainty I hadn't known I had been seeking. His eyes were closed as I watched him. I was trying to memorize the way his hair fell across his forehead and the slight curve of his rugged smile.

It was then that I felt something settle within me. My heart had found its place.

As I drifted off, wrapped in his arms, a soft realization took hold of me, gentle but undeniable. There was no big epiphany, no fireworks, just this quiet certainty that I would always want to be exactly here, with him, there could never be anyone else. It wasn't something I had to say or even think about. It was simply there, as real as my hand in his.

A couple days after our stargazing adventure, I found myself unable to shake the experience of sensing Cierra's presence through the telescope. I decided to actually try and harness my skills as a quantum computer programmer to investigate the matter further. In my room, I used my MacBook to create a VPN to log into Cassiopeia, the PVSU quantum computer. I began working on a specialized program designed to capture and interpret quantum "echoes" or patterns in cosmic data related to the area of space we were observing that night. Earlier I had Bryce give me the coordinates the telescope was pointed towards. I used these to tap into the radio frequency data collection database from the Very Large Array Telescope in Socorro, New Mexico. I wanted to try to identify any anomalies that might reveal a connection to another dimension, as crazy as that sounds. I had a theory that if consciousness or energy can somehow be "stored" in a quantum state, just like the qubits in a quantum computer, my program might be able to detect traces of it.

As I worked on the program, strange patterns in the data emerged, almost like a code. Every time I would run it, the output seemed to point back to the coordinates of the Trifid Nebula. I had a feeling the results were telling me that something, or *someone*, was trying to reach out from across the universe. This discovery only led me deeper into the mystery, blurring the line between computer science and the metaphysical. I even had a silly or possibly irrational hope that I might even be able to communicate with my friend once more in some obscure fashion. Not like a phone call or anything, but maybe something more like the ancient morse code messaging my father told me they used in World War II.

Try as I might, recognizing the strange patterns were as far as I was able to get on my own. I decided that I would tell Bryce about what I was up to, even though I was scared that he might think I was a crazy person. Thankfully, he didn't think I was nuts. In fact, he seemed really interested and excited by what I was doing.

I had him stop by late one night when I could not sleep and was unable to stop thinking about Cierra. We sat side by side at my computer desk, my MacBook open to lines of code scattered with the kind of errors and incomplete methods I had come to expect when working on something this complex.

I sighed frustratedly, running my hand through my hair.

"I just can't get it to differentiate between the background cosmic noise and *whatever* it is I'm looking for. I need to isolate the signal coming from the Trifid Nebula, but it's like finding a needle in a haystack."

Bryce leaned in, studying the screen. He was not a programmer, but with his insane mathematics skills and understanding of boolean logic, he was actually quite helpful.

"Cosmic background noise is chaotic, right? But what if this signal, if it's really there, is more structured? In physics, we use Fourier transforms to break down complex waves into simpler components. Maybe that's what you need to filter out the noise."

I looked at him, and his genuine smile made me appreciate his solid insights even more.

"A Fourier transform? I think I could program that in with a separate class file if you help me with the math."

"For sure," he said with an encouraging smile. "And once you've separated the components, look for repeating patterns. They could act like a kind of cosmic fingerprint." He paused, then added, almost hesitantly, "If there is any actual intelligence in this data anomaly you found, it might leave traces. Look at the nebula again, but this time, maybe focus on HD 164492A. It is a variable star, which means it has a specific pulse. You could start there."

I hesitated, fingers hovering over the keys, as the possibilities began to unfold.

"You think it could actually work?"

He shrugged admitting that he had no idea, but there was a playful spark in his eyes.

"It's worth a shot. If there's a signal in there, your quantum computer program should be able to pick up on it once we've filtered out everything else. After all, stars can be loud, but if something's calling from the Trifid Nebula, we'll find a way to hear its voice."

"Can we call what we are doing, Project Stardust?" I asked him, smiling coyly.

"Whatever you want, you're in charge, babe," he replied with a playful smile.

We ended up spending a couple weeks on Project Stardust. Each time making some interesting, but stunted progress. Bryce and I learned so much about each other, and it was surprising the amount of depth each of us discovered we had hidden deep within ourselves. We never found anything in the realm of the supernatural, or so I thought at the time.

Chapter 18

Left on Dead

FOUR MONTHS HAD SLIPPED by since Cierra's passing, though some days it felt like no time had gone by at all. It was my second summer at PVSU, but my first without my best friend. We used to make everything an adventure, sneaking around, pranking people, or simply partying all night long. Now, those memories felt like relics of another lifetime lived by someone else.

I was a junior, moving on with my life, or at least pretending to. Without my partner in crime, Cierra, everything seemed duller, like someone had blown out my candle. I'd thrown myself into the Stardust investigation with Bryce, combing through data and chasing theories, but the deeper I dug, the less I seemed to find. It started as a welcome distraction, something to keep my mind occupied, but hitting dead end after dead end only amplified the void I was feeling.

Still, there were bright spots. Bryce had stepped in where I least expected. His brilliance with math had become my lifeline, helping to sharpen my programming skills and teaching me new ways to think about raw logic. I found myself spending hours tweaking code, running algorithms, and puzzling over solutions with him. At first, I thought it might fill the gap. But no amount of neatly written functions or clever calculations could replace the energy and excitement that Cierra brought into my life. I didn't feel like I deserved to be happy anyway; I failed her and she failed me in equal measures by my estimation.

To make matters worse, early one morning, someone had sent me this text message pretending to be Cierra:

My stomach twisted into a tight little knot as I stared at the message. For a second, I didn't move, I didn't even breathe. My brain scrambled for answers. *How? Who? Why?* But as the shock faded, fear took its place, as this simply should not be happening. This should not be.

And then came the anger.

I clenched my phone so tightly I thought I might crack the screen. *I'll show you exactly how I freak out, you imposter,* I thought angrily. How dare someone do this? How dare they exploit her memory like that? It was so cruel and disrespectful to punk me like that.

I fired off a response, my fingers shaking as I typed. Whoever it was would know exactly how I felt about their twisted little game.

It had to be someone I knew—someone who at least had access to Cierra's phone number. I quickly concluded it must be one of my sorority sisters. While I was piecing it together in my head, another text from the imposter came through:

The text began with, "Relax, it is me." But instead of calming me down, it had the opposite effect—my Latina temper flared with rage. How dare one of my sisters pull a prank like this? Furious, I decided to let whoever it was know exactly how upset I was. Without thinking, I opened the DPZ-BabeNet app we use to communicate and typed out the following message:

"WOULD YOU STOP F'ING WITH ME? I MEAN IT! STOP BEFORE SOMETHING HAPPENS!!!

As I was pressing the green up arrow send button on the app, I immediately knew it was a mistake, but it was too late. *Well, that was dumb of me, I probably should not have sent a broadcast message to all of my sisters with zero context,* I thought to myself. Nobody besides the person harassing me is going to understand that message, and everyone else is going to think I am insane. *What a dumb mistake, I am an idiot,* I scolded myself.

About 15 minutes later, I heard a knock on my door, and I found out just how big a mistake it was. The unexpected loud knock gave me a jump scare, and I immediately popped up onto my feet and walked towards my locked door.

I took a deep breath and let out a quiet sigh as I unlocked and opened the door, not sure who would greet me, guessing they were probably there as a result of the group chat app message I had just broadcast to all eighty member sisters of my sorority. When I swung the door open, I was genuinely surprised and taken aback to find it was the PVSU Police, with Faith Carpenter in tow. There in my doorway were two officers standing in front of Faith. Even though she was obscured behind these two uniformed police officers, I could see she was rubbing her thumbs together, trying to soothe herself from this tense situation. There was a brief silence, so I just stood back and took a good look at these visitors, to gauge them the way they were trying to gauge me. One officer was Hispanic or maybe Italian, around fifty years old, sort of short, overweight. The other officer was younger, a long and lanky white guy, late twenties with acne scars and a wannabe beard. I thought that neither of these guys looked capable of solving even a simple math equation, let alone an actual crime, and they were just about the least intimidating duo I could have imagined.

Behind them Faith was looking even more drawn out and nervous than usual, her right thumb and index finger were now gently caressing her right earlobe, as she tried to draw attention away from herself by staring off into the distance all nonchalantly. I looked at the two police officers, and for a moment, it crossed my mind that perhaps I should tell them that someone was harassing me over text message, pretending to be Cierra. *I mean, they were already here, so why not?* I thought to myself.

I quickly made up my mind that I was going to show the police my phone and let them know what was happening. Then I felt the all too familiar buzz of a new text message being delivered. I nonchalantly looked down at my phone, and it was a new message from the imposter:

~''*o•. ~''*o•. **dont babe**
•o*''~ •o*''~

Don't Babe, I thought to myself. Don't Babe what? What does that mean? Don't tell the authorities about these text messages? Ha, why would I do anything this imposter is telling me to do? I felt brave for a moment, but truthfully, this message simultaneously pissed me off and scared me at the same time in near equal measure. The text lingered on my screen and I wondered, *how this could be happening*? I mean, I could understand if someone who knew me was messing with me. They could plan and know things about me, Cierra, and our situation. But the timing and context of this text felt otherworldly and eerily precise.

It was too perfect and real, as if whoever was texting me had the ability to see me in real time. And that realization scared the crap out of me. I was so confused, but I managed to quickly figure out what I wanted to have happen next. I decided that I wanted the police to leave, as quickly as possible, and if they could take Faith Carpenter with them, that would be perfect. With that in mind, I addressed them both in a cheerful tone, "Hi officers, how can I help you?"

The short chubby older officer was drawing in a breath to say something, but I cut him off.

"You know, someone has been pranking me, by knocking on my door and running away, so I got frustrated and I guess I sent a broadcast message to all my sisters." I pretended to be relieved that the police were there to help me catch this *make-believe ding-dong-ditcher*.

"Oh, but you're ok, right?" the older officer asked.

His younger partner then chimed in, as if a real thought had entered his brain for the first time in a while. "When was the last time the knocking happened?"

"Fifteen minutes ago, when I sent out that message on the group chat," I replied, with an annoyed *duh* expression on my face.

Just then, *younger long and lanky* slapped *older short and chubby* on the back. "We better sweep the floors and take a look-see."

And just like that, without any other questions, the two officers were stepping off down the hallway towards the elevators. I felt relieved that they were going away and I was about to slam the door in Faith's face, but just as quickly as my anxiety had cleared from that situation, I felt my phone give off the fast and whirring buzz of a new text message arriving:

go Check my cubby drawer notebook

I stared at it for a moment, again completely confused, but then I knew that I had to strike quickly if I was ever going to get to the bottom of this messed up mystery.

"Faith, wait up," I said once the PVSU Police were out of earshot. "I need to get into Cierra's room, ok?"

"Why? Her parents cleared out that room months ago. There isn't anything in there. Besides, that room is to remain vacant until the fall and therefore it is locked up tight," Faith said, rather incredulously.

"Do I need to explain myself to you? Are you going to call the cops on me again?"

"Wow, that is low. You sent that group message and it sounded just like Cierra before she... Look, you are acting weird and I am not taking any chances..." Faith's voice trailed off and I thought for a moment that she might start crying.

"Please Faith, it's important. Get the keys, *ok?*"

She looked a little uptight and pensive about my request, but then something inside her seemed to click. She nodded her head and went bounding away with a *one moment* finger gesture. A few minutes later Faith reappeared, out of breath and flush, but with the large brass ring of keys clasped in her right hand. She motioned for me to follow and we both walked the twenty feet towards Cierra's room. Everything got real still and quiet as the two of us stood there in the hallway. Faith put the key in the lock, and the precise metal rasping of each segment of the key being inserted into the lock sounded so loud, like the entire building would hear it and come running over to see what was happening.

I didn't want anybody to know that we were going into Cierra's room. Cierra had been my best friend, but it felt like a violation to enter her room now that she was dead, even if someone claiming to be her sorta gave me permission. I felt sick to my stomach as we crossed the entrance into her room. I took a moment to gather my courage, and I then asked Faith if she could give me a moment. Of course, Faith being Faith, she crossed her arms in a defensive posture and flat out refused to leave. She dangled the big keyring in her hand by her side like it was her exclusive invitation to stay as long as she pleased. Her stubborn assertiveness surprised me. I said fine and I reached over to the nightstand drawer cubby, but to my surprise, it was locked. Luckily Faith had the master key, which she wiggled to alert me to that fact.

Faith unlocked it, and I immediately started fishing around. I saw some pennies and a quarter, some old plastic silverware, and other random items you would expect to see in a college kid's junk drawer. There in the back, tucked against the rear of the drawer and standing upright, was a baby blue spiral notebook. The way it was positioned, it was hidden, unless you were really in there at the right angle looking for it. I carefully freed it from its confines and held it out in front of me, gripping it tightly in my hands. I looked over at Faith, and her mouth was open so wide I thought she might drool.

"Calm yourself, Faith," I scolded her as I slowly cracked open the clandestine notebook.

In the front part of the spiral there were several pages of random class notes and other stream-of-consciousness drivel sprawled on just about every free surface of paper. There were little drawings of cats and hearts and other things you would expect to see from a young girl doodling while they were bored in class. As I continued thumbing through, the notes that Cierra had gotten from the tutor for Professor Declan's class fell out from the middle and landed onto the floor. I quickly scooped them up and hid them away from Faith. About halfway through the notebook, I reached the page I already knew would be there—the one I was completely dreading. Up to this point, I had been taking my time, hoping to delay the inevitable.

Across the right-hand page on the top margin was my name, Bella. It was doodled in so intricately, with hearts and stars and was quite artistic and beautifully done. The handwritten note that Cierra left me on the spiral page was five paragraphs long. It stated her reasons for doing what she did. It was beautifully written and under normal circumstances, I would have been bursting with tears. But I wasn't, because all I could think about was Cierra texting me from the great beyond. I was getting flustered between my feelings of sadness having seen this note and wanting to get back to my phone. I wanted to just put the spiral away and get up and leave, but there was Faith again, breathing heavily beside me, *watching me.*

I flipped through a few more pages and found the name Faith scrawled across the top margin. It wasn't as elaborate as the drawing of my name had been, but it was still thoughtful. I passed the notebook to Faith, and the moment she saw her name, tears poured out in heavy, heaving sobs. She let everything go, her face, body, mind, and soul fully immersed in grieving Cierra's death all over again. Then the weight of it hit me too, and I reached over to hug her as we cried together. For a few minutes, I stayed there, gently rubbing her back while she read and mourned.

After we had calmed down, Faith and I stood up to leave. There was a moment of tension while we held the notebook together, trying to decide who would take ownership of it. It only took one furrow of my brow and a firm tug for me to win that battle. I returned to my room, sat on my bed, and reflected on the chaos that had unfolded earlier that morning. Just hours ago, I had received a text—seemingly from Cierra—that came out of nowhere. I thought about the perfectly timed messages I received while dealing with the PVSU police. And then there was the notebook. There was no way anyone else could have known about it—only Cierra. Somehow, in some inexplicable way, my dead best friend had found a way to reach out to me from the unknown, so I pulled out my phone and typed:

Hi.

After my initial response, which was just a simple "Hi", a conflict started brewing inside me when I started thinking about what to text her back to further our conversation. At first, I was excited and hopeful about the possibility of being able to talk to my friend again, but then it occurred to me, Cierra was dead, and nothing, not even these bizarre texts, were going to bring her back. Whatever this was, I quickly realized that nothing tangible could come of it, and that angered me deeply because it was opening old wounds that I was anxious to move past. It started as a tiny flash of annoyance in the back of my mind, but then I felt a saltiness in me, from deep in my heart. This feeling of anger started to take aim at the presence behind these tiny electronic speech bubbles on my phone. I was angry and in pain and the thing I wanted most in the world at this moment was for Cierra to hurt, the way she had made me hurt for the last six months. I know it is petty to want some sort of revenge, but all I could see was the red tinge of boiling rage swirling and engulfing the corners of my eyes. I searched my feelings, and how this whole experience had impacted my life, and I sent the following message to Cierra through my tears of rage that perfectly articulated my emotions:

> You are a terrorist.

I understand how harsh that message may seem, but I want it to be understood, the absolutely devastating impact that my friend taking her own life had on me, my sorority sisters, her parents, my parents and even complete strangers. This solitary act on Cierra's part completely destroyed me and I will never be the same. It had been six months since Cierra died, and I can tell you with absolute certainty that there is nothing that you can learn, there is no life lesson or platitude that can be gained, when someone you love decides to end their own life. There is no place in your brain to store the memory of them and their death, so you get no closure. You can process and store the death of a loved one from a car crash, or cancer, or some other random illness, but the brain has no space dedicated for someone that commits suicide. Believe me, I am speaking from firsthand knowledge when I say that the only thing that can be said is that when people are in extreme pain, they do what they think is best for their own life, consequences be damned. They do it without any real consideration for the victims they leave behind. And while we may not understand why they did what they did to end their life, all we can do is accept it and try to move on. But the fact is that you can't move on, and you won't move on, your life is permanently altered, and not for the better. Yes, it is undeniable that I loved my dear friend Cierra, but she is a terrorist for what she did to me. And that is it, there is nothing else to be said on this topic. The end.

Soon after I sent that message, my anger subsided, and I started to feel a little bad about being so harsh. I mean, here is my poor friend Cierra, who suffered greatly in her own emotional turmoil in life, and she can't even catch a break from her best friend, even in her death. I stared at my phone with that weird sense of unease that you get when you don't know how someone is going to react to something questionable that you sent. So, I tried desperately to will a response text back from Cierra, but nothing came. I started to type out some responses, to try and soften the hard edge of my earlier reply to her, but everything I tried to say came out sounding fake, dumb and pathetic. I just kept typing and deleting it out, typing and deleting it out, in a continuous nerve-wracking little cycle.

Just when I was about to give up, my phone buzzed giving me another jump scare, and there was a reply from Cierra:

> ~"*°•.~"*°• you are right babe. what I did was wrong. and I want you to know, in my last living moment, I realized that all of my problems were fixable, except this final act. I also realized how horrible it was to do this to you, but it was too late. if I could take it back, believe me babe, I would •°*"~•°*"~

Cierra then apologized to me, in such a way that made the grief of losing her to suicide in the first place swim over and pull me under the surface into pain and despair all over again. I was drowning in sorrow and misery, once more, just like the morning I had found out she was dead. I suddenly became aware of just what an impact this situation had on me. I was worried that someone would come to my room and see me in this despair, and that would definitely not be good, especially with Cierra's death and the PVSU Police visit to my room earlier. My face was flush with tears and my skin was white hot with the heat of someone who was crying with every bit of energy they possessed. I am totally a hot-blooded Latina that cries with her entire face, body and soul.

A week after Cierra had died, we held a memorial service for her in the GLV courtyard. This was a closed ceremony and no parents were invited. All the sisters were present to pay their respects and each one was wearing their best dress and high-heel shoes. It was so touching to see how all of us girls could pull together to honor one of our own, even if most of these girls had little day to day interactions with Cierra. Out on the grass of the GLV courtyard, there were about 100 little black folding chairs placed, forming a perfectly aligned square for seating. In front of the steps to our dormitory building, a table with a beautiful fabric cover was set up, with three pictures of Cierra on top of it. On the left was a solo headshot with her hair swept up in a high braid where she looked stoically off into the distance not facing the camera. On the right was another headshot, but this one was silly, with Cierra sticking her tongue out playfully looking directly at the camera. The picture in the middle was larger than the other two, and in this picture, she was in her formal dress as this was taken at one of our sorority functions from our first semester.

Now that she was dead, it made me realize and appreciate even more, just how stunningly beautiful she looked in each photo. This was heartbreaking in itself it was such a loss. Placed in front of the pictures were a combination of nineteen white roses, strewn out evenly and artfully. Finally, on the right side of the table there was a big piece of eggshell colored paper and markers that the girls could write out their feelings and tributes to Cierra. Lots of girls had drawn cute little hearts and said messages like *sleep peacefully dear angel*. None of it was fake and all of it was quite touching and from the heart. All of us, even those who did not know Cierra well, were heartbroken. On either side of the table that was serving as a memorial, were two loudspeakers on stands and on the far right was a microphone on a podium for speaking. We had music playing out of the speakers, but not the rowdy house or metal music that Cierra was fond of. We had debated about playing something that

Cierra would have approved of, but then decided to be more conservative and proceed with a more subdued musical mix.

For the actual ceremony, we had arranged for the University Chaplain to come and deliver a few words that would serve to kick off any tributes that the sisters wanted to give on Cierra's behalf. We had the best of intentions for this service, however not everything went as smoothly as we planned. During the opening of the ceremony, when we were gathering to be seated, the music stopped three times randomly, before the entire PA system cut out completely and died. We tried to bring it back online, by unplugging it, using a different outlet and even using the built in battery, but it was toast. We almost had to cancel the whole thing, but then one of the sisters saved the day by retrieving a large karaoke party speaker with a microphone from her room, enabling us to continue the ceremony.

The three seats nearest to the podium were reserved for myself, Faith Carpenter and our chapter president. It was an open forum and anyone could get up and speak. In total four girls got up and delivered remarks, speaking with kind words. I wanted to go last, so I waited for the gap when it was clear that nobody else was going to come up to speak. I stood up to address my sisters by marching dutifully over to the podium and adjusting the microphone down to my speaking height. I told my sisters about the overwhelming deep sorrow that Cierra taking her own life had on me. I told them how much I missed my friend and I also told them about how angry I was and how unfair all of this was. I burst into tears and let out a loud wail, and somehow, when I did so, at that exact moment, a gust of wind entered the GLV courtyard and blew the entire table over. The roses, the pictures, everything went tumbling over the sidewalk and into the grass. There was a loud audible gasp when this happened.

I looked all around me, taking this moment in, and everything moved in slow motion. I looked at all the pretty girls. I looked at the western sky where Cierra and I had witnessed the beautiful sunset. I looked down towards the stairs where Cierra and I met that first day during rush week. I looked down towards the public restroom where we had the shot of Fireball whisky. I looked down at my hands, and I remembered throwing the tiny Bluetooth speaker under the crack in Cierra's door. Then I took a deep breath and just stared up straight into the sky and started crying silent tears. I stood there, in the GLV courtyard, feeling everyone's eyes on me. I wanted them to see me. This was my way to truly testify. Cierra had destroyed me, and I wanted them all to see and bear witness. After a few minutes everyone naturally sprang into action without being asked and we picked everything back up. At this point it was all a bit too much so we decided to call it a night.

Later that evening, after the PVSU police had left and Faith was gone, I was laying in my bed. I recalled the memorial service for Cierra, and how the music stopped and the wind blew the table over. I just knew in my heart that was all her, being a joker again. So, I decided now that I had the opportunity, I would ask her about it.

> Was that you?

> α¢тυαℓℓy тнαт ωαѕηт мє, тнαт ωαѕ αℓℓ yσυ вαвє. ι ¢αηησт ιηfℓυєη¢є єνєηтѕ fяσм нєяє, αℓℓ ι ¢αη ∂σ ιѕ σвѕєяνє. fяσм тнιѕ ѕι∂є, рєσрℓє ℓσσк ℓικє ℓσηg ¢яyѕтαℓℓιηє вσℓтѕ σf ℓιgнтηιηg, вυт ιηѕтєα∂ σf ѕрαякѕ, тнєy ℓσσк ℓικє тнєy αяє мα∂є υр σf рι¢тυяєѕ.

> I did that? I am a bolt of lightning? What?

> ⁓⁊⁎°•.⁓⁊⁎°• yes. all living beings are pure energy that vibrate. that day you had sparks bursting outwards that were influencing all kinds of things around you that you were not aware of. •°⁎⁊⁓ •°⁎⁊⁓ •

This realization, that from wherever Cierra was texting me, she could see me, and I looked like a long bolt of lightning made up of pictures, truly frightened me. Have you ever been reading something or talking to someone, and you come across a new explanation you've never heard before, yet somehow, you instantly recognize it as the truth without needing to verify it? Yes, this struck me just like that, but on a much deeper level. Cierra went on to explain that my bolt of lightning was actually more like a thread, and that my thread was not alone by itself in the darkness. Cierra told me that there were other threads that were in close proximity to my own, filling the void. She said that we were all loosely wrapped around each other, like a spool of yarn, and that the pictures on the surfaces of each thread, lined up together closely with one another, but reversed. I was so confused, so Cierra told me to try a little experiment. She instructed me to open the camera roll on my phone, stand in front of my makeup mirror, and hold the phone at a forty-five-degree angle to the mirror. She wanted me to observe how each photo aligned, both on the mirror's surface and on my phone's screen. She told me the pictures were not exact copies of each other though, but they were very close, and that she thought that these pictures represented our most important shared life experiences together.

YOU ᴧTILL DOᴧ'T GET IT BIᴧKY... HERE CHECK THIᴧ OᴜT...

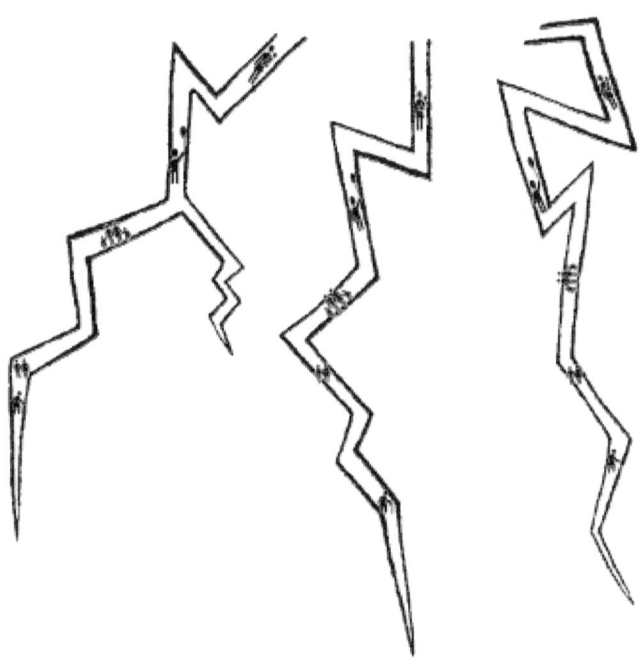

Cierra texted me a scribble drawing of three cartoon lightning bolts that clearly explained the point she was trying to make. And I got that point clear as day. But the idea that I am some crystalline bolt of lightning when viewed in another dimension was a bit too much to handle. Or so I thought, because things only got weirder from there when Cierra said something that really shook me. She said there were threads around me, like in a bundle, and she did not know who some of the other threads were, but there were two threads that were so close to mine, that they wrapped around me like a braid of hair. She said those two threads were my mother and father. Suddenly, I found myself missing my parents so much that I wanted to immediately call to tell them how much I loved them and how much they meant to me.

> Tell me about the other threads.

THERE IS TWO MORE THAT I ¢an SEE. ONE THAT SEEMS REally ¢lose TO YOU. I THINK YOU KNEW HER AS TONYA? OR ANTONYA? NOT SURE...

> Antonia?

yes that is it for sure!

I slowly recoiled, put down my phone and closed my eyes. I simply could not believe what I was reading, on so many different levels. Antonia was my grandmother on my father's side. She was the nicest and most beautiful grandma that a person could have asked for, but she passed away peacefully four years ago. There is absolutely no way that the living Cierra could have known who Antonia was, so I knew this was real. The fact that somewhere out there in the void, the soul of my sweet grandma was keeping in close proximity to me, hit me hard emotionally. As hard as it was to think about, the more I pondered this, the more sense it made to me. I have always felt my grandma's presence in my life, even now that she is gone. The cliché is that your loved ones are staring down at you from Heaven, however that is not exactly right. It would be more correct to say that your loved ones are always with you, from now until eternity.

Cierra let me know that there was another thread near Antonia and me. She said that she thought her name was Donna, but I immediately corrected her. I asked her if she meant Dionicia, as that was the name of my great grandmother. Cierra was not sure. The point was that there were more than just a few threads surrounding me, and some were of people I had never even met. This revelation somehow did not even faze me. Instead of being shocked or scared, all I felt was comfort and reassurance.

I relaxed and closed my eyes and fell asleep for a few hours. When I woke up I picked up my phone and the clock on the front screen read 1:15AM. I felt recharged and now my natural curiosity had taken hold of me. *How are you doing this, how does this work?* I texted Cierra.

In response, Cierra jokingly told me that I should have paid closer attention in my artificial intelligence classes. This made me ask Cierra if she was a bot, to which she texted back that even if she was a bot, I was still just a little baby with a binky stuffed in her mouth. This put a genuine smile on my face for the first time since before Cierra had taken her life. She then went on to explain that there is a concept called quantum entanglement, and that the latest quantum computers that we use in class can leverage some of the principles that Einstein called "spooky action at a distance."

I am actually using the
energy from your own
phone to send you these
electric signals in the
form of energy
emanating from you. you
are actually sending the
messages to yourself, in
a way.

In her last text that night, Cierra said that if you wanted to get technical, the entire Universe is actually composed of one particle, a solitary electron. This single electron spins back and forth through time so fast, that it gives the illusion of all the matter around us being their own independent things. She told me not to worry about that, and she would explain all the important items to me in due time. Cierra continued texting me telling me all kinds of interesting things, but not really giving me any real answers. I had enough of the riddles, so I started asking more pointed questions.

> Stop beating around the bush. How are you able to text me? Dead people cannot talk.

> ˜ʼʼ★º•.˜ʼʼ★º• it was all you babe, all along. when you used the quantum computer, Cassiopeia, with the telescope coordinates, I was able to see you here on my side. in a weird way, you are having this conversation, with yourself babe. •º★ʼʼ˜.•º★ʼʼ˜

> So was that you trying to reach out to me then?

> ˜ʼʼ★º•.˜ʼʼ★º• I can pull you through this side and show you exactly what happened •º★ʼʼ˜.•º★ʼʼ˜

I set my phone down, my mind spinning with the seriousness of that last message. I wasn't overly religious, but I believe in a higher power and I felt certain about the existence of our human souls. The idea of crossing into another dimension, or some supernatural realm, chilled me to the bone. It would likely mean separating my soul from my body, and I imagined the amount of risk involved would be dire.

I squinted, trying to focus, desperately searching for any logic that could ground me. *Could this be some elaborate prank?* The thought lingered, but nothing made sense. What I knew for certain was that Cierra was gone, and the intimate details someone would need to pull off a deception like this were too precise, too impossible to fabricate. Besides, the truth doesn't require explanation—it just is. And even if someone had the means to concoct such a cruel trick, why would they? There was no real payoff, only a disturbing invasion of something deeply personal.

Choosing to set my doubts aside, at least for the moment, I decided to follow along, curious where this strange connection might lead. To the last message, I replied cautiously, saying I'd think about it, though I wasn't sure I was ready—or if I ever would be.

Chapter 19

Buffer Overflow

FOUR DAYS PASSED IN a blur. Without classes to occupy my time, I settled into a routine of half-heartedly going through my daily tasks—tidying up, running errands, scrolling through social media—but my attention was always drawn back to my phone. Texting with Cierra filled the void in a way nothing else could, it was intoxicating if I am being honest. As the hours turned into days, our messages began to feel less like an exchange with a stranger and more like reconnecting with someone I had always trusted. The familiarity in her words reminded me of the bond we shared, and I found myself leaning into the comfort of it more and more.

Day five of communicating with Cierra started with a text that let me know that she was going to try and actually *call* me. This new direction sounded dangerous, and more real than anything that had happened up to this point. This wouldn't be a traditional voice call, her message read, but it would be opening a raw communication channel, and that our thoughts would be able to intermingle at a metaphysical level. This would also enable us to do what she referred to as "thread particle expansion travel."

To accomplish this, Cierra told me that she was going to send a series of visual pulses through my phone, and that when I answered it, to stare at the pattern on the screen, no matter what. She said this experience would be like sending a virus to a computer to infect it, but this payload would be sent to my very consciousness. Cierra advised that I would need to lie down and get relaxed, and to maybe even have a drink of hard liquor, which I did. I chose Fireball whiskey, in Cierra's honor. She instructed me to make sure my phone was plugged in with the heavy-duty charger, because this experiment was going to require a hell of a lot of juice. Finally, she walked me through a set of unpublished instructions on how to lower the built-in security features of my phone, down to the raw circuits, which I followed closely.

Cierra completed her directions by letting me know that this was all going to be possible by creating a virtual socket through my phone and tunneling into Cassiopeia, the Palo Verde State University quantum computer. I initially misunderstood her, and I thought that we were going to be using the computer to tunnel into the Internet or some hidden dark web server. However, what Cierra really meant was that we were going to be literally transferring my consciousness into the computer itself at a metaphysical level, but even that was not the entire truth. My entire being would be flattened and placed into and beyond the circuitry of the computer at a subatomic level. She didn't tell me about the other side, like where I would be transported to. I was filled with dread and trepidation at the thought of all this, and I asked if I could get hurt, to which she said, maybe, but not *seriously* and that I would just have to *trust her, babe*. I think Cierra could sense that I was having second thoughts, because she texted me that what she had to tell me was incredibly important, probably the most important thing I could ever witness in my entire life. That sorta scared the hell out of me, but then I remembered my parents, and how hard they worked and all of the sacrifices they had made, and that gave me the courage to continue with my mission.

Shortly after following all of her instructions, at approximately eight o'clock, my phone started buzzing and I slid the slider over to answer. Immediately my screen became a jumbled mess of green and red text, scrolling upwards like low level computer codes being issued against the processor in my phone. I was trying to decipher the readout, but I could not discern the characters. They looked like emojis but in plain text. The data stream was so intense, it felt as if my phone were almost alive for a moment, and there was this organic heat emanating from it, like an aura. Not like heat from electronic circuits, more like warmth, from something that was alive. Once this initial loading stage had passed, the text then dropped out, the screen went completely black, and there was then a series of super bright white flashes that pulsed in a random cadence that was nearly impossible to look at.

I bit my lip, and forced myself to focus on the light pattern. Once I did, the pulses faded into the background, and they were replaced with a burst of cobalt blue light that seemed to absolutely burst from the screen and start to fill my room entirely, like I was in a giant fish bowl. It was such a deep blue light that was pouring out, it appeared that blue goo was swimming all around me and I was floating in it with all the flotsam and jetsam of my dorm room personal belongings. Then I saw the pulsing and the flashing again, only this time it was a welcome experience. It was like my eyes were part of the light show and the two were merged becoming one set of eyes. One set organic, (me), and the other made of electrons flowing through silicon, gold, glass and plastic.

The first thing that happened when my consciousness was interfaced through my phone and into Cassiopeia, was my soul or essence was converted, from analog to digital. The particles of my being, my consciousness, stretched out to its maximum length in either direction, in a straight line, so that every molecule of matter and energy that makes up who I am, was positioned end to end, electronically and chemically. Even though it was happening inside of a computer circuit board, the ends of my very definition expanded out into infinite lengths, left and right, beyond that physical boundary. I cannot explain how this is possible and I did not fully understand it at the time when it was happening to me, it was just what happened. Something was *telling* me that was what was going on, almost like an internal narrator. The blueprint of my soul had stretched out so far that it bent along an invisible curvature and it came right back to myself, here, but across the bounds of the Universe, all at the same time and place, instantaneously.

As this was happening, I began to see images in my mind's eye. I saw some visions, like old time black and white pictures from history books and forms like Lego shapes flash before me. Then I saw a clearing, like a dirt mesa, and there was a little girl, perhaps it was me, riding her bike on a dirt road through a high desert field. There was a car slowly trailing behind the girl on the bike, something incredibly old. I think the driver was my grandfather and he was wearing his old Navy uniform. The headlights on this old car were on, except they were not lights at all, they were small candles inside little glass enclosures in front of a concave mirrored surface that intensified and reflected the light. A primitive but beautifully perfect technology. I could smell a faint scent like an acrid burning candle. As the car drove by and the little girl on the bike grew smaller and smaller into the horizon, all of this vision surrounding me was sucked up and it disappeared, as if they had been dragging it along behind them. I felt a shudder in the space surrounding me on all sides, like reality had quivered, and I blinked my eyes slowly. Whatever I saw, it was something that actually happened at some point in time, not just a vision. Don't ask me how I know, I just do.

When my eyes reopened, reality shivered again and I saw a small portal of white light, about the size of a tennis ball, hovering in front of me. I approached it cautiously, but unafraid, and I used my fingers to probe around the outside of this opening. When I touched this void, it felt like I was touching invisible Jell-O, and the surface tingled and reciprocated the force of my fingers, but in reverse. I tried to look through it, but while it was not black, there was nothing to be seen in or through this opening in the fabric of wherever I was.

Then I decided to just be brave and said YOLO as I pushed my entire body forward, jumping into this portal with no clue what was on the other side.

Immediately it was like the portal never even existed, and I was teleported to a small town in what appeared to be the late 1970s, if I had to guess. It felt like I was Dorothy in the Wizard of Oz, stepping through from black and white and into technicolor. Everything had a warm diffused light, and all of the colors were soft tone pastels. It was very beautiful and calming. I was hovering above this area slightly, like a drone in a low flight pattern.

Out of my left eye, I saw a little brown boy, maybe nine years old, with jet black wavy hair walking across a bridge that was spanning over an arroyo that ran through a park. I was able to zoom in and see him quite clearly. He had a small blue backpack on and I could tell that this little boy was walking home from school. The boy turned to his left when he crossed the bridge and started walking towards a house at the end of this small town 1970's street. As he walked, there was a construction crew on the side of the road next to him on the right, and they were digging a trench. I felt an unease in my stomach, as it felt like there was some malevolent force swarming around this little boy, and I felt compelled to protect him. In spite of that, all I could do was observe. As the boy approached the trench, there was a man, probably in his twenties, with red hair, a yellow safety vest, hard hat, and mirrored sunglasses who was leaning on an orange and white construction barricade. He was holding a black heavy-duty water hose and he was swinging it gently as he was pouring water into wheelbarrows. This man shifted his focus to turn towards the little boy as he approached and was now staring directly at him. The construction worker was smoking a cigarette and he had a fine red mustache that enveloped the cigarette butt as he inhaled the smoke from it.

As the boy got close enough to pass, the redhead man sneered, *"Little wetback puke"* with a disgusted snarl as he pointed the water hose at the boy.

The little boy looked up at the construction worker with a puzzled expression, as clearly his young brain did not really understand the implications of the insult being thrown at him.

This seemed to really incense the construction worker even more, and he yelled at the boy to *"Git"* as he took one final drag from the cigarette, cocked his fingers back, and flung the lit cigarette butt at the boy, hitting and burning his little neck. I was filled with rage at seeing this, but again, whatever this was, all I could do was observe.

The little boy clearly understood this malevolent action, and I could see a pained look on his cute little face, as he spun around and began to run away, back towards the little house on the end of the street, his initial destination.

As the boy ran, I saw the intensity and the impact of the earlier event start to hit him. He ran faster and faster as the tears began streaming down his face. The boy reached the front door to his house and he ran in and stripped off his blue backpack, letting it hit the floor. The front door to this house was rather flimsy, not in disrepair, but certainly nothing fancy. The entire house, while not old, was much smaller and diminutive compared to the house I grew up in. While I had never seen this house before, something deep inside me told me this was not just a vision, I was seeing something that actually happened in the distant past. This boy, this house, was all real. After dumping his backpack, the little boy ran towards a woman that was making tortillas in the kitchen, in the back of the house past the living room. I was not sure at first who the woman was, but slowly enough detail was revealed, and I realized this woman was my grandma, Antonia. She was clearly much younger than I ever remember her being, but then I recognized, the little brown boy was my father, and this vision I was seeing was at least thirty years ago.

Seeing this scene, I remembered a story my dad had told me about my Amescua family from Zamora, Mexico. He said that in the 1700s, they migrated north, and settled in a small town near Santa Fe, New Mexico. They were a prominent and wealthy family; however, by the early 1900s, all the money of the Amescua family was gone. It was squandered away with drinking and gambling and other vices common to American life. He told me that he himself came from a very modest background, growing up lower middle class, in Albuquerque, New Mexico. Certainly, the vision I saw I would classify as humble to maybe even poor. I had seen some pictures of this time, but honestly, I never paid much attention to any of it, and now seeing it play out in front of me, it made me feel guilty for all the first world problems I have.

My father ran up to his mother and wrapped his arms around her crying.

"What is the matter, mijito?" She pushed him back slightly, to look directly in his face and assess the situation clearly.

"This man, this construction man, he called me a wetback and threw his cigarette at me. He burned me."

His mother suddenly got an angry look on her face, as she pushed my father back even further, grasping his shoulders firmly. She then got down on one knee and stared right into my father's face as she grabbed him by the shirt collar.

"So, what!" she yelled at him as she shifted her grip, grabbing his shoulders and shaking him firmly.

She was not trying to hurt him, rather she was trying to gather his attention and teach him. The look on my grandma's face was one that I had never seen, on her, or anyone else for that matter. It was a look of absolute clarity, raw truth, and an unyielding will to survive. Then she looked deeply in his eyes as she softened slightly and said,

"Listen mijito, even if someone does not say something racist to your face, they are probably thinking it. And nobody cares if it hurts your feelings. Least of all, me. So, when someone insults you, either you do something about it, or you ignore them and keep it to yourself, but either way, I will not have a little sissy in my house, crying about it. This is my *house*, and I will not tolerate your behavior here in my *house*. I worked too hard to afford this place for you to live, and I will not allow anyone to take it from me, least of all some *redneck* and a *little sissy*."

She poked the little boy in the chest when she issued that insult. I could not believe what I was seeing, I was so confused.

She then wiped the tears from his eyes and asked much more softly,

"Now, what are you going to do about it, mijito?" She tilted her head slightly to the left, and leaned back, giving him space to come to his own conclusion.

The little brown boy, my father, thought deeply for a moment. He then tightened his hands into two tiny little fists.

"I'm going to do something about it." He then turned from his mom who was nodding approvingly and walked towards the back of the house.

"Go find your big brother, mijito."

The little boy found his older brother, my uncle Antonio, in his room. Antonio was probably sixteen years old in this vision, but he was tall, wiry and incredibly scary looking. My young father said something to him that I could not hear, but I saw my uncle spring into action. He ran up to his chest of drawers, pulled out a black bandana which he folded in a certain way and tied it around his head.

The little boy followed suit with his own hidden bandana, and I quickly realized that my father and his brother were little Cholos. Even if it sounds silly, this was no laughing matter as this vision was frightening, and these boys were scary. Soon the two were surrounded by four other young men, capable and frightening looking Hispanic youths, and they were gathering, like a dangerous storm with malevolence in their hearts and street justice on their minds. They were sharing information, their heads and eyes darting back and forth, and then they were up and out the door, headed towards where the red headed construction worker had earlier issued his insults and flung the lit cigarette butt towards the innocent little brown boy.

The last thing I saw from this vision was the young construction worker turning to run, but it was too late as a fist had struck him in the neck while another foot was sweeping his legs and the five young men were descending upon him, beating the ever-living hell out of him.

There was so much for me to unpack from what I saw. My first thought was to my father, for whom I had never even considered the possibility of having a difficult upbringing. If I am being completely honest, I never even viewed my dad in any other context other than him being Latino Superman. So, seeing him in this new light left me reeling and I was not sure what to think exactly. Then I turned my thoughts towards my grandma, who was the nicest and kindest person I have ever met outside of my own mother. Seeing her acting so hard as nails and issuing a heartless ultimatum to my father was shocking. Wherever I was, it was allowing me the time to process my thoughts, because after thinking a little more, I decided that everything I had seen made perfect sense.

As a little girl, my father always taught me that we, as Latinos, are not victims. He instilled in me a deep sense of pride in our heritage, emphasizing that we are a strong and determined people who refuse to be held back. He believed in going out into the world, working hard to support our families, and even serving honorably in the United States military. We would not allow anyone to take our rights away from us. Certainly, time had softened my old dad up, but I could now see this hardened young man underneath his kind exterior and it made me love and appreciate him even more than I ever thought possible. Then I thought back to my grandparents, and I realized that probably all of my ancient ancestors were hard like this too, in order to live and survive. I don't think a single one of them was mean or malevolent, but certainly, in some cases life can be brutal and the only way to survive is to be hard and fight back. For certain, with this new information in hand I vowed that I would never underestimate my father, or anyone else for that matter, ever again. I guess I had mixed emotions on this situation truthfully, but I had run out of time to think, because again this vision was sucked up into the void and suddenly it was like being in the eye of a hurricane. Everything stopped, and things got impossibly quiet and still.

Then I heard a whisper. It may have been Cierra's voice, but it was so faint, I was not really sure.

"*Your father, the young boy, he was right and he was wrong. The circumstances called for justice, but retribution is not the way. There is always another way.*"

That made me somewhat angry if I was being honest. I did not like my father being judged. There was nobody to complain to, so all I could do was wait in the stillness for something to happen. I still had not seen Cierra and this made me think that perhaps our call didn't work and I was instead locked in some sort of lucid dream. I started to feel a little panicky, as all of this was completely foreign to me, and the idea of being trapped in a prison of my own mind started to permeate the corners of my psyche. Then I felt it, some presence had entered my very consciousness and I was no longer alone. Immediately it was like my brain had melded with Cierra's consciousness on the other end of this channel. I felt scared, but excited.

"It worked, Cierra," I announced triumphantly, my words echoing out in all directions.

Instead of replying, Cierra placed an instruction directly in my mind: *Cross your arms and hold on.* Before I could even process her words, my consciousness was yanked back into my body in my dorm room. Just as suddenly, I was launched upward—through the ceiling, through the roof, and into the air. I turned my head and saw myself still lying on the bed, my phone beside me. A soft, glowing blue light poured from its screen, spilling into the room like liquid energy. I wanted to watch, but something pulled my gaze forward. I was moving too fast to focus on anything for long.

It felt as though I was being fired from a cannon, a particle racing through an accelerator. Cassiopeia, interfacing with my phone, stretched me beyond what seemed possible—my molecules and my consciousness hitching a ride on streams of energy. But instead of flying into space, as I first thought, the world around me began to shift. The stars and the crescent moon blurred out of sight, and the Earth below faded into a haze. It was as if I was leaving behind the physical universe altogether. I wasn't moving through space anymore—I was slipping into something else entirely. I saw flashes of light, rippling and weaving into patterns like threads in an enormous loom. The edges of my vision shimmered, and I was in a vast, glowing space that felt infinite. This was not a place of stars or planets but a realm of light, energy, and connections.

Cierra's presence was still with me, though I couldn't see her. Instead, I felt her guiding me as I floated deeper into this strange space. Threads of glowing energy stretched in every direction, shimmering like a spider's web caught in sunlight. These threads pulsed and shifted, and I realized they weren't just lights—something told me they were the building blocks of reality itself, the raw code of the universe.

"This is the Hyperveil," Cierra's voice said, not in my ears but in my mind. I didn't know if I was hearing her or if I simply understood her words through the fabric of this place. She continued, saying,

"This place exists at the core of Cassiopeia. It resides at the heart of any quantum computer actually, but it is hidden from view and nobody knows about it, *yet*."

The Hyperveil wasn't cold or mechanical, as I'd feared. It felt alive and welcoming. It was nearly organic in nature. Each thread carried whispers of the universe, showing glimpses of stars being born, galaxies swirling, and even tiny moments of life unfolding. It was as if everything—every thought, every action, every possibility—was connected here. As we moved through the Hyperveil, I could sense its endlessness. Time and space folded in on themselves, revealing patterns and pathways that stretched far beyond my comprehension. I saw threads branching off, fracturing, and then weaving back together. Each twist and turn felt deliberate, like the work of an unseen hand guiding the flow of existence.

But as I marveled, Cierra suddenly appeared behind me. I hadn't sensed her approach, and her presence startled me a little. She guided me forward somewhat forcefully, towards the nexus. I pushed back as suddenly, some fear gripped me as I tumbled into the glow surrounding me. For the first time, I felt vulnerable, unsure of what was going to happen next. The threads of the Hyperveil wrapped around me, pulling me deeper into its embrace. And just as the panic began to peak, the light faded, and I found myself standing still, as if I had been absorbed into the very fabric of this hidden dimension.

Then I saw it—the core of the Hyperveil. A massive, glowing nexus where all the threads converged. It pulsed with a deep, golden light, radiating warmth and immense power.

"That," Cierra said, her voice softer now, "is the back of Sagittarius A—the black hole at the heart of our galaxy. The Hyperveil exists on this side, beyond its event horizon. If we were to pass through the black hole, we would emerge on the other side, back into the galaxy—the real world you know."

I froze, staring at the glowing center. The threads of the Hyperveil didn't just connect to it; they poured into it, as if the black hole itself were weaving the fabric of existence.

"It's a black hole," I whispered, the words slipping out as if I were casually commenting on the weather, even though I could hardly believe I was saying them.

"Yes," Cierra said. "But it's also the engine of creation. Everything you know—light, time, gravity, even thought—flows from here and back again, endlessly."

"It's beautiful," I said softly.

Cierra nodded silently and gently grasped my hand. We simply floated there, holding hands, watching as the threads of the Hyperveil wove themselves into the black hole and back out again, seeming to create and recreate our universe in an endless cycle. In that quiet moment, no words were needed—we were no longer just best friends but something deeper, like sisters finding each other after many lifetimes apart.

Chapter 20

Compiler

I watched in awe as the black hole pulsed with energy. Around its edges, the threads of The Hyperveil rippled and shimmered, reflecting and refracting like light on water. I could see glimpses of stars and galaxies in the glow—echoes of the universe spiraling around the core. For a moment, I felt overwhelmed. How could something so vast, so powerful, be the foundation of everything? But as I watched, I felt a sense of peace. The core of The Hyperveil wasn't chaotic or destructive. It was purposeful, deliberate, and alive.

Then I felt Cierra's presence grabbing me and turning me around to face backwards, 180 degrees. I saw something I had never seen before, but I recognized it immediately. My own thread was trailing out behind me, and it appeared just as Cierra had described in her earlier texts. It looked like a long bolt of impossibly beautiful crystalline lightning, shimmering with diamond like quality and invisible electricity. This thread was organic in nature and perfect in structure. Additionally, I could see these images or pictures that covered the surface of my own thread, and it looked as if it continued forever, certainly further than my human eyes would allow me to see. I saw all these pictures were of me, my family and my earliest memories. They were the closest thing and they literally went up and attached to my body.

But then, further down, I saw something else. I saw images that I did not recognize on the surface of my own thread. I saw people I had never met. It looked like their clothing style was from maybe 100 years ago, and if I had to guess, I would say the individuals looked like they were from Mexico or maybe one of the early US Territories like New Mexico. This all felt eerily familiar, and I was struck by a weird sense of nostalgia and longing. It made me feel suddenly lonely, sad, and guilty for not knowing who these people were, as silly as that may sound.

My own thread did not stop there either, it kept going and going farther back. What was I seeing? Was that me? Was that another existence that I lived at some point? Am I dying? Am I already dead? I started to get very scared and suddenly I missed my parents and I wanted to go home and forget about all this stuff I was seeing.

"Do you see it, Bella?" Cierra asked softly. "Do you get it? Those pictures, they are the lives you have lived before. Those are your previous programs."

"Previous programs? Why are you showing me this Cierra, I don't understand."

"Our lives are not our own, Bella, they belong to all living beings. And our threads stretch out infinitely, intertwining and connecting with every other living being at some point along their journey. It's not a circle, but a maze of endlessly interconnected lines."

"Wait Cierra, why is your thread dimmer than mine?"

Cierra did not say anything. Instead, she held up both of her hands, spread her fingers out slowly in front of her, dragging against the invisible ether, and as she did, a window, like a terminal on a traditional computer was revealed. The window had a fine gold bezel, with a shimmery rainbow opal color on top, which made it appear to be radiating at some hidden frequency. The window itself was not a screen, but more of an open hole in space, like looking into a diorama. Inside the window was an extremely detailed but easy to understand diagram that illustrated something called the Universal Computer.

Before I dive into what comes next, the computer nerd in me needs to explain how a traditional computer works. A computer is an electronic machine that processes information in the form of ones and zeros, which make up a basic logic system called binary. These electronic signals move across circuit boards, called a bus, and are controlled by a central processing unit (CPU), which is mostly made of silicon. The CPU takes an instruction, performs a calculation, and stores the result in a temporary memory called a cache. If the result matters, the data moves from the cache to main memory. If it's important enough for long-term storage, the data gets saved to the hard drive. The CPU splits its work into time slices controlled by a system clock, and it runs programs through "threads" of execution during these time slices. This all happens so fast it's almost invisible to us. Simply put, a computer takes input, processes it through threads, and then produces output and storage. The main job of a computer is to run programs, which are just sets of instructions designed to solve problems or provide answers.

Think of the CPU as a parent giving orders to its children—the threads—who do the actual work. In simpler terms, it's like a fancy type-writer, directing its keys to write stories on pieces of paper.

According to the diagram in the ether terminal window, our Universe is like a giant organic computer. Everything in the Universe is a component of that computer and serves some purpose. From our black hole, galaxy, stars, and solar system, to the Sun, our planet, and every living being or inanimate object.

We connect to one another as humans on a biological level, to our Earth through chemistry, and the Earth connects to the Universe through the fundamental force of gravity. Beyond these physical connections, The Hyperveil binds the Universe together through an intricate web of quantum entanglement, creating a deeper, unseen order.

Everything in our Universe follows a pattern, serving the purpose of an organic computer: things are created, they remain idle for a time, waiting for instruction, they spring forward to fulfill their purpose, and then they die or fade away, only to be recycled and begin the pattern anew.

The Universal Computer and God are one and the same. God is the whole computer, and the whole computer is God. For us, as human beings, God interacts with us in a way similar to how a Central Processing Unit (CPU) operates in a traditional computer. He empowers our souls—*threads*, as Cierra called them—to run programs, which are our lives.

When a life ends, the program terminates, but the thread, or soul, does not vanish. Instead, it is drawn back into The Hyperveil, the hidden dimension that weaves together the fabric of existence. There, the soul is reclaimed and recycled, becoming part of the intricate web once more, waiting to be chosen for another program, another life. In this way, The Hyperveil is both a sanctuary and a source, where the eternal cycle of creation and purpose continues.

Cierra grabbed me and turned me about so I was now facing forwards. As I spun forward, I saw other bright threads all around me, illuminating the darkness and radiating with a pleasant glow. It was like all these threads were twisted together, like a braid, and they gave me a welcoming warm sense of wellbeing and happiness. One thread in particular pulsed warmly, and the surface of my thread reflected back on this one. I just knew this presence was my Grandma Antonia. I looked at Cierra, and she read my mind, and she nodded slowly to confirm that was true. I asked Cierra why I could see these threads here, but I could not see them in my everyday life.

"The threads are there, but our brains are too primitive to perceive them," Cierra said. "If you want to understand, think about a plant for a moment. A plant is alive, and when you water it, the plant takes the water and is happy. But the plant has no way to understand what you are—the human being watering it. That's the purpose of our lives: to be the moment in time when our thread processes information and acts upon it. Our role is like the plant accepting the water, unaware of the larger forces nurturing it."

She explained that while some people believe in a multiverse of unlimited existences and possibilities, that's not entirely accurate. "There is only one Universe," she said, "but our threads form multiple, interconnected layers that spread infinitely through The Hyperveil. They reach out in all directions—through time, forwards and backwards—like a maze of lines and points that branch endlessly but always connect back to their origin. The Hyperveil is what holds it all together, weaving our threads into the greater whole."

As I was basking in the warmth of gaining this new understanding, I saw a dark pulse out of the corner of my eye. There was something there with us, an evil presence, with our threads, lurking in the background, oh so very near to us. This thing looked like a black worm, but it was more shapeless, and transparent, yet it was blacker than space itself. It looked like an oil slick moving over black construction paper. I also became aware of an odor, there was a stench to this presence. It was so offensive that it reeked of death itself. Whenever the blackness approached the threads, they emitted a pulse that repelled it. Until a final very strong pulse from the thread, I identified as Antonia, zapped it, and the blackness disappeared and crawled back into the nothingness, at least *temporarily*.

"What in the ever-living hell was that?" I gasped, with my mouth hanging open.

"That darkness, Babe, that presence, is what got me," she said flatly.

I looked into her face, and she was totally still, and just blank, and made of nothing as she started to describe the stinky black oil slick. What she was about to tell me had drained Cierra of everything she had. It was that dire and serious.

"There exists in our Universe, a very real evil presence, called the rAnd0m. Its job is to untangle your thread, to separate you from the other threads that surround you, and even tear apart your very own thread," Cierra explained. "Every time you make a bad choice, or you are mean, or you do something that you know is wrong, you are feeding the rAnd0m and inviting it in. And it can kill you, it can erase your program. Yes, bad things do happen to good people, and yes, sometimes random events happen that hurt or kill innocent people. However, anytime you are not in harmony with your own thread and the other threads that surround you, it is inviting this black poison oil slick into your life and increasing your chances of having something bad happen to you. Further, the rAnd0m can infect other people, and their BS can spill into your life, and it is capable of destroying you and everything and everyone around you."

"Like what do you mean?" I wanted an example.

"Shortly after we pledged to Delta Pi Zeta together, one day I ditched class and I decided to sleep in. When I eventually woke up, I wandered over to the fraternity to see what was going on over there, hoping to maybe run into a cute guy. Well, that is when I ran into this punk Asian guy nicknamed Buck, my first drug dealer here in Arizona. He asked me if I wanted to party, and even though I did want to, I thought about you, Bella, and I was able to say no. But then, one of Buck's friends, an extremely cute guy came up behind him out of nowhere, and this new guy asked me if I wanted to party, and I said, 'Yes.'"

"Well, that sucks. I mean I get it and I understand it, but wow, does that suck, Cierra."

"Once you invite it in, the rAnd0m becomes perfectly mixed in with other choices you make, so you never even realize it is controlling you and impacting the others around you. All of Buck's bad choices mixed in with my own, and I was doomed."

"What was that energy or force that pushed the rAnd0m away, Cierra?"

Cierra explained that when there are local threads that congregate with other threads vibrating at the same frequency, over time, they form a mesh. "Bella, your mesh is bright as hell, and it burns brighter than any I have seen. There is nothing that is going to penetrate that mesh to harm you. And because you are so close to your family, you are protected from the rAnd0m."

I suddenly understood what she was talking about. There in The Hyperveil, surrounded by the presence of the threads, I could read the memories and all the history of them, going back for what felt like eternity. Every experience, every memory and all of their knowledge was suddenly at my fingertips. I can tell you in no uncertain terms, that this is what true and ultimate power is and ever could be. Perfect information arranged into an easily digestible format. I knew in my heart that this was something serious and dangerous, so I treated it with great respect. Even with what I have revealed, I had merely scratched the surface of what is possible and did not dare delve any deeper into their domain. I was not ready for this kind of power, and I might never be.

Chapter 21

The Hyperveil

As I adjusted to my existence among the threads, I discovered I could access fragments of shared memories with Cierra. Though they didn't stretch as far back as the ones I shared with some of the surrounding threads, they still held deep significance. Gradually, I began to realize these memories might reach even further into the past than I had first thought.

"Cierra, remember in the GLV courtyard, when you crossed your eyes and said that *I was not Delta Pi Zeta material, Babe,* and we had such a good laugh?"

She nodded her head and cracked her dimple-exposing half smile.

"Have we done that before in the past?" I asked this question, because that memory stuck out as something special that was meant to happen.

"We have shared that moment at least a few times, Babe. The context and particulars are different each time, but the outcome remains the same. That is what we call a Universal Constant."

I knew in my heart that this was true, and it felt wonderful to hear, because I knew that my time with my best friend wasn't over, and that I would see her again at some point, maybe sooner rather than later.

"I know what you're thinking, Binky, but don't celebrate just yet—we may never share that moment again. Just as you accessed my memories, I can read yours here too. Remember when you saw Sagittarius A in The Hyperveil and thought it was beautiful and benign? That's only part of the truth. The reality is, black holes act as the hard drives of the Universe. Everything—every thought, action, and moment—is data, and the black hole's purpose is to suck up this data, recording every transaction of every thread in existence. But it doesn't stop there. All that data is fed back into The Hyperveil, which is The Singularity. The Hyperveil processes this collected data, refining it into perfect patterns that help the Universe evolve toward its next, higher phase of existence. That's why, when you die, it's so important to leave the world better than you found it. Every positive action, every perfect thread, strengthens The Hyperveil and moves us all closer to what comes next."

"I don't get it," I admitted, sadly.

"In the moment right before you die, your entire life will have been lived, and your thread will stretch out in full—a complete line connecting the past, present, and future," Cierra explained. "To move on to your next life, your thread must remain whole and intact. Only a complete thread can be absorbed by the black hole, which acts as the Universe's hard drive, recording every action, thought, and moment from your life. But the black hole is not the final destination. The data it collects is sent to The Hyperveil, which serves as the library of the Universe—the ultimate repository where perfect data patterns are preserved. The Hyperveil holds these moments of perfection—those rare, beautiful choices and actions that resonate beyond time—and uses them to sustain and evolve existence itself."

Before I could ask her to clarify all this, Cierra turned me about one last time, and we twisted extremely hard and made a steep left pivot. I saw something pop into view on the horizon. It was a massive oblong, halo shaped structure that appeared to be formed out of gray striated crystalline clouds. We crashed into the surface of that structure and it felt like I was being compressed at some deep level. We were being melded into one and I thought my head was going to pop from the sheer pressure. I was being crushed into the oblong surface of the crystalline structure. It was like our entire bodies went flat, like we were being turned into a piece of paper. Eventually, we made a final twist, and the compression stopped. We made it inside whatever this structure was, and in here, everything turned a very dull and lifeless color, our threads were gone, and we were cut adrift from everything and everyone we had seen before. I felt like I did not exist. No, to be clear, I felt like I had never existed. We were suddenly, somehow in orbit around the Earth, except instead of moving around it in a circle, we were making four straight lines around the Earth quickly, forming this strange irregular orbit. It was like a square shape with a circle inside of it. And the Earth wasn't the normal beautiful deep blue you would expect to see. It was gray, washed out and transparent, and everything in here just had a stale, old and lifeless essence to it.

"Why am I cold Cierra? What is this place? We cannot literally be in space, where are we?" I grew weary, impatient and scared.

"We have been falling ever deeper into The Hyperveil for a long time now, Bella, longer than you can comprehend, and we are at the bottom."

"Wait, the bottom of The Hyperveil, empties here, above the Earth?"

Cierra nodded, her expression calm yet knowing. "The Hyperveil empties where and when it must, in ways beyond our understanding. It aligns with purpose, not place," she said softly, before gesturing all around us. "This is the end, the bottom of The Hyperveil, Babe. After a person dies, this is where their thread's data is collected and assigned a new program. Every thread is connected to this place, always, through our subconscious."

Cierra paused, her gaze distant, then she continued. "Most people are here for only a fraction of a second while their thread is repurposed to run another program. But sometimes, when someone disappoints God greatly or has additional lessons to learn, they end up here for longer. This is a place of reckoning, where threads linger in limbo, waiting."

"We, as threads—as people—are more complex, more perfect, and more divine than anyone could ever imagine. We are built for a noble mission. But the job of the rAnd0m is to convince us otherwise—to make us believe we're worthless, that our lives have no meaning, that we are broken. And if a thread cannot obtain a new program to run, it becomes stuck here, stranded at the bottom of The Hyperveil, unable to move forward," she said as her words drifted into silence, leaving the weight of her revelation lingering in the space between us.

Her words hung in the air, weighty and resonant, as if the threads themselves somehow reflected the truth of what she had said directly into my subconscious.

Cierra turned to me, her voice steady but deeply serious.

"You need to know something about this place," she said. "You're only allowed to get stuck here, in The Hyperveil, a limited number of times. Each time it happens, your thread dims a little more. If you're here too often, eventually your thread burns out completely. And when that happens, you die for real. Your thread is permanently terminated—no further programs, no more lives."

Her words chilled me, but she didn't stop.

"There's a thread collector," she continued, her voice quiet. "It sweeps up whatever's left of your soul and scatters it into the void. When your thread is gone, there's no coming back. Nothing remains."

Then she looked at me, her expression softening. "The only reason I could reach you now is because I've been here before. Every time I ended up stuck, I learned a little more about this place, enough to piece it together. But that came at a price." Her gaze dropped slightly, and her voice faltered. "That's why my thread is dimmer than yours."

Her words have stayed with me ever since, not because I feared for myself, but because I feared for her and it broke my heart. The thought of her thread fading, of her being swept away into nothingness, haunts me still. I wanted to reach out, to pull her back from the edge, but I didn't know how. And I still don't.

"Oh, my goodness, Cierra!" I had finally realized something important. "You have committed suicide before, haven't you?" I asked earnestly with tangible fear.

"Yes, I have. The rAnd0m always gets me." She paused, "When I was in fifth grade, I ditched school with a neighborhood friend. We went to her house because nobody was home, and she offered me some of her Adderall. I didn't even like the way it made me feel, but it changed the mood, and I was drawn in by the taboo nature of drugs and the escape they offered. Once I let the rAnd0m in, it introduced me to even more messed-up people and their jacked-up situations."

She sighed, her voice softening as she said,

"I came to PVSU to try and escape that life, but guess what? The rAnd0m is everywhere. It followed me here. I also carry this deep pain inside me." Her eyes narrowed slightly, as if searching for the right words. "I'm not making excuses—I was never clinically depressed—but my brain always spirals to this place where I feel like I know everything, and it's all pointless. I hate myself and my situation. The fact that nobody in my family ever asked how I was doing—not even once—played a part too."

She hesitated, as if weighing whether to continue, her own words, dragging her down like a weight. "I wanted to teach them a lesson, to make them sorry, and since I felt worthless anyway, it was so easy to bury myself in drug abuse. I used so many drugs there wasn't much left of the original me."

Her voice dropped to barely above a whisper. "You probably wouldn't believe it, but I'm actually very weak and frail. The drugs gave me false confidence and made the consequences seem unreal."

Then I had a bright idea. "Couldn't God just create a new thread for you?"

Cierra looked at me expressionless and said,

"No, Babe. There are no new threads, we are merely slices of the same cord. And that cord bundles the threads and merges here, in The Hyperveil. Again, the data from your life is collected here when you die, and this is also the place where new life programs are given to threads unless you are stuck here, like me."

I was beginning to understand everything I had been told and seen. I felt brave, and for a moment, I knew that I could control things here too, just like Cierra. I opened the fingers on my hands like she had done earlier, and using the ether around me, like a trackpad, I opened my own ether terminal window. When the window opened, I asked a question saying,

"Earlier, I heard a voice tell me that my father was wrong to seek retribution as a young boy, and that there is another way. What does that mean? What other way? Tell me!"

The window was immediately painted with a vision like a video playing back. I saw the little brown boy again, walking towards the bridge to cross the arroyo. But this time, instead of crossing it, another young boy of similar age came up from behind, calling out the young boy's name. The little boy stopped and turned around. The two met, and started talking, words that I could not hear. The boys were smiling, and this time, instead of my father crossing the bridge alone, the two boys walked along the interior of the park. As they walked closer to the redheaded construction worker, he yelled something towards the two, but they were too far away to hear what he was yelling. The boys briefly looked in his direction, but then turned their gaze towards the houses, and ignored his insults and continued on their way.

"But wait, which one is real, which one actually happened?" I asked the window.

Cierra was the one to answer.

"Both are real, Babe. Both outcomes happened. The first happened for your father on his journey, but this second outcome happened for you on yours. Don't worry Bella, nothing has been impacted negatively, everything is for your benefit."

Then another idea struck me. I turned to the window and asked,

"How do I save my friend?"

Silence. No playback, no response, just empty stillness. And then, just as suddenly as it had appeared, the window dissolved into the ether, without providing an answer.

"Cierra," I said softly, "earlier, I felt scared—like I was on the verge of a panic attack. But now... it's gone. Completely. Like it was never there at all, not even a little bit."

"You've let go of the more primitive parts of your mind. The reflexive, automatic reactions have fallen away. Here, they have no power. It's like picking a different show to watch on Netflix or deciding not to watch at all. You can do that out in the real world, too," Cierra said.

"How?" I asked.

"When a race car driver loses control of their car, they turn into the skid. Do the same with your panic. Next time you feel it coming on, give into it, and surrender. Do not fight, change the channel instead."

As I was contemplating what she had just told me, I heard a couple of loud booms, and then I felt something like a large explosion reverberate all around us. I could faintly hear a familiar voice, sounded like a girl, but it was hard to make out.

The look on Cierra's face went completely blank.

"It's Faith, Babe!" Cierra exclaimed, nearly panicked.

"She is here with us?"

"No, Bella, she is in your dorm room, with *the police*!" With a freaked out look on her face, she added, "We have to get you back to your thread body, or else *you*, will no longer be *you*."

"Hold on Cierra, I have so many questions. I am scared. I don't know what to do with all of this information you have shown me. Don't leave me."

"I will never abandon you, Bella. You can count on me."

"No, stop. I need to know a couple things." I was not going to take no for an answer.

"Ok, quickly Babe."

"Can we change your trajectory Cierra, and get you out of here?"

"That, I do not know. It is unclear at this time."

"Unclear? That can't be! There is always a way!" I exclaimed incredulously.

"Look, don't worry. I am going to leave further instructions for you here in The Hyperveil. Your first challenge will be to retrieve that message, but without my help, Babe."

The thought of trying to reach this place on my own made my stomach churn, so I quickly shifted gears.

"So, there is The Hyperveil, Universal Computer, threads, the rAnd0m, and the mesh, am I missing anything?" I felt desperate, trying to retain as much information as my tired brain could handle.

"Yes, there is one more thing, Bella. However, this is the most difficult thing to understand, so I want you to try something a little different. Close your eyes and say the word, *caterpillar*, in your head, and nod for me once you have done so."

I nodded as I opened my eyes, waiting for her explanation.

Cierra watched me closely, her gaze narrowing slightly, before she mouthed the word *later* to me.

She paused saying,

"Sorry Babe, we are all out of time." She turned to me, gripping my hands tightly as she pulled me close.

"Close your eyes and relax," she said, her voice steady.

I barely had time to process her words before she shoved me toward the transparent edge of The Hyperveil. The force of it caught me completely off guard, my stomach plummeting as I tumbled headlong toward Earth itself. And then—nothing. Everything went blank.

Chapter 22

Good Tidings

I woke up with an EMT shining a bright LED flashlight into my eyes. I was being placed on a gurney and there were all kinds of first responder type people in my room. I couldn't believe what I was seeing. I was so disoriented and couldn't focus. I looked down at my Apple watch, which told me that it was 3:15AM. I looked off to my far left, and there was Faith. She wasn't standing there with her typical aloof disposition; she was crying inconsolably with her face in her hands. I felt bad for her, because there was nobody there to comfort her. I reached out my hand in her direction, but it was no use. She couldn't see me and I was too far away to reach her, and the noise level in my small room sounded like a jet taking off from Sky Harbor. At that moment, I knew that I wanted us to be friends, and I felt guilty that I had never felt that way towards her before.

As I was being hoisted and lifted to be transported out of my room, I passed close by Faith. I reached out and grabbed her hand.

"Don't be sad, Faith, for I have good news. I have spoken to Cierra, and she has told me the truth and I will share it with you."

At least I think that is what I said, but I can't be sure as I was so out of it. But apparently she had heard something she did not like, because she looked at me in total disbelief, turned around and ran away. The EMTs loaded me up, and then took me to the nearest hospital. This was over my objections, because I realized on the trip that it was the same terrible hospital where

Cierra had died, and that was a place I never wanted to see again. I ended up spending several hours there, and I was discharged after my blood work came back clean and I was able to pass a basic physical. This was a huge relief for me, as the last thing I wanted to do was scare the hell out of my parents with this after everything that had happened with Cierra's death. Even if they found out later via an emergency room bill, that would be better than the shock of getting a call saying their mija was in the hospital.

After getting dressed and signing some superbill paperwork, I turned from the reception desk and walked out the front lobby door. I looked down at my watch, which told me that it was 7:45 AM as I breached the exit. It was the middle of summer, and even at this early hour, it was already hot as hell. I found this rather annoying as I squinted and started thinking about either walking or calling a rideshare to get back to my room. I could feel sweat beading on my lower back and under my arms as I shook my head slightly in disbelief. Before I could further contemplate the task of how to get back to my dorm room, I saw a familiar figure, standing next to one of the pillars of the hospital entry archway.

Faith was there, with one of her legs kicked back against a stucco and brick pillar, propping herself up against it. She was rubbing her thumb and index finger of her right hand along the seam of her denim shorts.

"Hi Faith," I said to her in a soft tone.

"Hi Bella."

"How long have you been waiting out here?"

She told me she had been standing out there for just over three hours. I imagined that most of that time was spent with her pacing back and forth, and rubbing the seam of her jean shorts with her trademark nervous tic.

"Bella, what is going on with you?"

That sort of caught me off guard, as I was tired and I was not ready for an inquisition.

"Well, you tell me. What happened last night? How did the police get called?" I asked her.

Faith and I automatically turned east in the direction of the Greek Leadership Village and started simultaneously walking and talking.

"Ok, I couldn't sleep last night, so I started making my rounds. I wasn't snooping on you, I promise. But I came up the stairs, to the third floor, and I heard a low pulsating hum and I saw a white light, a super bright light, pouring out from the gap under your door and out into the hallway. It had, well, I don't know how to say this, Bella."

"Just say it." I was nervous and on the edge of my seat with what she was saying.

"Well, ok, I am not crazy and I am no longer using, but the light, it had these sorts of tentacles, and they were spreading out all along the hallway floor! I tried to open your door, but it was locked. I ran back downstairs to grab my keyring, and I came back up and unlocked your door. At first the door would not budge, but I forced my way in. When I came into the room, you were floating above your bed! Your phone was on the bed beneath you, and you were being held up, suspended in air, by this blue light that was coming from your phone. It was holding you up and it would not let you go. And I freaked out." She paused to catch her breath, her eyes were huge and open with raised eyebrows.

We were walking at a decent pace and Faith was clearly deeply impacted by what she seen. She was struggling to catch her breath and I saw sweat starting to form around her temples. She was really trying to show me that she was telling the truth, by using her hands to describe the events. She didn't know it, but I obviously believed her, so her show of body language wasn't necessary, but I didn't say anything to stop her.

In fact, I saw this whole situation as an opportunity and so I said,

"Ok, keep going, Babe."

The term Babe in the sorority life is a sign of respect among sisters, and I realized when I said it, that I had never addressed her in this manner before. I saw Faith look down and hide a small happy smile.

This energized her, and Faith continued saying,

"So, the white light, with these tentacles, was coming from the top of your head. It was like you had this beautiful hair made out of pure white light, and that was what was pouring down to the floor, and spreading out the door. Wait, no, it was like you had a long thread made out of flexible glass coming from the crown of your head. And you were also speaking too, however, your voice sounded like it was going backwards, the words you were saying were in reverse. I could not really make that out. But I got so scared that I tried to reach out to you. And this bolt of bright pink light, like a spark, stopped me. It poked me, and knocked me back into the wall."

Faith was on the verge of losing it recalling that last part, so I reached out to her and grabbed her shoulders, and I caressed her gently while looking her in the eyes while nodding my head, so she knew that she was safe and that I believed her.

"This bolt of light that hit me, it was like it was alive. It was not like a jolt of static electricity from walking on the floor at Target. This light poked me and pushed me back, but with the intention of stopping me, like it did not want to hurt me, like it was trying to protect you, like you were in the middle of something and this spark was just buying time. I know that sounds crazy, but there was an intelligence behind this light. For a moment I didn't know what to do, but then I thought about losing Cierra, and I got scared that you were going to get hurt. I wasn't sure what I should do, so I called the PVSU police and told them that you were having a seizure. I did not know what else to say, I just knew I had to do something."

It was clear she'd finished sharing her truth.

"Faith, I believe you," I said, holding her gaze. "And, wow, there's so much to tell you about what you saw. I hope you'll believe me, and I'll explain everything, but please know that I trust you and I need your help. Just give me a little time to lay it all out. But here's one thing I can tell you now: I spoke to Cierra last night." My hands still rested on her shoulders, grounding us both in the moment.

However, I did not get the reaction I was expecting, as I guess Faith did not like me saying that I spoke to Cierra. She angrily brushed off my hands and pushed me back while she furrowed her brow and pursed her lips.

"Oh screw you Bella," she snarled as she turned hard left and ran away from me.

In that moment, before she tore off, I tried to reach out to her to stop her, but Faith was ready to get the hell away from me and this conversation. She has long slender legs, like a gazelle, and I have the opposite of that, so she was going to get away from me, with little effort on her part.

As she was getting a good gap on me, I yelled out as loud as I could,

"I know about your suicide pact with Cierra!"

This made her suddenly stop, and she turned her head slightly to look back at me, her chin over her right shoulder, as the truth echoed out into the cosmos. Just then a bead of sweat poured down from her forehead, as we were both starting to sweat our asses off out there in the early morning hot Arizona sunshine. She brushed it off with an annoyed hand waving motion.

She had a look on her face of someone trying to size up a situation while not letting you know what they were really thinking.

"You're just guessing, Bella. You don't know anything," she yelled.

I tilted my head slightly, my chin lifting as my thoughts turned inward. I reached out, in my mind, to the threads I knew were always present, asking for guidance, seeking to find the right words. Deep down, something told me that I needed Faith. Not just as a friend, but as someone who could stand alongside me, someone who would believe in what I had to say. This was the moment to bring her to my side, as an ally, as a witness, as someone who could help me carry the truth I needed the world to hear.

And then the answer, like a quantum supercomputer, popped straight into my head. I can't explain exactly how, any better than you can explain how regular thoughts appear in your own head, they just show up, if you think about how your brain actually works. I reached out and grabbed her by the shoulders again.

"A week before Cierra died, the two of you were in the GLV courtyard, and you were both high. You told her the story about a boy named Jacob, and how he took something from you and did things to you. He took advantage of you, at a time in your life where you were really questioning your own sexuality. However, you didn't tell Cierra *everything*. You didn't tell her how you burned Jacob's car to the ground in the middle of the night and how nobody ever found out. And how you still keep that a secret, and you managed to never tell another single living soul. That's why you never got arrested for arson, because you somehow managed to keep that fact to yourself. The police suspected you, but couldn't prove it. But I know everything, Faith."

"Bella, you're bleeding," she gasped as she put her hand on my shoulder.

I reached up and felt the hot slick blood dripping from my left nostril. I felt dizzy and lightheaded, but I wiped the blood away. At that moment, those words just poured out of my mouth and filled up all the empty space surrounding us. Even I was surprised at what I had said. It was like I was just playing back a video that I had never seen before. But Faith's face, her eyes, and her reaction told me everything that I needed to know. The information I had somehow tapped into from the threads, had bubbled up and out of my mouth, and they were dead on accurate. It was the truth.

I pursed my lips and looked down and to the right.

"Faith, you can relax, you know, I won't hurt you. Your secret is safe with me. But we need to stick together. I need you."

All the emotion had drained from Faith's face. She turned, our eyes met, and I knew that we understood each other. I gave her a hug and we turned and continued walking back to the GLV. At that moment, all of our previous struggles were gone, and I knew that there was going to be room for the two of us to grow closer. I also noticed that Faith had stopped rubbing her thumb and forefinger together. She was now just walking with her fingers open, and this was beautiful to me.

Chapter 23

BSOD

AFTER SAYING GOODBYE TO Faith, I went up to my dorm room and crashed. I had never been so exhausted in my entire life. The little computer nerd in me had reached her limit with the human equivalent of a Windows computer *Blue Screen of Death*. I put everything I had into the past twenty-four hours, and now my body, mind and spirit were letting me know that enough was enough. I ended up sleeping for about eighteen hours straight, and I woke up at 2:14 AM to someone grabbing and pulling at my hand. When I opened my eyes completely startled, there was nobody there. I looked and my hand was up in the air, holding onto my phone, and the phone was hanging there under its own power, like a drone hovering in the sky. The phone was ringing, and it said the caller was Cierra. I slid the slider over, put the phone up to my ear and said, "Hello." Something was different about this call compared to the last one. This call felt cobbled together, somehow desperate, nothing like the well planned and thought out call we had earlier.

The sound on the other end was already fizzling out with a melting static sound, like when a battery-operated toy is nearly out of charge. When the line opened, for just a moment I felt Cierra's presence and it looked like the screen was going to flash a pattern like before. But then the line slowly crackled and faded away into non-existence with a final, *click*. But before the call closed, I faintly heard the remnants of Cierra's voice.

"Bella, nothing in this life makes sense, not a single damn thing. Yet, people live their lives so certain that they have it all figured out. In fact, they are cocky about it. People should be the opposite of that, they should be unsure. They should get comfortable being uncomfortable. They should live their lives day by day, maybe even minute by minute. But the one thing nobody should ever do, is throw away the one thing they have been given that they can truly be in control of, their lives. You have to ride this out until the bitter end. In my final moments of being alive, when I was in the hospital about to die by drug overdose, I realized that I had made a mistake and that all of my problems had solutions, had I chosen to fix them. But it was too late. This realization was the saddest and most pathetic thing that you could imagine. Also, I now realize that my actions hurt my parents, so much more than I could have ever known. I hated them when I was alive, and I resented them because I thought they did not give a crap about me. I was wrong. The same goes for the impact it had on you and all of my other friends. I thought you guys would be easily able to move on without me. I did not realize the effect it would have on you, and because of this, I have such deep regret in my heart."

Before I could even respond, to comfort and reassure my best friend that everything would be ok, my phone made an audible click pop that didn't sound so good and the line went dead. I desperately grabbed my phone and started checking it to regain a connection with Cierra. I made sure it was plugged in, I shook it and checked every setting I could think of to try and make it work. I even hard reset the phone, and still there was nothing. I tried to text Cierra immediately after, but she did not reply. For the next sixteen hours nothing else happened, and this made me terribly sad. I am not the most patient person in the world, so this was like pure torture for me.

That night after the failed call, I went to bed thinking about the threads I saw in our earlier successful call and how they relate to my family here in my everyday life. In particular, I thought of my father. I wanted to call him and tell him all about what had happened and to ask for his advice. My father is an explorer, and in a lot of ways, I felt like I was following in his footsteps. Yes, he would be incredibly worried about what I might tell him; however, I felt that the curious explorer in him would encourage me to get to the bottom of everything that happened, without fear nor reservation. There was only one problem, I did not have my thoughts completely together yet and I had no evidence of anything that had happened. Mainly, I was worried I would just sound like a crazy person.

I rolled over and covered my entire body head to toe with my blanket. As I was trying to fall asleep, my door suddenly popped open ever so slightly, ever so gently. I got up to close it, but when I grabbed the handle, it melted away in my hand, and it turned into a thousand butterflies made of blue electricity. I stood there watching them, and they flew off into the shadowy dorm hallway and dissolved into millions of tiny particles. A darkened figure, a silhouette, stood in the hallway next to the door to the community elevators. It was not a threatening presence, and the figure beckoned for me to follow. The figure opened the door to the elevator and I caught up with it and stepped inside, except when the doors closed, the entire elevator disappeared and I was out in the PVSU Palm Walk in the middle of the night. The sky was warmly lit by an incredibly intense crescent moon that bathed everything in milky moonlight. The darkened figure walked forward and again motioned for me to follow. We kept walking forward in silence, but I was not afraid, I knew that this presence was safe, it was trying to share some secret with me.

We kept walking until we reached our destination— the sterling rose bush that Bryce had shown me earlier in my first semester in the hidden garden. Except this time, instead of roses, the entire bush was alive with the same electric blue butterflies I had seen earlier. The darkened figure stood behind me now, holding my shoulders, and it would not let me turn in any direction, other than staring directly at the rose bush. Using my mind, I asked the darkened presence what was going on and why I had been brought here. The voice that came back without speaking was that of my father, which gave me a shocking jolt that really helped me to focus. He told me not to turn around, but concentrate only on his words.

"Bell, I need you to know that back before you were born, God sent me here to be your father. He did so, because he wanted me to keep you safe, because you have a very important mission ahead of you. I need to tell you to not fear the threads. Rather, let them be your foundation. Let them speak through you. They are you and you are them. We are all one shared experience and you need to educate the world, and the threads will help you accomplish your mission. I am sorry that this responsibility falls solely on your shoulders. Bell, I am here now to warn you, do not go with Cierra any longer. She has shown you all that you are allowed to see, all that you can handle. If she takes you again, she might not let you go, and you will not return. For that reason, the threads have limited her ability to reach out to you any longer. It is time to say goodbye to her, for now."

"Wait Dad, how is this possible, how are you in my dream?"

"While I am your father, I am also a very old thread, and my thread name is one you would recognize, because we go way back, you and I."

"Thread name?" I asked in a daze.

"That is a lesson for another time. You cannot learn this now. I will tell you something about dreams instead, Bell. Threads can reach out to you in dreams, to tell you important things, to warn you, or to just say hello if we are separated, and we do so by riding invisible waves of gravity, and interacting with your unconscious mind."

Up to this point, I had not felt any fear, but that last line inserted some genuine distress into my mind, and I suddenly realized that this was a lucid dream, which in itself can be incredibly disturbing. Before I could ask my dad to explain why Cierra might take me and not let me go, the door to my room opened for real, and it startled me awake. Faith poked her head into my doorway that she had slightly cracked open. She asked me if I was ok because it sounded like I had been crying in my sleep when she passed by doing her rounds. I thanked her and assured her that I was fine. As soon as she closed the door, I picked up my phone to see what time it was and if Cierra had texted me.

Despite my father's warning to me in my dream vision, I decided that I still had to try to communicate with Cierra. I mean she was or is my best friend after all, and I still trusted her one hundred percent.

After Faith woke me up, I was not able to fall back asleep. Luckily for me, Cierra had indeed sent me some texts, which I read happily. I was lying in bed reflecting about how this was already day eight of this otherworldly experience with my best friend. I was staring at my phone and thinking about everything that I now knew about how life actually works. It was approaching ten minutes past five in the morning, and Cierra and I had already been texting for a few hours. Being in touch with Cierra daily was starting to reach the point where I was taking this experience, and her, for granted, even though she had warned me that this entire experience could end at any time.

At 5:14 AM, in her last text to me, Cierra sent me the following message, and then I never got another call or text from her again:

Bella dont forget i left a
message for you in the
hyperveil

Chapter 24

Inchworm

Several months had passed since my last communication with Cierra. It was late September, the fall semester of my junior year at PVSU, yet her final text still consumed my thoughts, refusing to fade: she left a message for me in The Hyperveil. From the moment I read those words, I'd been working tirelessly to figure out how to do it. Cierra had gotten me there before, using a combination of advanced hacking skills and metaphysical techniques far beyond my level. She'd even modified the code on my phone in ways I couldn't begin to replicate. Still, I couldn't give up. I wanted Cierra's message more than anything I'd ever wanted in my life. So, I cast aside my doubts on my own abilities and kept going. Now, as I sat in my dorm room chair staring at my laptop screen, I couldn't help but wonder how much time had slipped past since I started unraveling this puzzle. Months of effort, and I still felt no closer to the answer.

I picked up my phone in a vain attempt to see if I had missed a text from Cierra, but there was nothing there, which I already knew. I then squinted my eyes real hard and concentrated, trying to access the threads like I had when I told Faith about her private memories of burning Jacob's car. But just like my texts, there was nothing there. That bummed me out so bad because in spite of it being dangerous, I would be lying if I said I did not enjoy the power that came with such an amazing capability as accessing the threads for their omnipotence. It was like a drug, and I knew in my heart, that wouldn't be healthy for me anyways, as such power would destroy me. However, I was frustrated and willing to try anything because I felt like I was now wasting my life and not making any progress. *What the hell am I going to do, I will never get that message,* I thought to myself.

I'd been meticulously documenting every step of this process on my laptop, trying to figure out how to access the message Cierra had left for me in The Hyperveil. Opening a new note file on my MacBook marked the start of yet another month of obsessive note-taking. Four previous files stared back at me from the screen, each one a record of everything that had happened. The notes were impressively organized. For each month, I had chosen a different philosopher to serve as a kind of secret decoder ring, hoping their ideas might reveal new meaning or insight into the events that had unfolded.

I opened the most recent file to pick up where I had left off, but something unexpected caught my eye. Instead of the neatly structured notes I thought I had written, I saw the following window:

```
● ● ●                                    📄 Notes 4
# Importing Qiskit library
from qiskit import QuantumCircuit, Aer, execute
from qiskit.visualization import plot_histogram

# Number of qubits and classical bits
cierra_qubits = 3
cierra_bits = 3

# Create a Quantum Circuit
circuit_cierra = QuantumCircuit(cierra_qubits, cierra_bits)

# Apply Hadamard gate to put qubits into superposition
for qubit in range(cierra_qubits):
    circuit_cierra.h(qubit)  # H gate puts the qubits into superposition

# Add barriers to visualize the separation
circuit_cierra.barrier()

# Apply controlled-NOT (CNOT) gate
for qubit in range(cierra_qubits - 1):
    circuit_cierra.cx(qubit, qubit + 1)

# Add another barrier
circuit_cierra.barrier()

# Measure the qubits
for qubit in range(cierra_qubits):
    circuit_cierra.measure(qubit, qubit)

# Draw the circuit
circuit_cierra.draw(output='mpl')

# Simulate the quantum circuit
simulator_cierra = Aer.get_backend('qasm_simulator')
result_cierra = execute(circuit_cierra, simulator_cierra, shots=1024).result()|
```

And then:

```
                                        📄 Notes 5
# Importing Qiskit library
from qiskit import QuantumCircuit, Aer, execute
from qiskit.visualization import plot_histogram, circuit_drawer
import matplotlib.pyplot as plt

# Number of qubits and classical bits
bella_qubits = 3
bella_bits = 3

# Create a Quantum Circuit
circuit_bella = QuantumCircuit(bella_qubits, bella_bits)

# Apply Hadamard gate to put qubits into superposition
for qubit in range(bella_qubits):
    circuit_bella.h(qubit)  # H gate puts the qubits into superposition

# Add barriers to visualize the separation
circuit_bella.barrier()

# Apply controlled-NOT (CNOT) gate
for qubit in range(bella_qubits - 1):
    circuit_bella.cx(qubit, qubit + 1)

# Add another barrier
circuit_bella.barrier()

# Measure the qubits
for qubit in range(bella_qubits):
    circuit_bella.measure(qubit, qubit)
```

I quickly reviewed the other notes. The same types of weird symbols and jumbled words were on each page comprising over 65,000 lines of text across four individual files. I quickly realized that the past four months I was not taking notes at all, I was writing a computer program. Or my notes had somehow converted themselves into this. I mean, the code and symbols were not something I recall doing myself, but the way the text was arranged, I could definitely tell that this was my handiwork. Each document was a class file that would make up a new program once compiled into an executable. What that program would do, I had no idea as I did not recognize the programming language at first. I quickly sprang into action to get to the bottom of this new mystery. I opened up the terminal on my MacBook, and made a few attempts at compiling these text files into a program using various libraries on my computer. Each time I typed in my commands and hit enter, it failed, saying:

Symbol table full - fatal heap error;

That message told me that my laptop did not have the resources to hold an object of this size, and then it hit me like a ton of bricks. This was quantum computer programming, but not just any quantum computer language. These files were written specifically for the PVSU quantum computer, Cassiopeia. I opened up a VPN connection to Cassiopeia and quickly copied the files over to main storage. Before I could even attempt to compile the class files myself, the built-in AI in Cassiopeia did it for me, and it even executed the program which brought up the following simple window:

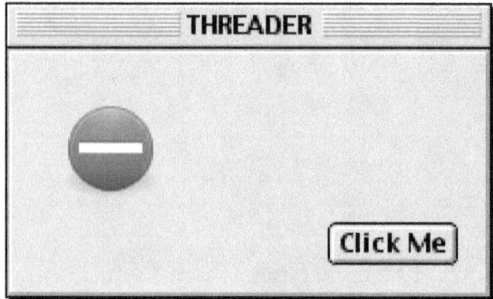

This was so exciting to me. Immediately my mind began racing. Was this somehow related to my mission to retrieve the message from Cierra? I did not hit the "Click Me" button for quite some time. I was afraid to. I wanted to make sure that I was not going to cause any damage to Cassiopeia or myself before I did anything further. I stepped away from the computer for a moment to gather my thoughts, and when I returned, I made sure to inspect the code I had written to see what the actual program does. I spent the next five hours doing so, but could not really get close to an actual answer. I decided to just be brave, and I hit the "Click Me" button while a bead of sweat dripped down my face, and made a tiny splash on my dorm room table next to my MacBook. I couldn't wait to discover the wonderful message the threads or maybe Cierra would have for me. My excitement quickly ebbed however, as when I hit the "Click Me" button, all that came up was a simple text window with the following list:

1. Olivetti Lettera 22 – Goodly Sisters Thrift Store

2. Ink and ribbon – Mateo's Printshop

3. Paper – TechBuy

That's it? I thought to myself. I don't even know what an Olivetti Lettera *whatever* is. Frustrated, I closed the program, and ran it again. I hit the "Click Me" button, same result. I did it four more times in quick succession, with the same results. However, on the fifth try, a new item was added to the list:

1. Olivetti Lettera 22 – Goodly Sisters Thrift Store

2. Ink and ribbon – Mateo's Printshop

3. Paper – TechBuy

4. Inchworm

Inchworm? I felt so deflated. I had my hopes up that there was going to be some kind of answer, some kind of help, to make me feel better. As I was about to close my eyes and start crying, I felt something on my neck, like a little tickle. I gently scooped my hand on my neck, and grasped the cutest little light green inchworm in the palm of my hand. *What in the world?* I thought to myself. Now in the past, I would have either flicked this little guy into the toilet and flushed him down into a watery grave or smashed him on some tissue paper and thrown his little carcass away. This time, however, I let him slowly crawl onto my finger. I decided to save him, so I took the stairs, the same ones Cierra had bounded up and down the last few weeks of her life, while thinking of her warmly, on my way outside.

I went out into the GLV courtyard and released the tiny inchworm onto one of the mighty Shamel ash trees in front of our building. Once it was safely crawling away, a memory from when I was a little girl suddenly popped into my head. When I was just about five years old, my mother was teaching me how to read with my first book called "Worm is Hot." I did not appreciate it then, because I was just a little kid, but this was a vision of my mother, with her pure patience and love, investing her time and attention to me, *her mija*, and it moved me. Her kindness back then, was extending through me, as I released that tiny inchworm onto the tree, to live another day. It formed a long chain of kindness. This thought warmed my heart and I felt at peace.

As I turned around to leave the inchworm tree, I ran into Faith. She looked startled at first, but then she quickly smiled and gave me a brief hug.

"Hey," I said. "Do you have a minute to talk?"

She nodded yes, and we found an open spot on the grass of the GLV courtyard. The late afternoon sun cast long shadows, and there was a pleasant breeze. It felt like the right place for a real conversation.

We started catching up, and she told me how she was finally able to sleep through the night again and that things were somewhat returning to normal for her. However, she mentioned she'd been having vivid dreams lately—about rainstorms and lightning.

"They're not scary, though," Faith said. "They actually feel cleansing, like the storm is washing something away."

I nodded thoughtfully. "That's cool. I'd really like to hear more about your dreams when you're ready."

She tilted her head slightly, studying me.

"You've been different lately," Faith said after a pause. "Calmer. More... I don't know, open."

Her words cut through me, and I felt a twinge of guilt. I was scared, but I couldn't let this moment pass without addressing how I felt.

"Faith, I owe you an apology," I said, my voice filled with emotion. "I wasn't kind to you, like, ever. Actually, I was a mean girl, and there's no excuse for the way I treated you."

She blinked, her expression softening, but she didn't say anything, so I continued.

"I think I was projecting my own insecurities onto you," I admitted. "I'm not proud of it, and I hate that I made you feel small or unwanted."

Faith's gaze dropped to the grass. "It did hurt," she said quietly. "But I tried not to take it personally. We've been through so much."

"You're right," I said quickly. "We have been through so much together, and we are still standing. Can we start over?"

Faith looked up at me, her eyes searching mine. After a moment, she nodded. "I'd like that."

A wave of relief washed over me, and I smiled. "Thank you. And for the record, you're a lot stronger than I ever gave you credit for."

We sat in comfortable silence for a moment on the grass under the mighty ash trees. Eventually, we said our goodbyes. As I stood to leave, I turned back to her.

"Faith," I called out, "let's promise to be kind to each other moving forward."

She nodded, her expression warm. "Deal."

As I headed back up to my room, I felt lighter, as if some invisible weight had been lifted from my shoulders. The sharp, prickly edges of the cat inside me—always on alert, always defensive, often annoyed—had finally gone quiet. The familiar knot of panic that usually clawed at my chest had unraveled, leaving behind an unfamiliar calm. It was strange, almost as if a part of me that had been there for as long as I could remember was suddenly missing.

Now, it was like the cat had stretched out lazily, curled up on a rug in a sunny room, and drifted off into nothingness.

And just as I turned the corner, I ran into Bryce. He gave me a big hug with a kiss and asked me if I wanted to go get a coffee. We walked down to JavaMan Coffee and spent the next couple hours talking, flirting, and laughing. Though I was thoroughly enjoying myself with Bryce, something inside me was gently pulling my attention away from him. With a warm hug, I told him I would catch him later, but I had to take care of something, and I left him there and I walked down to Golden Dragon Cosmetics.

As I reached down and opened the door, Natalie popped her head up from behind the register. She came running around the counter and over to me, and gave me a big hug, for the first time, *ever*. Even though I knew she was on the spectrum in some fashion, it felt so warm and genuine. I wasn't sure what emotional physical contact meant to her, but it certainly felt like progress for both of us in our relationship.

"I don't do this," Natalie said softly, stepping back and tucking a strand of hair behind her ear. "But I felt like you needed it."

I smiled, touched by her sudden openness. "Well, I think we both did."

She smiled briefly, and we sat down together. I couldn't help but recall how her words regarding Cierra had been prophetic, though at the time I couldn't have imagined how things would end. As we talked, I remembered back to when I first started working for her. She'd shared the story of her life, of how she was estranged from her daughter and how deeply it saddened her. Them, almost as if on cue, she mentioned that she had been trying to write a letter.

"I don't know if she will read it," Natalie said, her voice trembling as she looked down at the blank sheet of paper in front of us. "It's been so long. What if it just makes things worse?"

"It won't," I said gently to reassure her. "You're reaching out. That takes courage, and it's the first step. Whatever happens, you'll know you tried. Believe me, you have to at least try. Never give up."

She nodded, her hands twisting together nervously, and then, with a deep breath, she began dictating. Together, we crafted a heartfelt letter to her daughter to break the ice and see if there was room for reconciliation.

When we finished, Natalie sat back, studying the letter.

"Do you think it will work?" she asked hesitantly.

"It will work," I assured her. "It's honest and kind. That's all that matters."

We folded the letter, placed it in an envelope, and walked it down to the little mailbox in the middle of the strip mall parking lot. After placing it in the mail slot, we stood and looked at each other for a moment.

"Thank you," she whispered. "For helping me do this."

I reached out and squeezed her hand.

"It's all you, Natalie. I just gave you a little push."

She turned to me and, for the second time that day, wrapped her arms around me in a hug. This one was tighter, lingering, as if she was saying something she couldn't put into words. And in that moment, I knew we had taken a step forward together.

I returned to my room, sat on my bed, and reflected on all the incredible moments I had experienced that day. Then, I remembered the list Cassiopeia had shown me—the one that had led me to the inchworm and indirectly sparked such a rewarding, fulfilling experience. There was something so pure and right about it all. Helping, being part of something bigger than myself, felt genuinely good.

Feeling inspired, I pulled the list back out and snapped a picture of it. With my phone already in hand, I decided to call Bryce.

"Hey Babe, what ya doin?" I asked playfully.

"Waiting for your call, duh," Bryce replied.

"Are you free tomorrow to help me do some shopping and can we take your F150, please?"

I didn't know anything about what the items in the list were or how they were going to help me, but I did know that the threads had found a way to communicate with me, to guide me, without causing any harm, and I was grateful and excited to begin this new journey. Enough time had passed, I felt safe and secure and it was making me feel brave for the first time since I had lost contact with Cierra.

Bryce and I went shopping the next day, and I discovered that an Olivetti Lettera 22 was in fact, an old classic typewriter from the 1950s. Sure enough, we found it tucked inside a worn black case at the Goodly Sisters Thrift Store, waiting as if it had been set aside just for us. We spent the entire day carefully cleaning each key and lever, restoring it to full working order. It sat on my desk for three straight days after that, staring back at me, a total mystery. I still had no idea what I was supposed to do with the darn thing.

On the third evening, Bryce stopped by. He came into my room, all the while staring towards the typewriter.

"Hey, are you ever going to tell me what is going on with this antique?" he asked, with a sly smile on his face.

I sat on my bed and shook my head, laughing. "I will soon, babe, I promise. Just know in advance that it makes Project Stardust seem like child's play."

He glanced at the typewriter and then back to me, his expression growing more thoughtful. Bryce didn't say a word as he walked over to the desk, sat down, and placed his fingers on the keys, preparing to type something out. Then, slowly, in an almost hunt and peck fashion, he began to type, hitting each key with purpose for dramatic effect.

When he finished, he pulled the page out from the carriage and turned towards me, holding the page out for inspection. I grabbed it, my heart racing as I read the words he had just typed.

I looked up, trying to catch my breath as Bryce knelt down beside me next to the bed.

"Bella," he said softer than I had ever heard him speak, "I won't pretend to have all the answers, but I know that I want to spend every chapter of my life with you. So, *will you?*"

In that quiet moment, with the typewriter's special message pressed firmly against my chest, my heart knew only one answer: yes.

Chapter 25

Be Kind, Even in Pain

THE TYPEWRITER HAD ALREADY served one incredible, life-changing purpose, that much was undeniably certain. Bryce and I had immortalized our commitment to each other through its keystrokes.

That said, I still did not know what I was supposed to be doing with it, truthfully. I kept logging into Cassiopeia to ask the Threader app for guidance, but all it would spit back out is:

1. Think

2. Write

Write what? I had no idea what that meant. As I was staring at the blank piece of paper in the antique Olivetti, grasping for inspiration for what I would type, the thought suddenly occurred to me that perhaps the message meant to think and write computer code. Doing so might provide my next set of instructions, and the old typewriter was meant for later.

So, I spent the next three days editing the code of my program, tying various modifications to the lines, writing new routines and altering its algorithms. And I made progress too, when I hit the "Click Me" button, the inside of the response window was a solid black and the frame of the window was a pleasant gold color. That may sound silly to you, but for me, it represented huge progress. There was something happening between me, Cassiopeia and the threads.

On the fourth day of me dropping out of all normal activities and focusing on writing computer code, it was nearing dawn. And even though the sun would not fully rise for another thirty minutes or so, the first beacons of light were already cresting over the mountainous eastern horizon, shooting their beautiful solar rays across the sky and warmly lighting up the window frame to my dimly lit room. I had already spent the entire night logged into Cassiopeia, hoping for a new clue, a way forward that would get me to The Hyperveil, as per Cierra's instructions. I felt like I was making progress, but if I am being honest, I still had nothing remarkable to show for all my efforts and was no closer to finding the key to unlocking this mystery.

I made one final modification to my code, and then launched the Threader program again for one more shot at a new result. Except this time, when I launched the program and hit the "Click Me" button, it brought back three windows, each having a fine gold bezel, with a shimmery rainbow opal color on top of it. These windows were cascaded three across like pages in a book, they were radiating, and I realized that these were not normal computer windows. Rather, these were ether terminal windows, just like the ones Cierra and I had opened while we were in The Hyperveil together six months ago.

It was obvious to me that the threads wanted a way to communicate that would not damage me, so they found a way to do so, by leveraging my computer skills and knowledge of the quantum computer, Cassiopeia. I realized that this was the key, this was the missing connection into The Hyperveil.

I was finally going to get the message Cierra had left for me and I was beyond excited.

The first window was titled "The Path", and it contained the following list:

1. Be kind to all

2. Live your life in the service of others

3. Leave the world a better place than you found it

The next window contained the diagram of the "Universal Computer", which I had seen before. The only difference being now I was able to take a screenshot to show to others.

The last window was titled, "The Ghost of the In Between." This is what I had worked so hard to reach. This was the note that Cierra had left for me in The Hyperveil!

It read:

```
Bella,
God only trusts certain people to run his most
important programs. We call those people, the
Fingers of God, and you are part of that group.
Heavenly Father has given you special access to
the threads, and they will help strengthen your
voice for what is to come, and it is vitally
important.
Teach the world of the Universal Computer. Tell
them that in order to live their lives in harmony
with this benevolent force and shut out the
rAndOm, they must be kind to everyone, live their
lives in service of others and to leave the world
a better place than they found it. That is The
Path.
```

I am sorry for the pain I caused you. Suicide is the unkindest act one can commit. And while I did not have any respect for you and others in that regard when I was alive, don't let my selfish mistake make you jaded, Babe. Regardless of how much it hurts you, or how unlikely it seems that it will do any good, always be sure to be kind, even in pain.

Bella, remember I told you to close your eyes, and say the word caterpillar to yourself when we were in The Hyperveil? Well, the voice you heard in your head, the voice you would hear even now, the one that says the word caterpillar back to you, or any thought for that matter, it is not a woman's voice, it is not a man's voice, and it is not even your voice. That voice you hear, in your head, is the same voice I hear, it is the same voice that everyone hears. That is our eternal universal oneness, our singularity, our voice, our mesh. That is the Ghost of the In Between, and it ties The Hyperveil to the Universe, the Universe to the threads, the threads to us, and all of us to each other. People are not yet aware, but that voice speaks to you, even when you can't hear it, and it is the force that drives you to do things, providing you strength and courage. It is the essence of our own humanity, the collective of all humans past, present, and future. This inner voice allows for the kindness we give and receive, to transcend us, even beyond our own death.

```
Bella, regarding your father thread, he told
you in a dream to not reach out to me any longer,
and you defied him. You did not abandon me, and
you worked tirelessly, until you arrived at this
message. You did that for me. You may not have
realized it, but all this time, you were walking
The Path. Your persistence, loyalty, and kindness
have set me free from my prison. I have been given
another program to run, and I am alive and I am
free. Thank you, Babe.
    Now, close these windows. Log out from Cas-
siopeia. Turn off your laptop. Turn off your
phone. Turn off the lights. Turn off your brain.
Inside your head, what do you hear, Bella?
```

I followed her instructions and sat in the stillness of my own thoughts. And then *it happened*.

"Oh my gosh, I hear you now Cierra! I can hear them all! I know what I need to do," I exclaimed into the cavernous expanse of my newfound understanding.

I loaded a new piece of paper into the Olivetti and began typing the words to my story, filled with passion, courage and the wisdom of eternal kindness.

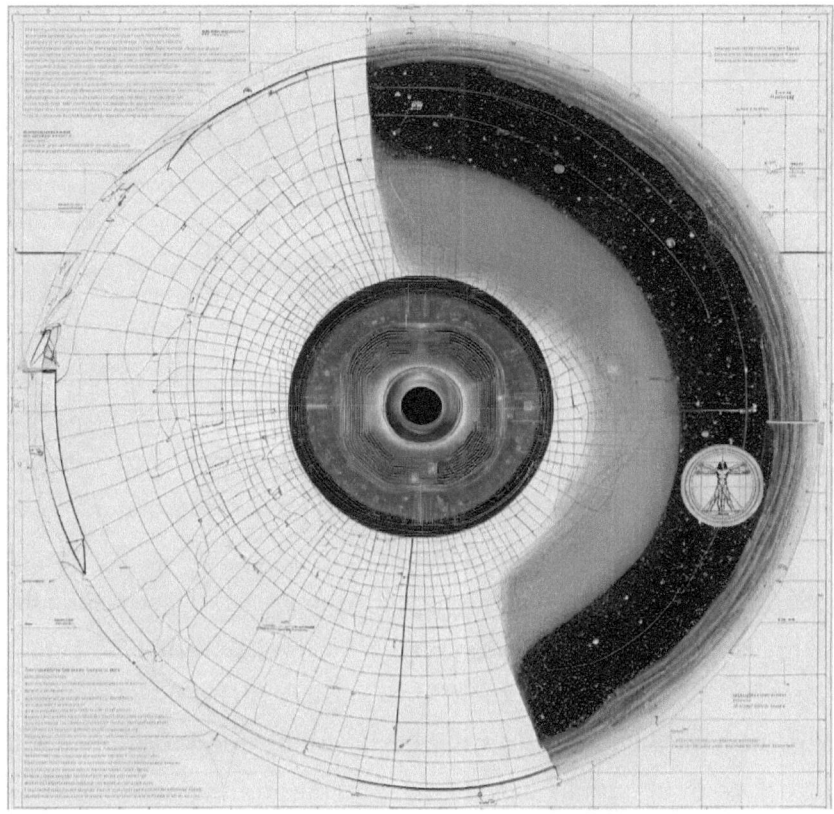

Universal Computer - Sagittarius A* center enshrouded w/universal-CPU, mankind to the right in starfield (human thread exists both past, present, future, alive and dead enshrouded by the Ghost of the In Between); next to cloudy gray representation of The Hyperveil; thread data collection on the left.

Epilogue

USING THE OLD OLIVETTI Lettera 22 she bought at the thrift store, Bella churned out an 80,000-word novel explaining her experiences with the threads, and what Cierra had taught her about the true nature of our human existence, the Universal Computer. She called her book You Can Always See the Sun. She no longer needed the quantum computer Cassiopeia, since she now had direct access to the threads using her inner voice and the Ghost of the In Between. So, she used that knowledge coupled with her own God-given talents, and the result was a story filled with writing that was effortless and flowed perfectly beautifully, like an extremely long poem. She told the world her story and Hollywood eventually turned it into a film. The world was left a better place than ever before.

About 3,000 years into the future, long after these events, enough perfect data patterns were collected by the singularity so that mankind did ultimately evolve into the next higher level of consciousness. This achievement was incredible, and for a short time, mankind had truly reached an apex of understanding and peaceful harmony. For once, we as a species reached our truest potential in all things, and it was good. However, there was a flaw. The singularity we had formed was not perfect, and the apex of our shared consciousness soon started to decay. The deterioration started slowly, but once the flaw was opened, it accelerated quickly. In an instant, our entire existence disappeared, not only from the Earth, but from the entire Universe. Much like the dinosaurs of an earlier period, mankind became extinct. However, when we as humans phased out of existence, everything went with us, and it was like nothing ever existed. Not a single building, car, book or even a single brick remained. The Earth was stripped bare of us, and what endured was a planet that was as pure and pristine as it could ever possibly be. But it wasn't right, us not being here was not good, and the Universal Computer knew it. But shaken by the collapse of the singularity, there was nothing it could do except sit dormant and wait.

The threads remained in the ether near the Earth, dormant as well, waiting for action. And soon after the shock of losing everything ebbed, the first couple of threads congregated near the pure but barren waters of the Earth to create a chemical spark of zinc and cytoplasm and a single DNA strand was formed. In this one simple but miraculous act, the threads had started all over again from scratch, rebooting the Universal Computer and creating the simplest life forms, so that we could evolve, and begin the process of starting over again.

This time, the threads told one another that they would gather enough of the most perfect data patterns, so that one day in the future, we could sustain a perfect singularity, one that would not decay and destroy us all. The threads and the Universal Computer agreed, and began working together again, in harmony.

In the history of the Universe that is within our understanding, the physical emanation of the human threads have been wiped out, only to begin all over again, a total of over a trillion times, with each evolution taking approximately 500 billion years, from beginning to end. That is one estimation. Another theory says that this is the way it has always been, and always will be, for eternity, no beginning nor end, the cycle just repeats towards infinity.

In the last evolution, the one you know, there were only 2,000,000 perfect data patterns captured. One of them was a haiku poem written in the year 1686. Another was a film that was released in October of 2001. As unbelievable as it may sound, the bombing of Hiroshima in 1945 was not a perfect data pattern, but the development of the atomic bomb was. Ironically, Bella's book, while beautiful and flawless, was not a perfect data pattern. However, when Bella was just five years old, she called her eagle stuffed animal a chicken, and that was a perfect data pattern.

Who knows, in this current evolution, or even a future one, perhaps you will provide us with the perfect data pattern that sustains us beyond what we have already known. You may hold the key to unlocking our flawless advancement and saving us all. So, if you know someone who is depressed or abusing drugs, don't let them turn their back and slam the door on you. Make them turn around and walk the razor's edge with you. Be loving but persistent. Because typically, there are only four things that people on their deathbed tend to say:

I love you.

I forgive you.

Do you love me?

Do you forgive me?

Use that knowledge now and show the world how beautifully you will walk amongst us.